MW01470228

MASTERMINDS

A Superhero Epic

JAIME MERA

ISBN-13: 978-1-941336-13-7
ISBN-10: 1941336132

Dedication

I dedicate this book to my friends Patrick Lawrence, Luis Monsalve, and Kevin Daugherty. You were an inspiration for me to see the best in people and believe in heroes.

Published books

A Superhero Epic Series

Creator (2004, 2014)

He Is Known as Ego (2006, 2014)

Guild Without a Name (2014)

The Galaxy Is Ours (2014)

Masterminds (2014)

Non-fiction

Doomsday Prepping and Survival: From Civil Disturbances to Biblical Proportions (2014)

Jesus and the Paint on the Wall: What Do People Live For? (2012)

Preface

The Eternal Champions were stronger in spirit and power after the victory over Ego, an interdimensional evil super being who tried to wipe out all life on Earth. Cindy, known as Mirage, was new to the group with the ability to be invisible and manipulate molecular particles. She was the group's part-time secret spy to find and fight criminals. Her past was veiled with mystery and death; but Richard, known as Creator and leader of the Eternal Champions, knew the value of trust and her part in a higher destiny which would change the future. Cindy's relationship to Joshua, a supreme superhuman, was also another reason Richard kept her close to him and the group. The truth which Richard hated was they were somehow being moved around like chess pieces, and to him destiny was another word for checkmate.

The Counter Espionage Agency (CEA) had their crosshairs on the Eternal Champions even though they were official superhero agents working for the government. Many people in the shadows hated superhumans and those who supported them. But the CEA was created and empowered to counter internal workings of all alphabet agencies in an attempt to neutralize a very high rise of hostile and criminal activity by superhuman villain groups and covert operations directed by national and international entities. Jean Lorenz, Director of the CEA, had a personal agenda to see the Eternal Champions fail as a group, and sanctioned illegal means to accomplish her goal. The Eternal Champions represented a halt to her attempt to take over the Special Investigation Agency (SIA) which had the resources to eliminate the people who killed her sister, and authority to keep her from taking revenge. It was a complex web of power, leverage, and cloak and dagger battlefields.

Jean reached out to superhuman mercenaries and tacticians to plot against the Eternal Champions. But her zeal invited the most ruthless and the most brilliant special black operations teams. Eibren Milows was one of those mercenaries who was only concerned about power and money. His anonymity as an assassin was delicately covered by the CEA after the SIA labeled him a threat to National Security. Eibren had no problem killing innocents, while the other operative team led by Jared wanted only to keep Jean from losing her soul.

The good people of the world wanted nothing more than to live in peace and happiness. Many thought superhumans were the key to this peace, while others blamed them for the deaths and escalation of violence on the streets. Legal issues arose over the authority of superhumans being allowed into law enforcement and government agencies. On the opposite end, others thought that vigilante methods were taken too far by superhumans, but it only mirrored what normal humans were doing in taking things into their own hands. The only difference was superhumans were more dangerous, and were naively expected to be responsible with their powers and actions. The legal system was scrutinized daily in an attempt to keep both human and superhumans protected and prosecuted without taking civil rights away from the innocent.

There were a few people who believed whole hardily in the many conspiracy theories at every turn and masterminds behind every evil plot to destroy our way of life. The majority however, believed whatever propaganda prevailed at the time which set the tone for justice. But it was unfortunate for the public, because the masterminds were real, and they were rooted in many of the smallest of cracks in established criminal, law enforcement, and political systems. SIA was the lead in destroying these criminal lords, with the help of superhero groups like Energy, Fire, and Light (EFL) headquartered in New York City, and the Eternal Champions stationed somewhere in Fort Lauderdale, Florida.

It wasn't enough that superhumans had to fight criminals on the streets, but also in the courtroom. The legal system was conflicted over the use of telepaths which the public thought was an invasion of privacy. The Supreme Court ruled against the use of telepaths, seeing it was an invasion of privacy under certain circumstances; but it was legal to use telepaths to get probable cause or linked to National Security. Jean wanted to eliminate the Eternal Champions using this legal loophole. But she would inadvertently initiate a historic nationwide event challenging the established legal system on the real balance of liberty, truth and justice versus what "We the People" demanded as righteous.

List of Characters

Richard Octavian / Creator – Leader of the Eternal Champions

Elizabeth A. Octavian / Isis – Member of the Eternal Champions

John Goodman / Mindseye –Member of the Eternal Champions

Susan M. Goodman / Pandora – Member of the Eternal Champions

Larcis G. Draven / Night – Member of the Eternal Champions

Cindy S. Owens (Samantha Brooks) / Mirage – Disciple of Joshua and Member of the Eternal Champions.

Erica – Member of the Eternal Champions (Super Artificial Intelligence computer)

Robert Dilinger – Head security guard for the Octavian Farm and supporter of the Eternal Champions.

Becky Ellington – Head veterinarian for the Octavian Farm and supporter of the Eternal Champions.

Alexis Mora – Secretary for the Octavian Farm

Randolph Maximilian – Director of the Special Investigation Agency (SIA)

Paul Rohan – Deputy Director of the Special Investigation Agency

Robert Thorn – SIA Field Agent and Lawyer, Superhuman Recovery Division

Senator Harleigh Summers – US Senate, (R – CA)

Jean Lorenz – Director of the Counterespionage Agency (CEA)

Jared Erickson – Special operative for the CEA

Natasha Erickson – Sister of Jared and special operative for the CEA

Eibren Milows – Mercenary and Special operative for CEA

Michael Stockwell – Archmagi/ruler of the Magistrate

Nick Phamos – Executor of the Magistrate, underworld of mentalists

Adam – Disciple prodigy of Michael, underworld of mentalists

Oliver Cox – Elder in the Magistrate, precognitive abilities

Starfire/Rebecca Emerson – Member of EFL and wife of Quatris

Starlight/Lynda Alexander – Member of EFL and wife of Hellfire

Judge/Deathstar/Fred Cider – Superhuman self proclaimed vigilante

Dr. Lethorn Harlov – Creator of Tantalumized Androids

SSG George B. Phoenix – US Army Military Police investigator

Malara Phoenix – Wife of George Phoenix

Honorable Judge Adam Cambridge – Florida Superior Court Judge

Charles Powell – Tallahassee District Attorney and lead prosecutor.

Joshua Marks (David) – All powerful Superhuman

Andrez Pobles – South American Councilmember of the Federation
Diego Gonzalez – South American Councilmember of the Federation

Eduardo T. Ramirez – South American Councilmember and Founder of the Federation

Estabon Ramirez – South American Councilmember of the Federation, and Captain of the Starship Andromeda

Jose Begestano – South American Councilmember of the Federation

Contents

Chapter One

❖---❋ ✪ ❋---❖

The Games Begin

Ellsworth Maine, January 19, 2014

A burning car lit the vacant gravel parking corner lot this particular Thursday night. Streetlights were broken due to vandalism, but it wouldn't have mattered if the area was lit up by the sun itself. The cold winter air with bitter wind chill kept many people close to the flames. The economy seemed to be bouncing back from a long recession, but it was no comfort to the people in the lot hoping they would see a good and fulfilling meal any time of day or night.

Over a dozen people gathered within yards of the blaze, while another crowd huddled next to a wall of an abandoned and gutted office building. The lot constantly attracted various drifters, but the police didn't pay too much attention since crime was higher in other blocks of the city. The building was occupied by many homeless, questionable wanderers and black marketing entrepreneurs. People were peddling drugs and comfort items in the street floor, but in the top stories of the building people exchanged blood for money. A handful of unshaven, smelly men with one woman lived with the population, but they were taking ampoule samples of blood and saliva for a fistful of wrinkled dollars. Normal procedure would be to use trial patients in a hospital, clinic or private business but that drew unwanted advertising and questions.

Reba accepted the labeled sample and scanned it to confirm the origin of the donor and the person who took the sample. The very small room was one of the few which didn't have small or large holes through the walls or doors. It was a dimly lit walk-in storage room now being used as a processing point. The black haired fifty-two year old woman's nose was running due to a cold she contracted, but she dared not wipe the mucus should she be contaminated by residue from the ampoule. The days were long with fatigue, she ignored added precautions leaving her mask off to the side. Gunter was in front of her and impatiently stuck out his hand to give her his sample, but Reba only stuck a hand up stopping him from placing it on a metal tray in front of her.

"Wait a minute. I need to clean myself." Reba tiredly stood up and move outside of the room.

Gunter turned to the side in the doorway letting Reba by him. Six other men stood in line behind Gunter. No one saw a sizable male figure floating an inch above the worn out tarnished floor in front of an opening where a very large window once existed. He didn't make a sound having slowly flown just inside the building from the cover of the dark sky and shadows.

The giant stood almost seven feet tall, wearing ash black padded body armor molded to his bodybuilder's physique. A dark gray under tunic covered his entire body except his head. A black rubberlike ski mask covered his facial features along with what seemed to be a headset or hearing protection underneath the mask. His eyes were dark in the low light with red eyeballs and black irises blending in with the pupils. He wielded a modified four barrel minigun with both hands, and there was a three foot drum-like backpack of ammunition on his back. A square shaped scope was attached on the middle of the weapon which displayed what seemed to be heat and x-ray signatures of whatever he pointed at. A flat black utility belt clung around his waist which stored a ten inch blade of a knife and Glock 30 pistol.

He was scanning the people in the room when Reba took a step beside Gunter and noticed him pointing the minigun at them.

Reba gasped in fright while the men in line turned their attention to the giant. "Deathstar." One of the men said, recognizing the locally famous masked vigilante.

The four inch display on the scope showed microscopic traces of a rare radioactive isotope in all of the people in the room, in particular Reba and half of the ampoule samples in the closet.

"My name is Judge." The giant replied with a deep voice and sprayed 7.62 mm rounds into the line of people.

The very loud bangs echoed throughout the block. Normally, gunshots wouldn't have been a surprise to the neighborhood, but machinegun fire was too much to ignore. People in and outside the building scattered in all directions, many down along the streets looking for a long stretch of land they could distance themselves from the block.

Judge, was the new name Deathstar was going by, having claimed to be a self-proclaimed and justified hero, a justice of the law. He had a short rap sheet fighting gang members and drug pushers in the past which gave him a reputation as a rogue vigilante using his juggernaut strength and daunting attributes. He had a track record of getting into altercations and fights, but today was the first time he'd killed anyone.

He seemed unconcerned however about his actions as he casually floated across the room above the mutilated dead bodies. He could hear people in the hallways and other floors yelling and scrambling to safety. Before he left the room, he scanned large body parts with his scope. The display showed two half inch scorpion like creatures moving inside the heads of Reba and a man. The man's head was partially decapitated and the creature was quickly trying to leave through the open neck. It moved like a cockroach, but not faster than Judge's Glock 30 as he unloaded several rounds point-blank at each of the creatures.

Judge moved swiftly through the building looking for more people but many had vacated a large portion of the floors. The few unfortunate souls that Judge encountered were shot first then scanned later. Four of the people, not instantly dead, were critically injured with no creatures or radioactive isotopes in their circulatory or digestive systems.

Judge floated an inch above the floor everywhere he went, but once he went outside, his feet touched the hard ground. The very heavy metallic boot impressions on the cold dirt and sidewalk sections indicated he must have weighed five to ten tons.

Three police cars with spotlights were waiting for him, but he ignored them and scanned the people who were bedridden on the side of the wall opposite the burning car.

"Deathstar, lower your weapon and get on your stomach with your hands on the back of your head!" A police officer commanded on the loudspeaker of a patrol car.

"They're going to get away, so leave me alone or I will hurt you!" Judge yelled.

Judge spotted an old man with high levels of the isotope, and was about to fire when six police officers opened up with a hailstorm of gunfire.

Over a dozen bullets hit Judge all over to include his head, but the police hollow points couldn't penetrate his superhuman skin. It was standard procedure and ignorance on the officers' part to think they could fight a bulletproof superhuman with standard munitions. But to their merit, the impacts of the rounds messed up Judge's aim, so he missed the old man by several feet.

Judge turned towards the police cars and lit up the area in a casual sideways sweeping motion. Three officers were hit while the others barely ducted or jumped out-of-the-way. Rounds penetrated the car doors and body, but to the officers' relief, their bulletproof vests kept two of them from instantly dying.

Judge was about to sweep a wave of rounds in the opposite

direction when three sonic booms broke many pieces of glass within a twelve block radius.

Starfire flew in front of Judge and melted the scope and barrels of the minigun with a red fiery laser beam from her hand so fast and hot that the minigun practically separated in two.

Ten rounds had left the muzzles and hit Starfire in the stomach area; but they bounced off with most turning into molten droplets of liquid metal before they hit the ground.

The shock wave of air would have pushed any normal person back several feet with deafening results but Judge was too heavy to be moved by Starfire's super fast entrance; nor did the deafening sound do much to injure or disorientate him.

"You're under arrest Deathstar. Do as the officers instruct." Starfire's mature and sultry voice clearly sounded through the cold air that the officers would've heard as if she were standing next to each of them. But instead, the officers heard a high-pitched whining sound from the effects of the sonic booms.

Starfire had long wavy and fluffy red hair which seemed to be on fire with red and yellow flames a few millimeters in length throughout every hair strand. Her eyes were also fiery red. She wore a red skintight rubberlike sleek suit up to her neck with yellow and blue flame designs around her neck, wrists, knees, and waist. There was also a thin red and black sash around her waist which extended down to her left knee.

"There's a monster in that old man and the other people in the building. Look at him!" Judge implored.

"Get down on your stomach now." Starfire commanded one last time, giving the superhuman a chance to cooperate or resist, not sure which one she was banking on.

Judge saw his explanation was being ignored and the old man was now not bedridden anymore, but was standing up and about to run away. His quick draw of the Glock 30 only caused Starfire to respond by punching him in the chest with an open palm. Judge flew backwards into the building he had just exited. Judge hit the building like a demolition ball another ten meters into the building.

The police officers stood at a safe distance, knowing Starfire had everything under control. Fortunately, city building codes had been changed to prevent mass lost of taxpayers' money because of superhuman collateral damage to property.

"Detain that man!" Starfire ordered the police officers, pointing at the old man and flying inside to apprehend Judge.

Judge was on his back with rubble all around him. His chest armored pads had been caved in but his body was unscathed. He tried to get up, but Starfire was above him now blocking his escape.

"You don't know what you're doing. The monsters will take over the country!" Judge pleaded.

"The way you're doing things isn't going to cut it. I'll look into these monsters, but you're through. If you continue to resist me, I will have to use lethal force." Starfire calmly replied.

Starfire was a foot shorter than Judge, but she was much stronger and faster. Rightly so, being a member of EFL and

Quatris' wife. She grabbed his wrist, pulled him up on his feet and pushed him from behind, forcibly leading him outside.

More police and emergency vehicles were on their way a few blocks away, as well as a helicopter being heard in the distance.

"What do you want us to do with Mr. Warren?" Sergeant Merda asked Starfire, referring to the old man.

"SIA agents will be here soon. Mr. Warren will go with them as will Deathstar here." She replied.

"My name is Judge." He corrected her.

Starfire slightly smirked. "You're lucky my husband wasn't here, he would have probably killed you when you tried to shoot Mr. Warren there, so you might appreciate it when the officers read you your rights."

The sergeant looked at Starfire with reverence; having never met any of the EFL members in his seven years as a police officer. They were the strongest superhumans he knew on the planet and their reputation to uphold the law without giving second warnings made the criminal underworld tremble. Starfire was very beautiful even with the intimidating fiery eyes and hair and to him; she seemed like a goddess from the center of a red star.

SIA agents and a swarm of emergency, law enforcement and media vehicles came on the scene. The agents quickly setup a perimeter to secure the area, looking for more creatures. The discovery was kept a secret, but the media however had a field day with the fact that Judge was giving superhuman superheroes a very bad name; having killed innocent humans and possible criminals without just cause.

Four months later, women's section, JCPenney, Fort Lauderdale, Florida.

Malara Phoenix passed her hands through a rack of maternity dresses. Her husband was overseas on deployment to Egypt, but he was expected back home to see the birth of their son less than a month away. She had plenty of dresses, but it was out of habit that she shopped in familiar store areas of the past several months. The baby section was on her mind as she walked down a wide aisle. Her silky black hair reached close to her shoulders complementing her slender smiling face and brown eyes full of joy. She pushed the plastic shopping cart along the sunlit floor, light flooding in from large windows in the high ceiling of the store.

A sleek shadow appeared on the floor as Malara heard a door slam and shatter in the distance. A few people yelled in surprise. The ones that didn't yell were too afraid to yell or run away.

Creator flew ten meters from Malara and stopped on the tiled marble floor. He stood in a hand to hand stance facing her. He was wearing his usual brown leather open vest similar to a three-piece suit vest, long black slacks, and white boots. His chest was exposed showing off his perfect chest and stomach muscles. He had two large wristbands made of metallic leather. His black hair extended down an inch below his collar bone which also covered his pointed Elven ears. His black Radon-like sunglasses covered his totally black eyeballs.

"I'm warning you, don't do it!"

Malara looked around thinking he was talking to someone else, but terror quickly took control as she saw Creator put his hands in front of him. The air vibrated similar to heat waves on a hot and long flat surface. She turned and ran for her life as Creator let loose a telekinetic bolt through the air from his fists. A loud thunderclap erupted as the bolt split the air ripping everything in its path. The almost invisible bolt hit Malara without mercy, tearing her in half. Blood splattered everywhere. Both halves of her body fell a few feet backwards but kept within several feet of each other; her infant utterly obliterated.

Several dozen shoppers and workers ran for their lives, fainted, or hid in absolute fear. A foot wide twenty meter long trench-like area of destruction could be seen through merchandise almost killing two other people by inches in the distance.

Creator looked on without concern, but after a second, he flew almost instantly to where Malara's remains lay. On his knees, he touched her head as if trying to confirm that what he was touching was real. He looked around at the terrified people, spoke into his wristwatch, and sat down away from Malara's split body waiting for the authorities to arrive. He didn't move for ten minutes, like a defeated statue, until the police arrived where he laid face down with his hands behind his back before they got within vocal range. The police handcuffed him and took him away from the horrific scene.

Night and Mindseye arrived shortly afterwards, but they were instructed to stay away, as Creator was placed in a squad car. Mindseye quickly scanned surface thoughts of the officers and saw the ghastly crime scene, but Creator's thoughts of Malara played a different picture. Mindseye wanted to scan deeper, but he sensed that Creator didn't want him to do a deep probe. Mindseye fought the emotional impulse to find out what was going on, but accepted his leader's wishes.

Two SIA vehicles came on the scene in response to a superhuman incident. The police officer in charge talked to the agents, and instead of releasing Creator into SIA custody; the agents escorted the police car straight to the police station.

Mindseye and Night received a call from Pandora, and the two heroes returned with heavy hearts to the Eternal Champions Headquarters, nicknamed the Eternal Domain (ED).

Safe House, Outside of Alexandria, Virginia

The four bedroom cottage estate was not very elegant compared to the surrounding properties. It was a moderate size property and wasn't suppose to stand out like most places in the area; being a vacation home as a front.

Jared Erickson was watching the news as the gate alarm went off. The four rings indicated that someone at the gate had entered the correct access number and was on the way into the driveway. Jared's hazel gray eyes jumped from across three television screens in front of the sofa to the front door. His light brown hair was wavy, curtained styled, parting in the middle and extending a few inches from his scalp. His face was very handsome and carefree for a thirty-one year old man. He raised a small remote control by his side and turned on an array of lasers in the house. The information the lasers gathered was fed into his ear implant microchip.

Jared was alone, his sister and partner, Natasha, was running an errand in Utah. The doorbell rang and he opened the front door knowing who was on the other side.

Jean was standing under the entrance overhang shadow. The sky was a beautiful aqua blue without a trace of clouds. It was late morning and cool, but Jean's formal dark blue business skirt suit made her look warm. Her ponytail fashioned pure white hair extending down to her shoulder blades. Her five foot ten inch height stood a few inches shorter than Jared, but her high heels compensated for the difference. Her dark blue eyes seemed to change color as she moved from the shadow into the house's natural lighting turning into crystal blue.

Jared met her with a closed lip smile, and she returned the same greeting, even though her gentle emotions were rarely displayed. "Good morning." Jared said as Jean entered the house.

"Yes, it is." Jean walked into the house living room.

Two of the television screens were turned off, the third in the center was displaying muted CNN World News.

"I take it you heard about Creator; but you already knew that since it's been on the news for over a day now. So, why the early visit on a workday?"

Jean sat on the leather single seat sofa facing the kitchen and dining room. "I need to know how you plan on keeping this from coming back to us."

Jared sat next to her on the long sofa edge. "I thought you read the fine print on the plan we drew up."

"It's too early to start with jokes Mr. Erickson."

"Mr. Milows was instructed to blame the Australian secret service as we discussed, and hopefully that's what he will do."

"We discussed a murder of a person, not a mother and an unborn infant." Jean's voice started to lower in pitch as her blood pressure began to rise.

"I didn't like it or approve of it." Jared looked straight into her alluring eyes. "Jean, I can't take back what happened, but I will exploit it so your objective is met."

"Why was she the target?"

Jared sat back breathing in deeply. "Creator has a strong bond to protect the helpless being the elderly, women, children, and infants. In addition, Isis gave birth recently, and the death of an infant will make him prone to stronger emotional disorder in the courtroom. Mr. Milows said he would make sure the trial, which I'm sure there will be one; is going to go smoothly. There is a failsafe which Creator might trigger if he focuses on the collateral damage instead of accepting that everything is not perfect. So, we are taking a big gamble, but you knew this from the start. In either case, I have already erased most of our tracks."

"So you're saying there's a chance all of this can go south?"

"There's always a chance Jean. A small one, but unfortunately, we're committed now and there's no turning back." Jared stated, but in the back of his mind, the chance was a big one, since it depended on factors out of his control; Mr. Milows, the legal system, and the Eternal Champions.

Any frame-up of superhero group members had to be done early on and with great care, before the group was firmly established with a solid reputation and safe guards against mental manipulations. The Eternal Champions had safeguards, but the three superhumans capable of keeping Creator from being mentally manipulated were strategically nullified when Creator started to patrol by himself.

Jared's abilities and his training of Mr. Milows was beyond any known telepath that he knew, but he had never had to directly test his powers or skills against Pandora or Ramus. Mindseye was a wild card and intelligence on his abilities were rumored to be stronger than Pandora, but it was preliminary since the new data and analysis was a few months old.

Natasha was the data gatherer which was one reason she was in Utah; having performed research in Ft. Lewis, Seattle, and was currently visiting old friends on the way back.

Jean looked around the room, and stood up. "I take it you're alone?"

Jared stood up with her. "Why did you come here Jean?"

"Is it possible for you to address me properly?" Jean moved towards the front entrance.

“When we’re alone, it’s impossible for me to call you director. But, stop trying to change the subject. Why are you here?” Jared commanded.

“I came to get your assurance that this operation is under complete control.” Jean said slowly walking to the front entrance.

Jared quickly stepped in front of her. “I don’t believe you.”

Jean looked at Jared’s gray eyes in defiance. “I don’t care if you don’t believe me.”

Jared blocked her path as she tried to sidestep him.

“What do you want?” Jean said as her white eyebrows tightened together around her slightly sun tanned face.

“I want you of course.” Jared said and grabbed her by the waist close to him.

Jean didn’t get angry or push him away, but instead grabbed his head with both hands and passionately kissed him.

They embraced for a while in erotic exchanges of pleasurable touching. Jean called work for the day, and the two enjoyed the first time they had alone without work or differences to get in between their new relationship.

Jared was ecstatic as he slept with the woman he loved. Likewise, Jean was at peace and slept soundly for the first time in many years. She awoke to Jared’s handsome face with his head on a pillow. His light brown facial hair was growing but instead of making him look sloppy and unshaven, he was masculine and strong in her eyes. His smile made her feel special and loved. He opened his eyes and she instantly kissed him before he could say a word.

"I should've kissed you many years ago." Jared said as they exchanged kisses.

Jean stopped and pushed him away from her so she could get a better look at his entire face. "Why didn't you?"

Jared smiled. "I thought you were going to fire me before I got my first assignment."

Jean relaxed her head on her pillow doubting what was happening to her. "Mmm, what are we doing?"

Jared rested with his face inches from hers. "I don't know where all this spy stuff is going to take us; but I have hope, that you and I will be together for the rest of our lives, if that's alright with you?"

"Well, you know that I'm not going to just leave my position as Director to settle down with you." Jean replied as if he was asking her to leave her job for him.

Jared smiled. "I don't want you to. I want my future wife to be President, if she decides to go for office. I don't mind being the First Gentleman in history."

"I won't be able to run for anything if Creator isn't convicted."

"Did you know that I can tell the future?" Jared stated, but Jean couldn't tell if he was serious or joking.

"Really? I missed that in your classified file."

"You'll be safe no matter what happens. I guarantee it with my life." Jared countered.

Jean wasn't happy with the reply. She had wanted to painfully hurt Jared many months ago with his rogue undisciplined behavior; but now she wanted him to live and the thought of him dying was daunting. Jared was the best at his job and they wouldn't be implicated, but if they were, he was sure to have a plan to change things around.

"Don't you dare talk about dying on me now that we've found each other." Jean said with a stern stare and tone.

Jared laughed. "I promise I won't my sweet and wonderful love."

They kissed and enjoyed the weekend together, planning their future as a couple.

Chapter Two

❖---✻ ✪ ✻---❖

Murder Trial

Broward County Jail, Interrogation Room Ft. Lauderdale; May 2014

The interrogation room was clear of police officers as Robert Thorn sat in front of Richard who was disguised as Creator. Robert was as tall as Richard, six feet two inches, but it was clear Richard's muscular definition made him look more formidable. Robert's eyes were hazel green, but his rounded and tapered brows gave the man a sense of added confidence and intelligence. Robert's dark gray two piece Armani suit, pristine black $1,000 shoes, and black Ivy League hairstyle complemented the look of a no-nonsense exceptionally successful lawyer.

Richard studied Robert before he had sat down thinking of many things. One was that Robert had many years in the past got him out of an incriminating situation with the University of Miami; but that was when he was Richard. He as Creator, they had never met. But yet, Robert was now here in front of him. Richard knew that the dean of the university didn't pull strings for just him or his father back before he graduated with a PhD in Computer Engineering. He always suspected that Randolph Maximilian was behind him not being blamed for the death of the people trying to assassinate him just before he started the superhero group; and Robert's presence sort of confirmed it. It was likely that Max had Robert come to represent him since Max was the only one in SIA who knew his true identity. The room's audio and video devices were turned off, allowing the two men to talk in privacy without compromising the criminal proceedings which the state of Florida didn't want to botch.

Richard was still in his Creator costume, except that his wristbands were not on him anymore. Not that it mattered since everything he wore was part of his shape shifting ability and articles like his sunglasses were in fact a part of him which he could remove at will or replace with a totally different face or wardrobe.

Robert introduced himself, and sat in front of Richard looking at him for a brief moment. Richard said nothing, waiting to see what Robert was going to actually say or do.

"I'm not going to color coat anything, so it will be in our best interest if we understand each other first. The investigators will ask you questions if you allow them to, with me being present, and you can make a statement if you wish. They are charging you with murder in the second degree, and willful destruction of private property. If you lie or impede the investigation, they can and will charge you with obstruction. It is good that you didn't resist arrest. If you tell me you didn't do it, I will support you until the end, even if you tell me you did do it. I just ask you not to lie to me. If you lie to me, I will be obligated to stop being your attorney, not because you are innocent or guilty, but because I don't play games. And if you want to play games with your life by lying, then you can find some other lawyer to help you." Robert stared intently at Richard's shades, waiting for a response.

"Did Max send you?"

Robert interlocked his fingers in front of him on the table. "The SIA is in a delicate situation and they cannot conduct their own investigation or use their telepaths; however, I and my team of attorneys can and will act on yours and their behalf; unofficially of course. But to answer your question; no, I volunteered."

Richard would have normally smiled seeing that Robert was truthful. But his heart was in deep pain and remorse as the vision of Malara's mutilated body to include her unborn child sprawled out on the department store floor was vivid and constantly embedded in the back of his mind. "What do you want to know first?"

Robert relaxed his hands and placed them on his stomach, sitting back into his chair. "I will ask you questions to clarify things as we go along; so what I want you to do first is, tell me in detail all the events that led you to go into the JCPenney store up to the police arresting you."

"I was patrolling the area when I received a message from Erica. She said there was someone killing people at the Galleria Mall. As I approached the mall, I saw police cars covering all the exits, but there was gunfire in JCPenney so I decided to enter. I could see through the walls of the store, and Deathstar, or Judge, whatever his name is, was shooting people with a minigun. I flew in there and stopped ten meters from him. He had not shot anyone since I arrived so I didn't attack him at first. Judge was going to shoot people behind the checkout counter, so I warned him not to do it. He didn't stop moving his minigun in that direction, so I shot him with a telekinetic bolt. He's a superhuman and I knew he couldn't be stopped by an aggressive push, so I used enough power to hurt him." Richard paused as he thought about what he was about to say.

"Judge moved to the side but I made sure I hit him center mass. That's when I realized that it wasn't Judge. It was a woman. A pregnant woman." Richard sadly stopped narrating.

"You're saying that you didn't see the woman until after you shot her?" Robert asked, knowing that telepaths could implant visions in people's minds, but not to this extent that he knew of on a superhuman working with the SIA. The SIA made sure all superhuman members working with them were trained and protected from mental invasions which would alter minds or perceptions.

"Yes, that's exactly what I'm saying. All the police and people who were killed by Judge, disappeared; and then I saw everyone in the store looking at me like I was a bloodthirsty killer. I touched the woman's body trying to figure out what was real and what wasn't. I called Erica and told them I had killed an innocent and needed help. I waited for the police, because I knew flying away would only make things worse."

"We have a problem then. SIA cannot use their telepaths

in this situation, and unfortunately, if any telepaths are allowed in this investigation, chances are that the judge will rule the evidence as inadmissible. Right now it's your word against everyone else, but maybe we can make a connection to what you reported to Erica, and the statement you said. We can also try to get the judge to get a sanctioned telepath to see if your mind was messed with." Robert explained options.

"You know that there aren't any telepaths strong or good enough to find out if my mind was messed with except maybe Pandora, Mindseye, or Ramus, and no one has seen or heard from him for the past three decades." Richard replied.

"That's the problem. No court proceeding will allow a judge or jury to view telepathic visions. If you had killed a government worker on government property, telepaths would have been admissible under a federal, military, or SIA led court. And even then, the chances of a telepath finding and confirming telepathic mental domination or illusions would be very hard to prove, if not impossible."

"I'm assuming Pandora or Mindseye can't visit me." Richard said, seeing that telepaths were going to be kept away from him or anyone related to the upcoming trial. Not that they needed to be near him to mentally communicate with him, but that was something only his group knew could be done with ease. But Richard had thought about the situation before and didn't want to be mentally communicated with just in case a telepath did scan his memories and say there was foul play involved.

"Correct, but before we go any further. I know you would say no, but I must give you the option of pleading guilty and not get the death penalty." Robert said.

"When I agreed to be a superhero, I agreed to uphold the law. I can easily disappear and become someone else and live another life without anyone knowing except my wife, close friends, and me. I didn't kill this woman out of evil or otherwise intentions. I was framed, and I will not plead guilty or insanity because someone messed with my mind."

"I understand your convictions; but the only ones who allow deep mental projections or telepaths in a courtroom judgment are South America, Australia, and the Union States of Africa. If there's a hint of telepathic influence in your defense at the trial, it will cause more problems than we want. In the eyes of the public you may lose support by them and the government. There will also probably be a mistrial which means that any favorable evidence may not be used later." Robert explained.

Richard had been in situations where telepathic meetings were what kept his group together, and Susan from being framed for attempted murder. The problem was it was done in a SIA facility and he had the power to dictate the evidence in the form of telepathic disclosure. There were many reasons why telepaths were not allowed for court evidence; the main reason being depending on the telepaths, any memory or thought could be altered or manipulated to the point of if seeming real or fake. There wasn't enough legal support to regulate telepathic visions just like the court system had historically struggled to regulate video and audio evidence certifying that it was authentic, altered, or even admissible.

"I am guessing you want to start a defense strategy. But before you do; I ask you allow Night to visit me. He's the only one in the group who doesn't have telepathic abilities." Richard asked.

"I will see what I can do; but any conversations you have with him will be monitored, and anything you discuss about this case will be used against you." Robert explained.

"Don't worry Robert, I know this. But in case this trial starts to go bad, I highly recommend you arrange my group to attend. I don't think this trial will be the last, and I promise that I will not instruct or suggest Pandora or Mindseye get involved; but I'm not their keepers. So, I suggest you get information to them so they don't start digging into peoples' minds before the trial." Richard warned him.

"I will talk to them." Robert was a little worried that this trial could turn into a legal circus with Pandora or Mindseye disobeying the law; but all he could do was hope that they would not make things worse.

"One other thing; what's the woman's name that I killed?"

Robert breathed and thought about what to say. "Her name was Malara Phoenix. She was eight months pregnant. Her husband was expected to return from the Middle East in two weeks for the birth of their son." Robert told him what he thought Creator should know.

"Thank you." Richard sadly replied.

A few months passed with many visits by Robert and Night. The media had a flare for the dramatic and advertised

Creator's unknown future along with the tragic new life of George Phoenix, husband of the victim. The headline news introduced critics and many activist groups to assemble for many weeks once it was announced that the trial for the murder of Malara Phoenix was scheduled less than eight months after her death. It was vague as to why the trial had been processed so quickly, but speculation in the media said that it was the State of Florida and SIA who pushed for a quick trial. Creator had pleaded not guilty during his initial hearing without any bail. The concern was not that Creator would skip town, but it was on his request that bail not be allowed. The public saw this as a way to hide from facing the public, but Richard wanted to make sure no one had an excuse to blame him for meeting telepaths or organizing a mental conspiracy. It was better to sit in a jailhouse and minimize gossip.

US Court House, Tallahassee, Florida, 2014

The Attorney General's office was on egg shells as the day had finally arrived in the first murder trial of an official superhero superhuman. They wanted to make sure they obeyed every procedure and make all evidence count. Several experts were expected to testify, along with twenty-four witnesses. Security was a major concern, not that anyone could hurt Creator, but that people trying to take matters into their own hands would only cause confusion, maybe hurt other people, and delay the trial. There was a level of dislike for superhumans in the past several months, and the actions of Judge and Creator didn't help the image. The trial was televised which helped greatly in keeping the press from exaggerating things and feeding the crowd of people around the court house with rumors and lies.

Jury selection started early in September, with the Honorable Judge Adam Cambridge presiding. Judge Cambridge was sixty-four years old with close to twenty years experience as a superior judge. His short black hair was covered with sporadic strands of gray, which gave him a sense of wisdom; but maybe it was more of his squared off face and straight mouth which gave him an added sense of authority. His dark blue eyes and very slight Irish accent complemented his robe and demeanor as a man of knowledge. He stood five feet six inches, but the chair he occupied put him above everyone in the courtroom.

Charles Powell was the lead prosecutor. He had a team of lawyers behind him as the jurors were questioned. The courtroom was an elongated square shape with the jury box on the far right side as people entered the courtroom. Charles was in his forties but he was very young looking as if he just got out of law school. His African American complexion was smooth and vibrant indicating he took very good care of his skin and general health. He stood tallest out of the group of lawyers in the room, up to six feet four inches. He wasn't stocky or thin, but his custom-made suit made him look wider than normal. His deep voice carried well in the room which was filled to max capacity of spectators and administration.

Larcis, known as Night to the public, was present. He wore his completely white formal costume covering every part of his body except for around his lower mouth area and around his eyes. Silver lightning designs wrapped around his waistline, extending towards all his limb extremities. His was thin, but muscularly defined through the rubbery like fabric. He sat in the rear corner, wanting to see the entire room. He didn't see faces of most of the spectators, but that didn't matter to him. He didn't like surprises from behind him, and he could react to anything in front of him with his lightning speed and superhuman reflexes. It was habit for him having been taught by Richard many things about security and counterintelligence. Susan, John, or Elizabeth were not there during the jury selection process, primarily because they had telepathic abilities and didn't want anyone to accuse them of fixing the jury.

Robert Thorn had his team of three lawyers and four assistants next to him. Across from the table, Charles and his team were positioned. Jury selection went fairly quickly and painlessly. Both men and the judge were in complete agreement with the selection and the fact that the jury would be sequestered from the very beginning. There were precedents the jury could be exposed to telepathic influence and being such a high profile trial the decision was not argued upon by Robert or Charles.

Judge Cambridge allowed the prosecution and defense a day to prepare for opening remarks, which also allowed the jury to settle into their new temporary secure home.

Richard and Robert talked much about the evidence the prosecutor had, since half of it was pertaining to the character of Creator. Richard's exploits in Complex San Francisco was the major issue which Richard was somewhat ashamed of. There was apparently a witness that would testify he murdered an inmate in cold blood. Richard couldn't deny the incident, but it wasn't out of a cold calculated heart which it occurred and it told him someone was lying. Not that he had not killed an inmate, but that the witness saw it. Robert understood the situation, and was going to try to get it dismissed on the fact that the operation was classified. In addition, the witness was not as credible as was thought, having lied in court in the past. But Robert knew it was a maneuver by the prosecutor to get Richard to admit or try to deny it, if he did go up on the stand. Either way, the two men sat down on the first day of opening remarks prepared for a trial that would change both their lives with or without a favorable verdict.

Susan and John, publicly known as Pandora and Mindseye, were there on the first day of trial with media already starting to report people objecting to their presence. Pandora wore a completely black rubbery like outfit with a red triangular design on her upper body like an arrow pointing to her belly button. Her arms were red except her gloves changed color back to black. Her long black hair blended very well with the red and black attire. There was an engraving of a cubed designed metal box above where her heart was situated. Mindseye also wore a black and red rubberlike fabric except his long sleeved gloves and boots were the only red parts of his costume. His sandy blonde hair was covered by a skintight hood, just like Night. An engraving of an eye was above where his heart was positioned.

Richard told Larcis to tell the team what had happened, exactly what he told Robert on the first day they met. The team had been conducting their own investigation in the matter, but couldn't find any leads or proof that Richard was mentally manipulated; but that didn't mean he wasn't. Susan and John both wanted so much to look deep into Richard's mind, but that would only prove his innocence to them, not the jury. There was also a good chance that it would work against Richard since it would be tampering with possible evidence and the trial.

John was a lot more powerful now that he had absorbed a large portion of a nuclear explosion with his cosmic energy ability a little more than two years ago. His powers had not only exponentially increased but he could alter his abilities to create new powers, just like Susan. The public and even SIA were unaware of their new abilities, but Richard knew and was at peace knowing they were both in the courtroom. Elizabeth didn't attend, but it was only because she was babysitting their almost two-year-old baby boy who was strong enough to accidently break the bones of a normal human caregiver's hand or arm.

The courtroom was again filled to capacity which included two television camera crews stationed on opposite sides but in such a way that the jury was never captured in their fields of view. There were six rows of twelve theater style seats on each side of the center aisle. The prosecutor and his team were seated along two rectangular tables making up two rows of additional seating on the left side as someone faced the judge. The defense was seated on the right side and also in front of the witness-box. In the center before the judge was a table. Seats surrounded it for the administrative personnel in charge of evidence handling and setting up presentation aides, where the lawyers had also sat across from one another during jury selection.

Security was tight with twelve uniformed police officers stationed around the room, eight other officers in plain clothes and in uniform ready to enter the courtroom if a major disturbance occurred. The carpeted floor was light gray and there was light cider wood finishing on the divider railing, judge's table, jury and witness boxes. The ceiling was fourteen to fifteen feet high with many dome light fixtures. The walls were soft white and audience seats were a darker gray than the carpet with maple wood trimming.

The murder trial of the State of Florida vs. Creator, started promptly at 8:30 a.m. October 9th, 2014. Judge Cambridge gave instructions on the proceedings and opening remarks were presented by Mr. Charles Powell.

The summarized version of the remarks was simple. Creator was a superhuman working for the SIA, but on that particular day he had shown his true colors and deliberately killed Malara Phoenix fully knowing she was pregnant, out of a wanton desire to release his frustrations. The prosecution was going to prove beyond a shadow of a doubt that Creator's character was not that of a true hero. One who desired dominance and had contempt for life being covered by the guise of a leader of a government sponsored official superhero group. The evidence would show that Creator had killed in the past, and now he had equated his past exploits in the name of law enforcement, to his own sense of right and wrong being reckless in his method of expressing his uncontrolled temper.

Everyone was very attentive to the speech Charles gave, with close-ups of Creator on camera. Richard gave no room for emotional facial displays throughout Charles' remarks. Robert had done well in coaching Richard about not letting the media and in particular, the jury to see he wasn't frustrated or emotionally unstable.

Richard did however; show some emotions of sadness which Robert had hoped would portray Richard as a person with feelings and not some emotionless calculated killer. Charles talked about the evidence brought forth by the prisoners of Complex San Francisco and reports about Deathstar and Creator two years ago in Dadeland Mall; but that was no surprise to the defense.

Robert's time was up, and he began the opening remarks with Creator did in fact kill Malara, but was fooled to think Malara Phoenix was Deathstar also known as Judge. Telepathic abilities and the use of telepathic mediums were going to be put to the test with non-telepathic witnesses and counter witnesses. But Creator's character was the focal point in the prosecutor's strategy to show Creator as a villain and murder. The defense would show that Creator did not willingly seek out and kill Malara and her unborn son because of an emotional break down or evil intent. Creator was and has always been a person of morals with a strong desire to fight for the helpless and protect the public from crime and evil. His actions after the death of Mrs. Malara Phoenix was not a show of regret, but a response to a situation where he took responsibility knowing after the fact that he was mentally manipulated to think Mrs. Phoenix was Deathstar. Deathstar, also known as Judge and a killer, was killing people in the department store. Creator's actions were not done out of a murderous mindset or incompetence. His actions were in response to protect the public, and without telepathic evidence, the defense would show evidence that he was mentally manipulated into believing Mrs. Phoenix was Judge.

The remarks weren't extremely long, so Judge Cambridge ordered a recess for lunch and then Charles would be able to call his first witness for the prosecution.

The three Eternal Champion members didn't need to eat, but they left the courtroom to give the impression that they were like everyone else and could us the break. The entire time, Susan mentally linked the three heroes and they talked throughout the remarks and afterwards. The three didn't know who were going to be witnesses from Complex San Francisco or SIA to testify against Richard's character. But the problem was they could only guess what the testimony was going to be since they didn't have access to the information before hand like the defense had. Either way, Night was a character witness for the prosecution and they knew Complex San Francisco was going to be a topic of discussion even though it was a highly classified operation.

The District Attorney's office had contracted telepaths to ensure the jury and witnesses were not coached by sensing mental projections inside and outside of the courtroom. It was a passive measure and could not guarantee that the witnesses or jury were not mind controlled prior to the trial, but there were other measures in place to detect such activity. It was sort of hypocritical since telepathic evidence was not allowed, but telepathic measures to prevent tampering were, which in the state of Florida was legal and constantly under legislative attack. If the trial was under federal jurisdiction, telepaths would have been allowed to indicate truthfulness of a person; but it was only under consent and in particular circumstances. Since the defendant was a superhuman, a telepathic scan would probably not be admissible in a federal court since most superhumans tended to be resistant to mental scans and proof of reliability was lacking. However, the outcome of this state trial would set the tone for the outcome of any possible federal trial, or appeal. The Eternal Champions and Robert knew that they had to get a not guilty verdict. They couldn't show mental manipulation with telepaths and wouldn't be allowed to use telepaths in an appeal with any verdict. A guilty verdict would however strengthen the business as usual method of criminal trials without telepathic disclosure.

Lunch recess was over quickly for many anxious people even though it was a little over an hour long, before the first witness was called to the stand. Louis Jones was a shopper and witnessed the death of Malara from twenty feet away. The story was exactly how Richard told Robert except it was from the perspective of the shopper and not what Richard saw in his mind. Robert asked questions confirming that Creator's only words were, "I'm warning you, don't do it!" before he cut Malara in half.

Five other eye witnesses testified with the same story. Three other witnesses didn't see Creator kill Malara, but they heard his warning and saw the aftermath effects of his attack. The day ended with a very bad looking note for Creator's defense, even though the spoken warning seemed to indicate Richard saw Malara or someone as a threat. Richard anguished the first few hours of witnesses reminding him of the events, but it was consistently erroneous from his perspective. That didn't comfort him much thou, because he knew that he was the one who was mentally fooled and Malara and her son were dead because of it.

Susan and John carefully monitored the mental projections in the entire block, looking for any possible telepathic foul play. To their disappointment, no one was using telepathic powers to manipulate the witnesses or anyone else in the courtroom. The contracted telepaths were the only ones actively doing their job, passively alert to telepathic activity. It was Susan's and John's experience and mental powers which kept them hidden from the contracted telepaths. This presented a problem because it was possible to mentally fly under the radar of the contracted telepaths, if there were experienced and powerful enough telepathic villains involved.

'I don't think anyone needs to mess with the witnesses since they probably did see things exactly like they saw it in the store. The only one who was mentally messed with was Richard.' John mentally told Susan and Larcis.

'So what should we do?' Larcis asked as if he could mentally do anything about the situation.

'John and I will lay low, and let things play out. Hopefully, the bad guys will get involved with the trial. If not, then we might have to step in and show everyone what really happened.' Susan replied, not really knowing if they could prove that Richard was brainwashed. Showing people the truth was not always a guarantee that the judgment would be fair.

'Whoever framed him will show up.' John confidently said, knowing statistically that narcissist criminal minds like to see their own handy work up close and personal when possible. If the mentalist was strong enough to manipulate Richard, then he or she would probably think they would not get caught by him or Susan. They were considered telepaths, but not super telepaths like Ramus who at one time was a celebrity, but disappeared in the late 1980s, rumored to have been killed or retired on an island paradise.

The three heroes knew there were super telepaths out in the world, and it could be an unknown disciple or relative of Ramus who had framed Richard. Whoever it was, John and Susan were extremely certain they could take care of any superhuman villain.

The next day continued with emergency medical personnel on the scene as witnesses attesting to Creator's post actions and Mrs. Phoenix's death and mutilation. Expert witnesses came that day to testify on the cause of death which all pointed to Creator's telekinetic energy bolt. By the end of the day, SIA witnesses were called forth to testify on Creator's character, trying to make Creator look like an egotistical person with little regard for authority.

Robert extensively questioned the SIA witnesses. He was in many ways disappointed that they said negative things about Creator, since most of them only saw the interactions between Creator and the agents in the Oakland SIA center in California. It was the first mission the Eternal Champions received from SIA which saved the lives of a dozen citizens, thousands of inmates, prevented a war with South America, and forced the reform of Complex San Francisco. Creator and his team of three were new to SIA and had challenges in following procedural orders which Randolph Maximilian relented to in the end. One of three SIA witnesses said that Creator took it upon himself to defy international treaties and almost started a war by allowing South American special operation forces to operate inside Complex San Francisco.

Robert felt it as a stab in the back being an SIA agent

himself in what he considered a family, and no agent should be speaking half truths against other agents or those who worked for the agency. Richard however saw it differently. Richard had lived as a government spy in MI-6 and the CIA many decades ago during WWII and Vietnam. There were many good men and women whom he had no problem trading his life for theirs; but he also saw the pitfalls of politics and personal gain. People would be people, and the SIA agents only reported what they knew at the time; being forced by subpoena to testify for the prosecution under penalty of perjury and other criminal related charges and allegations.

Richard thought it was normal to see SIA agents being called out from the past. Whoever framed him had intimate knowledge of it and knew which agents would testify against his leadership style at the time. The witness that would testify he killed an inmate was the one witness he was interested in seeing the most. He knew for a fact that the witness was lying, because when he did inadvertently kill the inmate, there were no eye witnesses around for a thousand meters. But there was a possibility he was wrong, and there was a witness he failed to notice with his vision which could see through objects up to that distance.

The evidence was stacked against Richard, and he knew that Robert didn't like the idea, but Richard was going to have to get on the stand in his defense. It was a calculated and dangerous move, because it opened Richard up to questionable behavior in Complex San Francisco. The hope was that the jury would see the possibility that he was mentally manipulated without telepathic evidence. Their goal was to show the good side of his character and the fact that his actions were reflective of someone who seemed not to be in rage or delirious before and after he shot Malara. The prosecution had to show beyond a shadow of a doubt that Richard was completely out of control or killed Malara and her child out of malicious intent, incompetence, or malicious ignorance.

The fourth day of trial came with the awaited witnesses from the former Complex San Francisco. Charles was very direct in his questioning as not to allow for a possible response where Robert could object due to the classified matter. But unknown to Charles, Randolph had told Robert he could use whatever information he wanted in the trial. Robert understood and would try not to reveal too much since it wasn't that classified information would now be revealed; but that the operation was authorized by the President through Senate oversight and Randolph himself. In other words, Creator was given the green light to use deadly force against prison inmates and anyone else who would place the survivors of flight UA 0292 in lethal danger. Keeping classified information on weapon capabilities or SIA surveillance capabilities from leaking was not a concern for Robert. If those topics did come up he could divert it to Creator's team capabilities which would allow him not to disclose those agency secrets, but keep the information available to the jury and public.

The third SIA witness, Rick Tyler, was questioned on the operation itself. Agent Tyler was the agent in charge before Randolph Maximilian arrived to the Oakland command center. He summarized the operation which Creator, Night, and Mindseye undertook. The news revealed the outcome of the rescue operation, but didn't have all the details about the events. Charles was able to set the scene for the jury, which sounded favorable for Richard. The operation was a success, which Charles hailed as a good thing, out of respect for the achievement.

The last witness from the complex was Carl Odeh, a prison inmate at the time of the rescue operation. He was still an inmate in Los Angeles Redford Corrections Facility, which was evident by his orange prison uniform. He was a skinny old fellow, but his Asian complexion made him look young at the age of sixty. He spoke rough as if his throat had been burned and scarred. Both his parents were Philippine, but he was born in California only to join a street gang at an early age. He had a long rap sheet of illegal activity to include two murders. His testimony was not part of a plea bargain, but was favorable for him inside the prison where many people would give him special privileges because he testified against Creator.

The long story of Creator flying towards an inmate after being attacked by a hundred inmates was exactly as Richard remembered. The inmate Creator interrogated wouldn't tell him if the survivors had been captured, and he unintentionally squashed the inmate's foot. Creator flew off to investigate unidentified armored personnel carriers, and left the unconscious inmate to die of shock and blood lost. Carl said he was a hundred meters to the north inside some rubble when he witnessed the incident.

Carl didn't hear any conversation, so his story was simply that he heard a large explosion, and investigated since it occurred near his block. Shortly afterwards he spotted the unknown inmate who was part of a patrol for Sargon, and Creator was holding the inmate upright by the neck. Words were said, and Creator stepped on the inmate's foot. The incident occurred in maybe a ten second time frame when the inmate screamed in pain and Creator flew away. Carl waited for the coast to be clear behind building rubble and when he got to the unknown inmate a few minutes later, the inmate was already dead.

Richard held his tongue as Carl told his story. He was sure no rubble or buildings were within two hundred meters from his location when the incident occurred. In addition, the SIA bio-scanner indicated no such life forms in the area prior to him putting the plasma rifle on overload and throwing it at the attacking mob of inmates. He wondered if Carl was getting paid to testify or if he was mentally forced to believe what he was saying. He could see jury members lean forward as Carl said that Creator left the inmate to die, and then saying that his foot was squashed to the point of the man's ankle being torn off.

"Mr. Odeh, were you roaming around on the south side of the complex during this same time you claim you were in the west side of the complex witnessing Creator kill this unknown inmate?" Robert asked as his first question, once Charles finished questioning his witness.

"No Sir, I was in the west side of the complex." Carl replied, his thick black eyebrows slightly rose with doubt, but his brown eyes showed certainty.

"So you are saying that you weren't trying to escape the area with inmates Dan Rankin and Brittney Wills that night?

Robert asked.

"No, Sir I was by myself that night."

"Can you explain to me why these two people say you were with them that night and your signature is on this roster indicating where the FBI picked you up that night? At the southern perimeter area before Sargon was taken into SIA custody? Robert introduced the document as an evidence exhibit to the clerk, judge, and Carl.

Carl looked at the roster with intrigue.

"Is this your signature which is above your name, which you signed?" Robert asked.

"Yes Sir, it is." Carl said a little distracted as if in deep thought.

"After seeing your signature, are you sure you were where you said you were that night during that exact time?" Robert asked.

"I remember being with Dan and Brittney, but that was the night before."

"If you were with Mr. Rankin and Mrs. Wills the night before, how is it possible that the FBI found you on the south side of the city with both of them on the same night Creator was in the complex?" Robert continued to force decisive answer.

Carol was confused now. He couldn't explain how he saw Creator and at the same time ended up six miles on the other side of the city.

"I don't know."

Charles let out a slight relief of breath under his mouth as Carol for some reason didn't know what to say. Even though they had gone over what Carol should've said, which was he didn't know how his signature appeared on the roster; him being obviously confused only made whatever his reply was seem unreliable to the jury.

Contracted telepaths had vouched for Carol being truthful, but that only helped Charles in deciding to use Carol on the stand. Since telepathic disclosure was not allowed, Charles couldn't just get a telepath to confirm what Carol was saying was true, and had to rely on Carol's answers; which seemed to have backfired.

No one saw the emotional or intellectual displeasure Charles had for Carol's uncharacteristic confusion, except for John who sensed every biological aspect of all the people in the room. John wasn't trying to see if anyone was lying or telling the truth by monitoring biological fluctuations, but it occurred by chance because he was looking for a possible telepath who was hiding in plain sight. A telepath might be able to alter mental reality by use of illusions, but it would be hard to hide physical aspects of circulation and breathing which the telepath was performing should the telepath be physically in the room. There was a possibility that the telepath was invisible like Cindy Owens; known as Mirage, a member in his superhero group, but it was unlikely the telepath was able to be completely invisible and be a super telepath at the same time.

Night was called to the stand right after Carol stepped down from the witness box.

All eyes turned to the back of the room as Night moved forward to the front of the witness box.

Night faced the back of the courtroom as he swore in. He thought it was weird to see Richard in a suit as if he were a businessman. Richard wasn't wearing his sunglasses, but his eye balls weren't totally black either. His irises were blue, and his facial features slightly resembled that of Brad Pitt. Being a shape shifter, it was all for show as his real identity as Richard was still a secret.

Charles asked Night about what happened in front of the bank where supposedly Creator killed the unknown inmate. Night was unable to tell a lie and Charles was hoping he could use that to his advantage.

Night told his side of the story which basically ended with the tossing of the SIA weapon into the mob of attackers. After the explosion, he flew away towards the suspected unidentified APCs; so he never saw what Creator did or didn't do to the inmate. Night was pleased to say what he said, but things changed once Charles' first question made him comfortable.

"Has Creator ever lost his temper and damaged inorganic objects?" Charles carefully asked.

"Yes, one time." Night replied almost not wanting to.

"One time that you know of?"

"Yes."

"What did Creator damage, that one time?"

"He was upset that Isis was in a coma so he smashed a chair into submission."

"What do you mean by smashed into submission?"

"Uh, there was a wooden chair and he used his fist like a hammer and bashed it into several hundred pieces."

"Does Creator lose his temper most of the time?"

"Argumentative." Robert objected.

Judge Cambridge sustained.

"Has Creator gotten very frustrated as leader of the group more than a few times?"

"Yes, like any other leader."

"Did Creator go against SIA orders more than once because he didn't like the legal system keeping him from getting his man or woman?"

Night thought carefully. "No."

"So you're saying Creator followed all of the SIA orders given him."

"SIA never gave Creator orders since he and the team are independent agents. We follow recommendations, not orders."

Charles wasn't expecting such a response, but he kept his cool. "Even though SIA is attesting to your authority as crime fighters; you are telling me that you don't take orders from anyone in SIA or law enforcement?"

"We follow the law, and do take orders from the President

of the United States." Night countered.

"So if SIA ordered your team to stand down and retire, you have no obligation to obey that order, unless the President of the United States gave that order?" Charles asked.

"We serve the public and if the president ordered us to stand down we would do so out of respect; but if the public is in danger we will continue to serve and protect them."

Richard was happy to hear Night speak his mind. He had worked in the shadows for decades fighting for the weak and helpless. But now that he was in the spotlight, doubts started to creep in as the collateral damage of his superhero activity had raised to one too many people. Which at this point were at four that he really felt bad about: the inmate in San Francisco, his friend Mark, Malara and her unborn son.

Susan sensed a mental probe move into the entire jury. It was so subtle that she barely saw it as she paid attention to the proceedings. The contracted telepaths were completely unaware of the probe as someone was getting surface thoughts from the jurors. Susan mentally spoke to John alone, wanting to make sure no one else knew about the probe.

John didn't try to confirm what Susan sensed, but he did strengthen his constant link to Susan so they communicated exclusively to each other. She could instantly report anything to him guaranteeing the contracted telepaths couldn't find out what was going on.

'If the telepathic probe is used to control the jury let me know. I will scan the people outside of the courtroom and see if I can find the source.' John told Susan.

'What makes you think the telepath isn't in the courtroom?" Susan replied.

'He or she is good enough to bypass the other telepaths, so smart enough to know to stay outside of the room. I would.' John explained.

'Hmm, what if they want us to use our mental powers to cause a mistrial and then telepathic evidence will definitely not be allowed?'

'It's a good thing I passed the bar exam last month.' John joked.

'Don't let it go to your head Perry Mason.' Susan mentally laughed.

John slightly smiled in the courtroom, but no one saw it.

Night was leaving the witness box, when Judge Cambridge motioned the counselors to approach to the side.

Richard, Susan, and John could hear the conversation with ease; not that they were trying to ease drop, but it was their enhanced hearing which they couldn't just turn on and off at will.

Judge Cambridge wanted the know if Mr. Powell had any other witnesses not on the list and rest his case; otherwise, Mr. Thorn was going to get to call the defense witnesses on the next day. Charles had no other witnesses and Robert was prepared to start calling his witnesses.

Judge Cambridge broke up the huddle and Charles rested his case. The jury was instructed on what was going to happen for the rest of the day and they would convene back in the courtroom the next day; when the defense would present their case.

The mental probe ebbed off of the jurors as they stood up and walked out of the courtroom. John stayed seated as his mental scan found a busy mind a block and a half away in a Starbucks café table. The courtroom was empting out, but the three superheroes stayed seated.

Larcis thought they were waiting for the crowd to leave before heading out, but then he looked at Susan. She was paying attention to what was going on in the courtroom, but John wasn't. He seemed to be resting his eyes since they were both closed and he had his head slightly looking up at the ceiling as if in prayer.

"Don't ask." Susan softly told Larcis.

"Don't tell me I put him to sleep."

Susan smiled and put her hand on his lap. "You did good. We just need to wait a minute before we go."

"Oh, Okay." Larcis relaxed on his seat and calmly waited, but in the back of his mind his hopes were on a speedy end to the trial with a not guilty verdict.

John opened his eyes and slightly smiled with approval. He turned towards the two and spoke to them, "All of this court stuff is boring me, let's go," but at the same time he mentally spoke to Susan alone. 'It's a male illusionist. He seems to be implanting subconscious commands into the jury so he can enter their minds easier later.'

'Can you track his activities from now on?' Susan asked.

'Already on it, but we need to do things as nothing has changed and leave the area. I will need to probe deeper tomorrow and find out what he and others are up to.'

'So you know he's not alone?' Susan asked.

'It's a gut feeling, but I will find out the details to include motive tomorrow. There's no sense in following him and maybe revealing that he's compromised. He'll be back.' John causally walked out of the courtroom.

Chapter Three

❖---⁜ ✪ ⁜---❖

The Rest of the Story

Industrial building, Chattanooga, Tennessee

Theodore Patterson sat at a workstation processing accounting information. His African-American complexion was moderately dark and he had grown out his hair into a four-inch afro. He wore slightly tinted glasses as if they were prescribed, and he had grown out a full beard about two inched thick. A large mole was clearly visible on his upper left cheek. His casual attire matched his hazel eyes when he took off his glasses or peered over them. His clean cute business look of a government agent was all in the past and his modified disguise was only for people he met. He avoided all cameras whenever possible and made sure he never stayed at one place longer than needed.

His tedious task of crunching numbers was a cover as he communicated with his inside contact in the CEA. An unidentified operative was tasked to survey the Eternal Champions, but he knew that Eibren Milows had caused the incident with Creator. It was a simple deductive process of elimination, since the only two CEA agents not on the books with the ability to frame Creator were Eibren and Jared. Jared would have preformed things differently, unlike Eibren who had a warped desire for evil, wanting to kill or destroy people's lives on every mission.

Theodore knew very well that Eibren was affiliated with the Magistrate, an underworld of mentalists who's one major goal was to dominate the criminal market of superhumans and political arena. Jean had told him, that her plan was to use Eibren later as a way to get inside the organization. He didn't know why she would want to get inside the organization, but he assumed it was another angle for her to gain power in the law enforcement regime by taking down the criminal empire. Jean was keeping the enemy close to her, because unknown to Theodore, the Magistrate were the ones responsible for her sister's murder. Whatever the case, Theodore was banking that Jean would have to kill Eibren which would bring the Magistrate down on her shoulders.

He was tracking the trial very closely and searched for an opportunity to convey a message to Pandora whom he considered to be the one most capable of acting on the information he wanted them to know. Jean had attempted to kill him, and his own underhanded greed had saved him. He had learned months before Jean tried to kill him, the standardized plans she had in cases where she wanted an operative quietly eliminated. When he was sent to the photo studio, he knew he was heading into a death trap. It was ironic because he had wanted to quietly erase Jean in like fashion and take over her operation if his caper to send her to prison failed. He had made contingencies for the event and faked his death. He had been in hiding for over two years looking for the right leverage to point the finger in Jean's direction so she would face justice. In the end, he wouldn't be able to return to the CEA or any other government agency, but that didn't matter to him anymore. All he wanted was Jean's downfall, and a retirement location in an unknown warm sunny island.

A carefully prepared thumb drive and envelope made its way to the courtroom for Pandora that morning. The messenger was paid four thousand dollars, no questions asked, with the intent of getting to Pandora before she entered the courtroom. The middle-aged messenger maneuvered her way in front of Pandora, quickly introduced herself as a fan and handed the small brown envelope as if asking for an autograph. Susan read her mind as the messenger walked away without the autograph, but only saw that the envelope was dropped in front of her doorstep with cash and instructions. Susan saw the thumb drive through the security paper with her enray vision and then placed it in one of her costume pockets with past combat situations teaching her to have a way of securing important small items. The thumb drive may have been a way of pleading for them to take on an investigation. Or perhaps, it was related to the trial, but at the time she and John were focusing on the mentalist who was telepathically monitoring minds in the courtroom the day before. She would tell John and they would make time to read the information, hopefully that morning.

John walked with Larcis, ahead of Susan, but he noticed that the woman had given her the thumb drive. It was a note he placed in a section of his memory universe. Most people imagine a house or well-known location, some a city, to store and organize data bits in their brain, but John's house of memories was that of houses, cities, nations, planets, and star systems. His world of recalling information was massive. He was constantly being filled with endless information down to the slightest details ever since his control of cosmic energies was stabilized in his near death experience with a nuclear explosion at ground zero. His energies allowed him to manipulate his essence which meant he could create powers he never had in the past and also massively increase powers he originally had before he met Susan. A test run of his and Susan's power extremes occurred over a year ago when they had to stop a rebellion in the Argonian empire high command, led by Her Royal Highness Toluvis Cammeth. The Argonian Empire dominated the Milky Way Galaxy with Susan as the new queen, and John as the new king by default. They had not taken the throne on a fulltime basis, and to many aliens it was unclear why they were spending their time on Earth. Many things had to be done to stabilize the royal families and races that were anxious not knowing what the new leaders were going to do once they did make Argonia their new home.

John had adapted his vision to be able to see through objects, so he could not only find the mentalist in his mind, but physically see him from where he was seated in the courtroom. It would not have been necessary to be able to see him, but it helped Larcis and Susan know exactly where the mentalist was physically at. Susan and John had a plan and it did require that they were completely aware of their surroundings. Once the mentalist made his move, John would control the crowd and trial, while Susan assisted in neutralizing the mentalist, and outside influences.

Larcis didn't have anything to do if everything went as planned, but if need be he would run physical interference should a superhuman physically be trying to stop John and Susan from fixing things.

The thumb drive was easy to spot as it was metallic and plastic as opposed to cloth, flesh and bone. Many metallic substances were in the human body, but John saw every detail and automatically filtered the information. Seeing everything as solid and yet transparent zooming in and out at will up to several thousand meters. It was similar to Richard's en-ray vision, but a lot more detailed and vivid. John didn't always have his vision as such, being it was distracting at times seeing everything and his flexible energy powers were mainly configured for other things like flight, telepathy, energy manipulation, telekinesis, mental domination, and his other four senses. But the situation today required that he make his special vision active as well as his mental domination abilities.

The standing crowds outside of the courthouse were motivated to display their many visual aids. Most of them, condemning Creator and superhumans in general; saying Creator was a villain, was thinking he is above the law, or was a murderer of the worse kind. Three fist-a-cuffs had occurred during the few days of the trial between supporters of both sides. The majority of the crowds were against Creator and unlike most normal humans, Richard heard their loud comments even though he had not stepped outside of the courthouse since the start of the trial. The courtrooms were sound proof to a certain degree, but not enough because Richard could hear the echoes of sound come to the windows near the courtroom entrance double doors and courthouse jail cell. Larcis, John, and Susan could also hear the comments outside, but they had heard them since the beginning of the trial as they entered and left the courthouse along with every other commuter. The trio was hoping Richard wouldn't pay attention to the crowds, but it was wishful thinking and maybe too naive on their part. For the few years the three had known Richard, he was rock solid in his convictions. He was leader for many reasons, and one of his best quality was that Richard feared nothing and placed truth and justice above public opinion or legal red tape. They fought for the public, and it was expected to have negative things come out of situations. But protestors were people with feelings, whether justified or not, their actions and comments ate away at Richard's grief for the death of innocents on his watch.

The morning was tense, but Robert was the most at ease, as if he were walking along a calm beach with warm sand massaging the soles of his feet. He greeted everyone with a warm smile and firm shake, especially Richard. It was in the schedule that Richard would get on the witness stand that afternoon. The character and expert defense witnesses were to set a stage for Creator to tell it as he knew it. The evidence so far was up in the air, meaning it was up to interpretation by the jury members for a verdict. There was no doubt Creator killed Malara in Robert's reasoning of how the jury saw it. But the circumstances behind it was the determining factor in a jury believing that Creator was mentally fooled enough to kill her without knowing before the fact.

The first witness that day was Randolph Maximilian, Director of SIA. Randolph never appeared before a public grand jury in his life, but this was an exception he owed Richard. He had many times been to Senate Hearings, but this was different since a Senator could be easy to appease; but an experienced lawyer, that was a challenge. He stood six feet tall and was very well-built in his late thirties wearing a twenty thousand dollar modified two-piece black suit. He wore specialized bulletproof and elemental resistant undergarments, but it was unnoticed except to John, Susan, and Richard. His dark brown hair was semi-short and combed backwards as usual. He had a short but well trimmed beard like a classic G.I. Joe action figure. He walked majestically towards the witness-box, as everyone looked on at the historic event.

The Eternal Champions had only taken one emergency mission for SIA since Ego was destroyed over two years ago. Randolph was not about to admit it, but he felt guilty for not informing Richard about his friend who was killed during Ego's demise. So was the case that SIA and the Eternal Champions were not on the best of terms. SIA was also having their own problems with international agencies, superhuman villains, and partner governmental agencies. But this day view was not about how SIA was fairing, but how law enforcement and the public had faired because of Creator.

Richard looked on as Randolph introduced himself and chronologically spoke of the achievements the Eternal Champions had performed with Richard's leadership. Thirty-eight murderers and ninety-five thieves were captured, ten kidnapped people were saved, and over thousands of people were saved from industrial to home disasters. The country and planet had been saved twice and it was Creator's leadership which made the difference. Creator's character was of the upmost quality of a leader, and moral standing as Randolph described. Complex San Francisco was mentioned, and it was clear Randolph took all responsibility for ordering the team to use lethal force as needed, and supported Creator's actions, even how he questioned the inmate who inadvertently died. Richard had forgiven Randolph over a year ago for keeping secrets from him and the group. But the birth of his son, Susan and John's trip to outer space forced him and Larcis to pick up the slack of crime fighting. Doing missions for SIA would only add unwanted work on their plate which was why he had not volunteered to help them out for the last year. So the supportive words which Randolph said were gladly received in Richard's heart giving him a boost of encouragement to persevere.

Charles Powell cross-examined with his focus on getting Randolph to talk about why the Eternal Champions had not helped out SIA for the past year, but it backfired as Randolph explained they were not needed by SIA at the time. The Eternal Champions were already taking on investigations and tasks which SIA approved of before they even had to ask or request to task.

Four more witnesses came to the stand that morning attesting to Creator's care of people. One witness was Timothy Ison who was saved from an armed robber with a gun to his head and explosive vest. Creator changed into a normal police officer and talked the robber into a trade to take Timothy's place. Once the exchanged occurred, Creator made sure the store was clear of people before he overpowered the robber and absorbed the vest into his own body. The testimonies were favorable for Richard, and lunch time quickly arrived.

The intruding mentalist probed the juror's minds once Randolph started his testimony. As did John, who was shadowing Eibren Milows through a maze of memories and thoughts of his own and the twelve people in the box. Lunchtime brought a different aspect to the mental workings of Eibren's plan. The jurors were being coached into reforming memories of what was said on the stand to go against Creator. It was subtle in making Creator seem like he was a leader who was fighting crime for fame and jumping into a fight so that he would get the credit before anyone else. A full change in thoughts or convictions would have been noticed by the contracted telepaths, so Eibren slightly modified what they perceived and short-term memories.

John performed the normal physical actions a person would by standing up and moving out of the courtroom to go eat lunch. But Susan was telekinetically assisting him by helping him physically move his body to include any short phrase speaking. Deep inside John's mind, he was busy inside Eibren's mind gathering information and staying invisible to Eibren's mental consciousness.

Twenty minutes into lunch, Larcis had picked up the food for the group and was serving it at their table. John reached for his turkey club on Rye sandwich and started to eat. Susan knew he was in complete control of his surroundings now, having gathered all the information he needed to proceed with their plan.

"So what's going on, boss man?" Larcis asked, not using the usual title of Boss, which he reserved exclusively for Richard.

"Mmm, this is a good sandwich." John replied.

"Well for starters, I think we should look at the envelope." Susan stated.

'You are so right my love.' John mentally spoke to both of them as he enjoyed his meal.

Without reaching for the envelope John transported the three of them into a mentally created room with a glass table and chairs, with the walls, floor, and ceiling completely white. John scanned the thumb drive with his vision and in the mental room the three viewed what was in the thumb drive as if there was a large video screen above the table but only the image appeared.

Several videos on special overt projects, top secret plans of CEA operations, Jean's audio recordings of the destruction of the Eternal Champions was laid out along with an introduction video by Theodore. He explained the failed previous plan on assassinating Elizabeth in order to get Creator to go rogue and commit a crime. Theodore didn't say his name or credentials, but his knowledge of the incident inside SIA Medical Center indicated he was a reliable source to at least what he claimed had happened. He continued to explain that Jean Lorenz, Jared Erickson, and Eibren Milows were the ones leading this endeavor to destroy the team and Creator in particular. John's interest increased when Eibren's name was mentioned and also appeared in one of the project document.

Eibren Milows was a slim man in his late forties, with a Bruce Lee look hairstyle. His hair was pitch-black and thick brows were partially covered by very dark rimless geometric glasses. His face was usually unshaven due to a skin condition, but it was mild and under control at the moment. He didn't spend much time in the gym with his focus on mental disciplines and mystic lore, which didn't give him a habitual desire to be the athletic type. He did however eat a stable diet and constantly drank fluids. Eibren had an extensive criminal and agent portfolio, which confirmed John's in-depth probe into Eibren's mind. Jared Erickson had trained him to use mental illusions in conjunction with imbedded memories and emotions. It was Eibren who implanted the fake Susan in the minds of the SIA agents in the past to frame her in Elizabeth's assassination attempt. It was also he who implanted the illusion into Richard at JCPenney. Eibren was the tool, but Jared was the trainer and Jean was the higher authority for a go to the mission which wasn't sanctioned by the President or SIA.

John knew that Eibren was affiliated with several other organizations, but the one with the most influence was the Magistrate. The Magistrate was led by a council of Archmagis which was his source of criminal upbringing and strong desire to follow the dark underworld of mystics and magis. The gleamed information John got from Eibren's mind was enough to confirm the directives of the plans Theodore was stating as fact, incriminating the Director of CEA, several CEA agents, and proving Richard was framed. But, John knew better; the information would not be sufficient since the author and narrator of the accusation would not testify, and the information was obtained illegally or was of telepathic origin in some instances. John mended his thoughts with Susan and Larcis so they could see Eibren's memories as John saw them in the past several days. Eibren never met Jean, so the only personal memories he had of the agents involved was Jared alone. Eibren was hiding something in his subconscious, but John couldn't see it without blatantly invading his mind, so at this point he had to wait to see what Eibren was going to do further in the trial.

The three heroes mediated on the information that was poured out in the mental conference. 'So when do we spring Richard from jail and go home?' Larcis asked as if they had already won the trial.

Susan smiled, 'Be patient speedy, we need everyone to see the truth and let Eibren Milows make his big move.

'What if all he does is watch? The jury is already thinking negatively about Richard?' Larcis countered.

'He's not going to take any chances with the jury deciding on negative emotions or memories. He will want to get Richard to say something incriminating; at least enough for him to alter the memories of the jury and make him look like he confessed guilty.' John said.

'How are you so sure?' Larcis asked, Susan didn't say anything, but she had her doubts as well.

'Eibren has manipulated so many people, and he wants to prove himself worthy of being an Archmagi. He can't help himself not to.' John said and even though the conference was in a mentally created room, his expression of certainty could be felt in their souls.

'Since you put it that way, let's get back to lunch, before everyone wonders why we are daydreaming at the table.' Larcis joked.

The mental conference concluded as quickly as it started

lasting fifteen minutes in their minds, but in the physical world it was less than a minute.

Larcis slowly ate his nachos and cheese. “So, when are you going to tell Creator?”

John looked at his bright eyed friend. “After the verdict when we’re back in ED.” John knew Larcis was referring to the assassination attempt on Elizabeth and framing of Susan.

“Isis won’t take the news very well.” Susan commented.

“Yeah, that’s why we’ll wait until they’re both together.” John replied, and they finished their meals quietly as time was approaching for them to head back to the courtroom.

The attendees were back early and eager as the trial commenced without delay. Creator would be taking the stand before the end of the day. An unexpected witness was brought up to the stand as a rebuttal to an expert witness in a claim that Creator’s blast was lethal at any intensity or pattern. The testimony lasted two hours with a very detailed explanation of how Creator’s telekinetic blast had been used in many cases to stun a criminal or push heavy objects weighing from five hundred to twenty thousand pounds. The prosecution didn’t try to counter the testimony since it was already established that Creator’s blast did kill Malara. The jury understood it was not lethal all of the time, and that was all Robert wanted the jury to meditate on, even though it was lethal in this particular instance.

John could sense Eibren enter the minds of the jury all at once. The ease in which Eibren entered their minds made it seem like the contracted telepaths didn’t exist. Eibren made the jury think over and over how Creator's blast was intentionally made to kill Malara. Eibren was not holding back on his actions now and John knew that he was sure to do something once Richard got up on the stand so we waited patiently, as did Susan.

Creator was finally called to the stand. Richard sat down and calmly answered Robert's instructions with the routine verbal declaration of his name. "My name is Creator."

Eibren Mellows didn't waste any time in entering Richard's mind. It took more effort and careful finesse on his part, but John skillfully shadowed Eibren's mental probe. The contracted telepaths were severely out classed and not a single one could have imagined how much mental activity and manipulation was occurring under their noses. John noticed that Richard's mind had been entered in the past which made it accessible to Eibren, like a back door password on a computer. He had never considered searching for such a mental command or trigger since there was no indication Richard had been probed by other telepaths beside Susan or himself. Even then it wasn't an intrusive subconscious probe, but more on consented surface thoughts as the mental conference they had during lunch time.

Robert's questioning started from the beginning of the distress call to police officers dispatched to the report of Judge killing people in JCPenney. Erica, the Eternal Champion's Super AI, had never made such a call, but Richard insisted that he did get the report from Erica. John could see that Eibren had created the illusion so Richard thought the call was real. What the jury heard was a contradiction and the only one who could confirm Richard's claim was him alone without telepathic disclosure. John could feel Eibren's satisfaction as if a mental smile were in the darkest corner of Richard's mind, yet Richard sensed nothing.

Robert knew that contradictions would be heard because Creator's story was for the most part different than what witnesses saw, except for what was said prior to the blast and what happened after Malara was dead. He was banking on the fact that there was plausible doubt that Creator was reacting to what he claimed, by virtue of logical reasoning. And he would have been right, except that Eibren was now manipulating Richard's mind.

"Did you go into the JCPenney department store with the intent on killing Malara Phoenix?" Robert asked.

But what Richard heard, due to Eibren's manipulation, was "Did you go into the JCPenney department store seeing Judge killing people?"

Richard answered Yes, which took Robert and many other supporters in the room and television audiences by complete surprise.

"Okay, it's time." John said out loud to Susan and Larcis.

In an instant, John appeared in front of Judge Cambridge's desk and the witness box. Everyone saw him, except those viewing the trial through video broadcasts and cameras. There were several people, mainly the police officers, who wanted to stand up and react to the situation, but no one could move a limb or speak as they desired. The contracted telepaths were feverishly attempting to stop Mindseye from interrupting the trial, but found themselves as if they had no powers. Everyone in the building floor could see what was going on in the courtroom even though not everyone was physically in the room.

"Houston, we have a problem." Mindseye said and smiled, "I've always wanted to say that."

Everyone heard it audibly as if watching a television show with no distractions.

"I apologize for this change of setting Your Honor and jury, but unfortunately, this trial has been tampered with for the past two days. I am not going to say some mumble jumble Matlock excuse or quote law which allows me or doesn't allow me to interfere, simply because justice will not be blind to the truth today. And everyone will get to see the truth and decide on what they should do." John paused for a few seconds.

"Now, the rest of the story. Everyone who is present in the courtroom and everyone who must see and hear what's going to occur for the next hour or so, is mentally linked together at this time. The contracted telepaths are all also mentally linked. Don't worry, if you had an urge to go to the bathroom, you will go in the physical realm, but nothing will change here in this virtual courtroom."

Many of the attendees and many new viewers could not but wonder in awe on how real the virtual courtroom was. They could feel, see, and smell in their limited movement of their virtual seats and hear every word everyone said or thought, with restricted guidance or allowance by Mindseye. The contracted telepaths were trying to use mental drills and searching for a way to make their powers manifest, but they were in no position to overpower Susan and John's hold on their minds and bodies.

John spoke loudly into everyone's minds. "Many of you are wondering how you can hear thoughts of this person or that; but don't be alarmed. I am not going to allow you to see everything everyone is thinking, otherwise this trial would not be impartial and justice would not be served as a people with freedoms and individual rights. Your Honor, I will start by narrating from the start of the trial and fast forward through all of the witnesses. What they saw and heard from day one; up until Eibren Milows started to enter the minds of the jury. From that point on we will all see what I saw as Eibren altered what was going on in the minds of the jury and Creator.

Eibren Milows lost connection with all of the minds he sensed in the courtroom, in particular Richard's mind after he answered Robert's question. Before he could move out of his seat or look around in the café, Pandora's voice clearly rang in his ears from behind him.

"It's time for you to make a court appearance Eibren." Susan said as her iron like fingers gripped his arm.

Eibren felt the warm hand and relentless pressure on his arm, and instinctively attempted to stand up and pull away. His mind raced frantically trying to dominate his own thoughts and split reality from illusions.

Susan slightly smirked as she noticed Eibren thought he was being mentally fooled. "You're not thinking clearly for an Archmagi want to be."

"You're not real. You're not here, you're in the courtroom right now." Eibren said and turned his head looking at Susan's eyes and then at the customers in the café who were now obviously paying close attention to the two of them.

"No Eibren, this is real and you are powerless." Susan replied and they both instantly disappeared into thin air with café customers wondering what had just happened, thankful that Pandora was gone, or disappointed they didn't get an autograph.

John's mental narration lasted five minutes in the physical world, which included an out of body experience for everyone as if they were inside of invisible cameras and angles, of the things that occurred in the courtroom since day one. But when it came to Eibren's mental probes on day three, all of them entered the probe with Mindseye, seeing exactly what Eibren was doing to the jury members.

John showed everyone what Richard perceived to be the exact verbiage asked by Robert, after Eibren's manipulation. The narration stopped there, and John was the center stage once again as a lawyer at the front of the courtroom, dressed in a black suit but yet with his Mindseye disguise covering his face and head. "Now Your Honor, and jury, we will continue with the trial except Mr. Powell will be allowed at this time to bring back any witnesses he wishes before the defense continues to present their case. Also, Your Honor, I would ask that you take a few minutes to contemplate the proceedings which you can stop, or allow to continue. You know, as I do, the legal and political repercussions of allowing or stopping this trial with what has been revealed."

John changed audience and addressed the entire audience.

"You all might be thinking that this is fair, justly provoked, or just plain wrong, then I would tell you it's not about being right or wrong only. There is a dark war coming and I as King of the Argonian Empire must ensure justice is met, even here. So, don't place me as under your legal system as if I must obey your procedures which only apply to you in this country or planet. So am I illegally interfering with this trial? I say, not to worry about the little things, and look at what you will do now when you know or will know the facts and truth.

Judge Cambridge spoke, "I will give everyone an answer shortly. Mr. Powell, please prepare your list of witnesses you want to recall." Judge Cambridge glanced at John, stood up and retreated to his chamber, but in fact never left his seat in the real world.

John could sense the majority of the people were perplexed to the twist in the situation, and could only but sit back and see what would happen next. There were a few however who were angered to what was happening because things were being manipulated by a superhuman and the law was being broken. To them, there was no excuse or cause to get involved even though Eibren might have actually been illegally interfering with the trial. According to their logic, Mindseye could have exposed the interference and allowed a mistrial with the murder trial to be continued later. Others thought that the mental manipulation by Eibren was probable cause for Mindseye to go as far as he had already gone. But in the end, John was determined to set things right because he believed that the people and Malara's husband deserved the truth, not just Richard as Creator being given a fair trial.

Judge Cambridge's nerves were steady, even though his courtroom had been trampled on by three people as far as he knew. The compulsion to stop the trial by declaring a mistrial would cause Creator to be kept in jail much longer. Even though he was inclined to see that Creator was probably innocent of first degree murder, the law had to be upheld in all aspects to include courtroom procedures. But this was no normal proceeding and the criminal activity by Eibren that interfered with the trial was cause enough for him to see where the evidence would take the trial in the end. The prosecution would probably request a mistrial or at least someone would condemn him for going forward with the trial, but he was determined to stay the course and interpret the law for the people and for justice.

Richard kept quiet, even in his mind, having mentally closed off sections of his mind like Susan taught him many years ago. He saw how Eibren had invaded his mind and robbed him of free will. The nine months in jail for him was stolen time, but he valued spiritual freedom more, and Eibren's mental coercion hit a deep emotion in him. He wanted so much just to get up and leave. Leave to calm down and not let his anger take irrational control. He wanted to rip Eibren apart limb by limb, not because of the mental scam, but because Eibren was the cause of Malara's murder. He turned to look at George's face. George was young with a clean dark haired crew cut look; but the months after Malara's death, his eyes had aged a decade. Creator could tell even in the virtual courtroom, that George had shed tears everyday during the trial. It wasn't in the courtroom, but in the men's room during breaks. Sadness filled his heart a lot more than before knowing that more than two people died and suffered nine months ago, even now.

John didn't see what Richard was thinking, but he felt his sadness, risen anger, and efforts to control them. He mentally sent a message to Richard, as if he were standing next to him and no one else could hear him.

'Richard, it'll be alright. Take a breather and trust me.' John comforted him.

Richard took a deep breath, even though it really didn't do much since he didn't need air to live or synthesize energy. The feeling of it was relaxing though and helped change his self-loathing thoughts. 'I have made a big mess of things.' Richard replied.

'There's nothing you could have done. Eibren could have made you kill someone simply by making you fly into them, or making you think you were grabbing a tank and tossing it. It's my fault for not probing to see if someone had hacked you.' John explained.

John could feel a regretful frown from Richard. 'I have fought injustice, only to find people being happy they can condemn those who truly try to fight for what's right in the right way. Freedom isn't free, yet they want to take things into their own hands in order to dictate their own sense of freedoms for select people.'

'What are you talking about?'

'The only people that are grateful about me fighting for justice are the ones who were saved. Everyone else is only looking at face values or their own fears, so they call me evil. I'm tired of fighting against the people I try to help.' Richard answered.

'Hmm, keep that thought. I want you to see the truth, and not lose hope my friend.' John countered and broke off his mental dialog with his friend and leader. John had many things going on at once and he had to address all of them in this mental virtual world he had created, one being the judge.

Judge Cambridge's thoughts were clear to him as the judge spoke in his virtual chamber. 'Mindseye, I have decided to have this trial continue, but on one condition. There must be order in the court and you must support my judgments. Can you make it so court procedures will be adhered to by allowing the prosecution and defense to present their cases with and without telepathic evidence? In addition, witnesses must be allowed to speak and think freely without any coercion. I understand that lying will be or should be almost impossible, but the 5th Amendment was created for a reason and it must be honored.'

'I understand your Honor, and I agree to help in these matters. My intent was never to make your courtroom a spectacle, but I just can't sit back and let a mentalist dominate his will on people and your courtroom.' John stated.

'Don't think I'm not opposed to your methods, but since the Supreme Judges are involved in this fiasco now, and you seem to be ruler of another planet, I'm inclined to let you slide this one time.' The judge replied.

'Yes, your Honor, I apologize once again, and hope to make it up to you one day. I would ask you give Creator some latitude, he seems to be under a lot of stress now that he knows who was responsible for his mental rape. He's tired of the false accusations by the people outside, and is questioning his future as a superhero.' John informed him.

Judge Cambridge could only speculate on what degree of latitude John was asking for. 'I will keep that in mind. Alright, let's get this trial going. I assume the prosecution and defense are ready since time is not really a factor in this mental world we're in?'

John smiled in the real world. 'Yes, you're correct Your Honor. Let's get started.'

The judge returned to his chair and Mr. Powell was ready to start recalling witnesses. The testimonies were practically the same as before, except this time everyone was able to see what each witness saw, heard, smelled, and touched during the questioned periods. The testimony by Mr. Carl Odeh was different however, now that the truth of his mental coercion was revealed. He was in fact with his two friends on the other side of Complex San Francisco when Creator was trying to find the survivors of the downed flight. The testimonies of the witnesses in JCPenney were also the same except once again, everyone was able to see the events in high definition through the eyes and ears of the witnesses.

The time had come to question Eibren Milows, which Robert initiated, but Eibren clung to the 5th Amendment when asked if he had manipulated Creator's mind, or if he was in the vicinity of JCPenney during the death of Malara. The judge backed up Eibren's rights, and Robert changed tactics.

'Your Honor, in this situation, I would ask the court allow the testimony of Mindseye, who shadowed Mr. Milows' mind during the trial and in past situations.' Robert asked wanting Mindseye to take the stand.

Charles objected to the request, even though he was convinced Creator was innocent; but it was his duty to object since the witness was also the one dictating the unusual situation the trial had morphed into.

Judge Cambridge denied the objection on the basis that it was the defense's right to call a new witness even though the witness was in charge of linking all thoughts to the entire audience. It was all a formality to him, since the jury and audience had already seen what Eibren had done and couldn't force the audience to forget what was placed directly into their memory. Now it would be put on record as the recorder was typing away in the real world what the testimonies and actions were in the virtual courtroom.

Outside of the courtroom FBI, SIA, and Florida police officers were feverishly attempting to enter the floors on and around the courtroom, but it seemed to evade their every attempt. A SWAT team would get to the elevator door and force their way inside only to find out they forced themselves into a closet which was also a fake closet. Any attempt to enter the building by law enforcement not inside during the trial only ended up in entering another building, blocks away from the courthouse. Susan had teleported Eibren to SIA headquarters where he was taken into custody, but apart from that, her mental illusions were keeping anyone from interfering with the virtual trial John was conducting. It was something Jared would have been very impressed with, but he wasn't near the courtroom or State for that matter, knowing this frame attempt had to run its course without him.

Everyone saw what actually happened with Creator's mind being manipulated to think he was stopping Judge from killing other people. The virtual courtroom returned to normal once the defense closed their case. The mental projections people saw were gone and everyone was only seeing what they could perceive in the material world as they knew it since birth. The television broadcast resumed, with many messages coming in from outside the courtroom asking what was happening. Judge Cambridge pounced on the gavel bringing the now not so quiet courtroom to order.

"Officers, will you notify the authorities outside that everything is under control." Judge Cambridge turned to the camera. "For those of you who were watching, the trial was performed in a virtual courtroom. All that occurred is recorded, and the closing remarks will now be given. I assume Mr. Milows is in SIA custody?"

"Yes, he is Your Honor." Charles Powell replied, having been informed by John to that fact.

"Well then counselor, let's continue."

Closing remarks were given, but it was very hard for Charles to come up with a strong basis for declaring Creator guilty of 1st degree murder or manslaughter. His main focus was to state that because Creator had taken upon himself to fight criminals with the use of his super powers and government backing, it was a given that Malara Phoenix and her unborn child were used as the victims for a frame-up. Charles considered asking for a dismissal, but that would not go well with the people nor was it justly warranted for George Phoenix's sake. The trial had to go to completion and the jury would have to come up with a verdict, if the District Attorney's office were to keep some semblance of control and power in the justice system.

Robert knew Charles was doing what he could to let the jury perform their duty and appreciated his professionalism in a delicate situation. Robert's closing remarks was confidently stated with a request for the jury to make a not guilty verdict and allow Creator to return to crime fighting; however, towards the end of his statement, everyone was surprised to hear Creator speak.

"I know I shouldn't be speaking right now, but I need to have some time for myself." Richard said, stood up and started to walk outside of the courtroom.

There was an awkward pause, even from the judge.

"Creator, this is not proper procedure and I must ask you return to your seat." Judge Cambridge said.

Richard stopped in front of the two officers in front of the courtroom entrance, and turned towards the judge and jury. "You have seen everything there is to see. I'm tired of being called a baby killer, so you do what you want with your procedures, but I'm going to go outside to get some air." Richard turned to the officers. "You really think you can stop me from leaving?" Richard walked past them with little effort as the two men knew there was in fact nothing they could do to prevent him from leaving.

"Your Honor, if you may. Allow me to speak to Creator in private for a moment." Robert asked as he stood up and quickly walked backwards while facing the judge.

Judge Cambridge was about to slam the gavel once again, but he remembered what John told him earlier. In addition Mr. Thorn seemed to understand that contempt of court was something Creator was now playing with. "I will give you ten minutes counselor."

"Thank you Judge." Robert replied as Creator had already left the room.

The two police officers at the entrance had the double doors opened for Robert.

Richard stood in front of the large windows looking out to downtown Tallahassee. It was a few hours until sunset, but it didn't matter since the sun was shining into the corridor as if nothing could stop its beauty. Richard touched the metallic window frame in deep thought.

Robert walked up beside Richard, but kept quiet as if he was also captivated in the moment of the scenery.

"Are you here to convince me I should let justice take its course?" Richard broke the silence.

"You asked me why I took this case, and I lied to you." Robert replied.

"And that's coming from a lawyer I put my trust in?"

"I volunteered because I met a man a long time ago who had no fear in doing the right thing. You have been an idol of mine for many years ever since I met you in Miami."

Richard turned slightly towards Robert, but didn't look into his face. "So Max told you who I was?"

"No, Max never told me, and he doesn't know that I know. I put two and two together, since I had access to your incident at the university, and then all of the sudden a new superhero group turns up with the SIA. Yeah, it wasn't hard... I volunteered because I believe in you and the group. If I had your powers, I would have tried to do my best to fight crime as you have. But I know you are one of a kind and I couldn't hope to come close to the heroic job you've done and will do."

Richard sensed that Robert was honest and once again the thought of everyone not knowing his true identity popped up in his head as a lost cause. "I saw how some of the people see me, even though they have seen the evidence, they hate that I'm out there fighting evil. George has lost his family because of me, or people like me."

"You can keep feeling sorry for yourself if you want, but one thing I know in my heart is Malara would not want you give up. There are many more families you have and will save from suffering and death. Be the man I know you are, not just the hero everyone expects." Robert said and left Richard's side. "Everyone is waiting, don't let the bad guys get more leisure time on your watch."

Richard saw Robert's reflection on the glass as he returned

to the courtroom. The usual lawyer quick stride was now more of a casual walk into a grocery store. Richard felt much better now, he wasn't sure if it was because of Robert's confident motivational speech or the truth of the matter. Retirement was high on his to do list, but now it was a forgotten impulse. He thought about George and his extended family. Richard breathed under his breath and promised he would find closure for them and himself.

The courtroom was quiet as Richard returned to his seat, and Judge Cambridge instructed the jury to return to the jury room where they would be expected to deliberate and reach a verdict. John was abreast to everyone's feelings and thoughts, but he kept all the secrets to himself as if he knew nothing. He was very relieved that Richard was not depressed anymore, and Robert was there to help him. But what everyone, except Him and Susan, didn't know was that this was only the beginning of a chain of events which would cause criminals to fight harder against a wave of vengeance and fact finding by the good guys.

Judge Cambridge allowed Creator to wait with the defense team instead of a holding cell in the courthouse. Mindseye and Night were there with Creator as they waited for the jury to come to a decision. Susan left to stay in SIA headquarters to ensure Eibren didn't injury himself or attempt to escape. Robert's team was running around trying to gather administrative documentation and authorizations for wrapping up the case with a verdict, and a possible hung jury. But it was due to the intervention by Mindseye and Pandora that they had to jump through hoops, trying more to stifle gossip and confusion as many calls came into both sides of attorney teams and courthouse offices. Robert and his right hand woman, Kelly Rivers, were inside an office with Richard, John, and Larcis as they sat waiting for some take-out food. Robert hadn't eaten lunch and was hungry, but Larcis was the one most anxious to see food enter the room. He wasn't hungry or needed to eat, but he wanted something to do besides sitting on a leather sofa looking at book shelves and pictures on the wall of a law office.

"Robert, whatever the outcome, I want to thank you and your entire team for supporting me." Richard said after Kelly finished ordering the food.

"No thanks are necessary. I think you have done more for me than I have for all of you." Robert replied glancing at John and Richard.

"Well it's true that Mindseye here did a lot of work, but true support comes from people that care, I appreciate it very much and would always be there for any of you, that includes you too Mirage." Richard stated and looked at an unused spot on the second sofa corner.

Everyone looked in the direction of Creator's attention. A woman covered in a mixture of military style camouflage designs of all the colors of a massive paint pallet appeared out of thin air. The woman was very young by the smooth skin texture of her mouth area which was the only part of her body that was not shifting multicolor. Her hair strands were alternating colors ever so slowly putting a colorful computer screensaver to shame. She was about five feet nine inches tall and had a very sexy-athletic physique.

Kelly and Robert were surprised for a brief moment even

though they had dealt with the abnormal in the past; they weren't prepared for an invisible woman to appear in the room.

"How did you know I was here?" Mirage asked, her soft mellow gentle tone confirmed her youthfulness.

"It's a secret." Richard said. "Robert, Kelly; this is Mirage, the sixth member in the Eternal Champions.

"It's nice to meet you." Robert walked around the desk and extended a handshake.

Kelly followed suit, while Richard asked them to not reveal that Mirage existed. It was a rare event that Richard would reveal her identity to them, and they felt honored to have been so privileged.

Cindy hugged John, and Larcis who were like adopted brothers to her.

'How did you know she was there? I didn't sense her in any way.' John mentally asked Richard.

'The great Mindseye is clueless, who would have guessed.' Richard mockingly joked while he laughed in the mental message.

'Hey, Cindy is really invisible to all the senses, and mental perceptions, how did you know?" John pleaded.

'I'll tell you when we get home old friend.' Richard replied and started a conversation with Robert. "So Robert, what have I missed in these past nine months?"

Robert filled Richard in to world and local news, but most importantly he was able to tell Richard how George had been living his life along with Malara's extended family. It was not in great detail, but Richard was going to find the details in time, wanting to do something for George and Malara's parents out of a desire to help them short of bringing Malara back to life. He didn't feel obligated, but felt a desire to give them favor out of love for life and the life they had lost.

An hour had elapsed when the group got word that a verdict had been reached. Mirage instantly turned invisible and followed the group back to the courtroom. The deliberation was extremely quick for a murder trial which put many people on edge. Robert was confident that Richard would be exonerated, but was uneasy knowing that his time with SIA had come and would completely change. He was already famous for defending Creator and a non-guilty verdict would definitely place him as one of the most wanted lawyers in America. He guessed Max knew that the outcome would place him in a position to leave the agency with full retirement, or continue to work for them solely as a litigator. But his options would be many and he needed to take things one day at a time.

It was early evening when the jury in a unanimous decision declared Creator not guilty of all charges. The people in the courtroom were for the most part at ease with the verdict, even George who eyed Richard closely while the verdict was being read off. Judge Cambridge concluded the trial and congratulations were exchanged.

Richard was attentive to his surroundings and made his way to George who was on his way to the exit. "Mr. Phoenix, I would like to speak with you." Richard called out as people made an opening for Creator to get close to George.

An officer was next to George waiting in case he didn't want to speak with Creator, but the officer was dismissed by George's approving nod. "It's okay." George whispered.

"I cannot bring your wife and child back to you. But I know from what Mindseye has found out, Eibren Milows wasn't working alone. I give you my word that I will find everyone responsible for their deaths and keep them from hurting others."

"You will make them pay?" George asked in a cold monotone.

"Yes, they will pay." Richard stated without delay.

"I will be looking out for good news then." George replied and continued out of the courtroom with a weary gaze.

Robert interrupted Richard's attempt to continue outside with the rest of the crowd. "Creator, it's suggested you leave once everyone else has vacated. I have sent out my assistants to answer questions to the media, but it is only preparatory. If you don't want to make a statement now, just let me know and we can go out through a rear exit. Or you can fly away from the roof."

"I want to make a statement, so I'll wait." Richard replied and watched the crowd leave the room. John and Larcis both joined the pair, as well as Mirage who was constantly by Richard's side the entire time.

Richard seemed happy, but not overjoyed like many people who had just been pronounced not guilty of two capital crimes. He was more in deep thought as if he were a head coach brainstorming the next play in a football game.

Richard was quickly processed out of the State's custody, which was when he turned back into his normal Creator costume image, instead of the suit and Brad Pitt look a-like face.

It wasn't long before Richard as Creator, stepped outside in front of a makeshift podium stand with a microphone. Camera flashes increased once Robert Thorn announced that Creator would be making a statement.

Creator's glasses disappeared, but his black eyeballs were very obvious and ominous. "As you know, the verdict is not guilty, and I'm not here to say I'm happy about it. I was framed by a man called Eibren Milows, but he wasn't alone. So for the record on public television, I want to tell you people responsible for the death of Malara and her son, I am coming for you and you will pay for the evil you have done. All of you."

Kelly and a few people in the background showed a slight facial expression of surprise and apprehension. Robert kept his cool as legally it was a very bad idea to announce a threat on national television, but it was a bold first move on Creator's part to take the fight to their doorsteps. A roar of questions erupted from the more than forty journalists and special investigators.

Creator pointed to one of the reporters.

"Creator, WCNX News, Who are those people you are threatening?"

"They know who they are, that's all that matters right now." Creator replied and pointed to another raised hand.

"Debra Gale, TCC Gazette. Do you have anything to say

to Malara's family, for the record?"

The dark glasses materialized back on his face. "Yes, Debra. I have spoken to George Phoenix, but would like to extend my deepest regret for their loss to all of the families and friends involved, and promise to bring closure to them as well as to me."

The audience roared again with Creator's name, trying to get his attention.

Creator pointed to another reporter, "One last question."

"Tom Klain, WHC Network. So do you accept some responsibility for Malara's death even though you were found not guilty?"

"I accept that Eibren mentally fooled me to kill Malara, but rest assured I take responsibility for bringing the real criminals to justice. Thank you for your questions." Creator said; walked to the side, bid Robert and his team goodbye, and flew away along with Mindseye, Night, and Mirage at his heels.

Richard flew out of sight and John took over by teleporting all four of them to the Eternal Domain battle room. The extent of John's powers were not known to the world and Richard wanted to keep it that way knowing that the less the enemy knew about them, the better.

Chapter Four

❖---⁜ ✪ ⁜---❖

A Lasting Impression

Windsor, Canada

A heavy weight seemed to press down on Jean's chest. Project Outlaw was initiated many months ago and SIA headquarters and resident offices were being monitored 24/7. The verdict of not guilty and Creator's statement for finding justice placed Outlaw at risk of pointing incriminating evidence to her and the CEA. The Magistrate was also bound to make things personal and eliminate her because she was the source of Eibren's situation and their own downfall under imminent attack from the Eternal Champions. She constantly tried to plan things through, and find a way to destroy the Magistrate without the CEA or SIA and yet keep her and Jared together. Jared was very confident that he and Natasha had covered their tracks. But it didn't matter to her since the Magistrate and the Eternal Champions were not concerned about incriminating evidence and didn't have to follow legal procedures in finding them since they were out to seek and destroy. Now that telepathic evidence was in Mindseye's favor, giving Creator a reason to shoot first and then take prisoners later was the probable outcome facing whoever was linked to Eibren. Jean had not gone to work in over a week and the safe house Jared provided for them would not be safe for long. The Magistrate had a very large network of contacts and in many cases unknowing sources of people with access to large amounts of information on things in the streets.

Mentalists were different from normal telepaths or psychics. Mentalists were telepaths with added skills as con artists, thieving, assassination, and/or expert illusionists or controllers. Eibren was a strong illusionist, but Pandora and Mindseye were far stronger than what was on file. The Eternal Champions would find her in time, and she would not be able to defend herself, physically or mentally; that was if the Magistrate didn't find her first.

Jean awoke in a cold sweat. Her pillow and sheets were wet as if she had a bad fever. But she was in perfect health, except for her nerves which were being brought to their limits. Jared sat up and hugged her softy.

"It's okay Jean."

Jean turned toward Jared and hugged him back as they lain-back down. "We can't hide forever."

"I know. That's why we are going to take down the Magistrate as fast as possible."

Jean was comforted to hear Jared say that without her having to command or suggest it. She never admitted to it, or told

Jared, but he knew already that the Magistrate was always her enemy and it was them she wanted revenge on, if it was her final act in life. "What about the Eternal Champions?"

"I have a plan which will work, but you must trust me. Whatever happens, you must not give them any reason to attack you when they find us. But for now, Natasha will be here soon so we can move somewhere safer, and start planning to take the Magistrate head on. Okay?"

"So far your plans haven't worked out very well." Jean commented with a slight sarcastic sneer.

"The plan to get Creator to retire was sound. He chose to fight back instead of living in his sorrow. It was a gamble, but the best one. I knew that the frame-up was a long shot, and I knew Eibren would probably be caught. That's why I had no problem with him being lead operative and helping him, when he was selected to take the mission. The Magistrate will look hard for us and spread their resources out. They will also be expecting the Eternal Champions to come to their doorsteps, not us. But you know my best plan did work."

"What plan was that?" Jean stared at him with strong anticipation as to what he would say.

"I planned for us." Jared smiled.

"Really? So your plan was for me to accidentally not kill you." Jean laughed.

"Accidents happen in plans sometimes." Jared replied with a kiss.

They enjoyed each other for a while before a tall slender woman entered through the security door downstairs. Her long black hair was very wavy and stylish like a super model. Her wide eyes and well placed makeup, pure white blouse, blueberry single button jacket, black silky tight slacks, and high heel Carven bow back jungle-print court shoes distinguished her as a very wealthy or classy young lady. She didn't carry a purse, but it would have been expected since she wore a forty thousand dollar assortment of neck, finger, and wrist jewelry on top of the expensive clothing.

"Brat, I'm home." Natasha yelled with a slight European accent.

"We'll be right down in a little while!" Jean yelled from upstairs.

Natasha wasn't accustomed to hearing a woman reply for her brother, but considering the situation, it brought up a warm happy feeling she hadn't had in a long time. She walked into the open kitchen floor plan and helped herself to a glass of water and fresh fruits on the breakfast table. Her entire flashy attire changed into a long sleeve dark gray cotton shirt, faded black jeans, and candid pump shoes as she sat down at the table. Her long wavy black hair shorten to her collar bone, but its silky shine remained. Her brown eyes changed color to sky blue. Her bone structure even changed as if a completely different woman was in the house. There was no morphing of clothes, sound, or colorful bright lights; the clothes appeared instantly in a blink of an eye. She reached in her back pocket and withdrew a deck of playing cards. She spread out the deck and shuffled it with one hand while eating an apple with the other. She eyed the deck as if she were going to cut it, and she did cut it, but the top card on the half of deck still on the table showed an ace of spades facing up. With a flick of her thumb on the half of deck she had picked up, the three remaining aces flipped out onto the table revealing all four aces.

It was a magician's card trick, but to her it was more than that. The cards disappeared in an instant and were replaced by four platinum credit cards and a deck of various social security cards, personal photos, and driver's licenses. "As easy as taking candy from a sleeping baby."

Natasha smiled, "No, it was much easier than that." Jared had taught her well and the people she encountered physically gave the cards and photos to her as if she were the ATM, social worker, cashier, business associate, friend, or a police officer. She carefully looked through the cards and set more than half to the side, knowing they would be useless for their purpose if not used within the next twelve to twenty-four hours. Once the person found out their card was lost or stolen, then they would deactivate the cards or inform the proper authorities. Jared had instructed her to find specific people for his plan to work. Stealing someone's identity was very easy with their powers, but using that information was hard since the implementation of AI safeguards countrywide. The added safeguards were due to the super killer virus incident a few years ago making it so they would be found out quickly should they use credit cards or try to get money. Illusions helped in bypassing many safeguards but they had a small window, and Jared was hoping that the targets would not report their lost documents because of who they were. In particular, the drug pushers and pimps from downtown Detroit who would hesitate to report such loses or notice before they were taken advantage of.

Jared and Jean eventually made it down to the kitchen, each with a relaxed and cheerful aura about them. “Did you find what we needed?” Jared asked.

“Since when have I failed you?” Natasha quickly replied.

Jared signed. “Well there was that one time. Oh, never mind, that was somebody else. Okay, anyways, let’s see what we have.”

Jean sat across from Natasha as they both exchanged a goofy half smile at Jared’s weak attempt of a joke.

“What are these going to do for us? We don’t need money.” Jean inquisitively asked.

“No, but we do need real covers for our people to go into a police recruiting station with a complaint, in distress or asking for information which is something the magistrate won’t expect.” Jared explained.

“Alright, but why so many? There has to be more than fifty people here?”

“Because, we need more than twenty decoys in case we are compromised and when we do make our presence known. This recruiting police station on West Fort Street is flooded with magistrate disciples, and we need to be able to start distractions on the spot as we move in and out.”

“So you know where the leaders are?” Jean asked seeing that his plan was an attack plan, and not one to gather information.

Jared moved his chair away from the table, looking at both women. “I had an idea a year ago, but I wasn’t for sure until a few months ago.” Jared replied and turned his head towards Natasha.

“My illusions aren’t very strong, but they don’t have to be when you’re looking for a paper trail.” Natasha said as she reclined back on her chair.

“The Magistrate mentalists are so preoccupied in covering their minds and criminal deeds, that they ignore the digits and routines of people they use to finance their living expenses. So I was able to track the expenses of janitorial and food consumption habits to this police station.” Natasha started to explain.

“It’s normal for large amounts of money to be budgeted for food and TP.” Jean interrupted.

“Yes, but you wouldn’t believe how much a health nut would spend on a diet made specifically for mentalists. There are maybe over 150 people eating there with a mentalist diet used by Michael himself; all eating out of the station.” Natasha grinned with pride.

“Really?” Jean’s eyes widen with approval.

“Michael won’t be there, but it will bring him out of his fortress.” Jared added.

“So he losses all those disciples; he can make more.” Jean said with disappointment after hearing Michael Stockwell, the leader of the Magistrate, was still out of their reach.

“His elect prodigy is there at the moment. Michael will want to surface to get his revenge in person.” Jared stated.

"Alright, so what are we looking at?" Jean asked thinking they would make plans in the kitchen.

"We need to move to our staging area first. Are the crews ready?"

"They will all be there in ten hours fourteen minutes, and counting." Natasha replied.

Jared picked up all the cards from the table and everyone sterilized the house. They worked quickly and thoroughly even though the maid service was scheduled to arrive within the hour to clean some more for the real residents who would return to their home that same evening.

Jared's mental illusions were perfect and the occupation of homes was easy for him, making it so the homeowners left for a vacation or outing having obtained money prices, or real vacation packages and the like. The Magistrate were too spread out with mentalists to be able to sense Jared's ghostlike movements, and they were not prepared for Natasha who was capable of moving around their contacts and scouts without their knowledge.

The trio moved to the staging area in a basement of an old Canadian paint processing plant across the river from the recruiting police station. Jared laid out the plan to infiltrate the recruiting station to include the adjacent four story gutted out building which was used as a training site for the recruits. An underground complex was below the building no more than three years old, but it was aged with neglect since the disciples were always focused on enhancing their mental powers instead of caring for the complex.

Natasha would distribute the identifications to a group of volunteers who only knew they were being paid to act parts in a con. Jared would cover the three of them with his illusions and get a lieutenant or leader to gain access to the complex under the building next to the station. The prodigy mentalist was Adam, a young but ruthless second in command of all of Michael's disciples. Not all of the disciples in the recruiting station were under Michael's vow of allegiance, but the one disciple that mattered to Jared was Adam. It wouldn't be easy because if Adam was worth his weight in gold, he would know how to counter Jared's illusions or at least sense them. But Jean was there, and as long as Jared guided her, she could neutralize and kill Adam without any major problems. The unknown variable in the plan was they didn't know how many controllers were in the complex or aboveground buildings.

The controllers were the mentalists who were Magis, being proficient in mental domination. The normal humans in the recruiting station would have definitively been brainwashed several times over by them as to keep any suspicion fall on the activities of people moving in and around the area. Jared assumed there would be at least three controllers, since the complex had been operating for a while. Two controllers were sufficient for their needs to mind control people as desired. Non-magistrate recruits that passed the training would be controlled to be happy to request specific assignments, and instructors would be held on a very short leash. Jared was sure another controller would be there shadowing Adam as a bodyguard. The controllers might be able to command them to lower their defenses, or fight each other; but Jared was prepared for up to five controllers and Adam.

The blueprints of the complex were unwillingly drawn up from the mind of one of the builders. Jean wondered how Jared and Natasha were able to get the information, but she knew better than to ask someone who could alter reality in the minds of people. She wasn't certain, but she had a feeling that Natasha was able to read minds to a certain degree which gave her the ability to make people see realistic illusions. Jared on the other hand was able to force his illusions into the minds of people that were so real they could kill. Fooling someone to print out or draw blueprints was probably a very easy task for them.

Jean remembered how Jared kissed her in the past with his illusions, and it was as real as any other time to her, no matter how much she knew it was an illusion. It was creepy because Jared could make someone believe a fake history. Even though there could be physical proof to the contrary, the person would not be able to disbelief or forget the memories without some sort of mental intervention by a very powerful telepath.

"There are living quarters and meditation chambers all throughout the six story underground maze. The higher ranking mentalists are housed closer to the surface. Most of the larger rooms are for training, and life support. Adam will likely be in these sections of the complex, or probably in the Commodore's office area in the recruiting station itself." Jared explained.

"Why isn't Adam with Michael?" Jean asked, feeling as if she were the odd person in the group, not knowing already.

"Adam has been visiting the station for the past few years, screening new recruits and strengthening his powers by using the recruits as human experimental subjects. He arrived yesterday along with a new iteration of cadets."

"I'm assuming he's not a push over." Jean commented.

"He's Michael's prodigy disciple so he will know how to sense my illusions and maybe even be able to fight back. But that's where you come in." Jared eyed Jean. "I will neutralize the controllers, Nat will confuse the disciples, and you will freeze Adam to death. Simple."

"Simple for now, but what's going to happen after Adam dies?" Jean asked.

"Michael will travel to the city and hunt us down once he hears that we're hiding here."

"Detroit's one of Brat's favorite places. Michael will think we'll hide among the factions and mafia. He'll look hard and walk into our trap." Natasha said, Brat meaning brother from her Polish upbringing.

The three worked out the details of their backup covers, and timeline. Jean was accustomed to knowing secrets, but the fewer she knew, the less she could unwillingly expose in a deep mental scan. There would definitely be a mental scan of everyone entering the building, but that was only if a person was known to have entered.

It was evening when the three of them crossed the river by boat and stood near the railroad tracks and cars behind the recruiting station. Lights covered the football field size area, but the three of them were invisible to the camera. Natasha's light illusions were perfect and soon they were over the fence line and on police property.

A metro bus rolled down the street colliding with the meshed metal fence, nicking the recruiting station and continuing into the training building corner. Several fence poles and mesh were dragged into the building as the bus caved in a good portion of its concrete structure.

People started to pour out of the station in response to the commotion. People seemed to stream out of the bus, but in fact most were never on the bus as they stood waiting along the sidewalk for their queue. The surveillance cameras only saw the bus plow into the building, and not the nearby walkers who jumped into the bus and then pretended to have been in the bus. The actors were well paid and their memory blocks were strong so when they intentionally hit their heads or bruised an arm, the fact that it was intentional injury was forgotten. The driver was unconscious and stuck in between rubble, the front dash, and his chair. Over a dozen police recruits and station officers rushed in like heroes getting twenty-one passengers to safety.

Jared concentrated on the people outside and just inside both buildings. There was a large hole which was created by the bus but barely allowed for a person to enter in between the bus and wall into the training building without using the front door or windows. The mentalists outside and even one controller couldn't see Jared, Jean, and Natasha crawl single file through a gap just seven feet from where the driver's seat was. There was no visual, audio, odor, or mental indication that the three had entered the training building.

Jean walked behind Jared while Natasha covered their back. She could see Jared walking casually as if he worked in the building going directly to the third staircase on the west end. The first floor was more or less an open bay with metallic and concrete pillars supporting the floors above. The east end was built up with walls, and four people burst out of an opening rushing toward the bus. Two men and two women dressed in Detroit police department uniforms quickly assessed the situation and acted more like firefighters by getting a water hose and figuring out what pillars to start reinforcing. Jean stared at them thinking they would be found out, but the illusions Jared was creating made them invisible. However, Jared waited for a moment as if he was examining them, grading their actions.

Jared had told her not to talk while they moved around, so she held her tongue and they all stood watching the scene. A few minutes passed and Jared motioned them with a wave of his hand to follow him. They entered the staircase and worked their way downward. Jean was sure that Natasha was making them invisible with her illusions, so what was Jared doing?

"Follow my lead; you will be Cony, the brunette. Nat, you will be the blonde." Jared said to them as they walked down the staircase.

Jean wasn't for certain of what was going on, but it seemed that Jared examined the people on the first floor so he could get enough information about them to use them for an illusion. The covers they memorized were covers for their minds and not the actual people that they were impersonating.

"There's a controller on this floor. I sense eighteen

people." Jared said as they stopped in front of a key locked door two floors from the very bottom of the staircase.

Natasha got in front and started to pick the lock on the door. Jared looked around, but mostly at Jean. "I love how your makeup is always so perfect." Jared joked.

"Hmm, I don't have any makeup on." Jean smugly countered.

Jared's eyes and mouth widen in surprise. "Really? Wow." He turned back towards the door and his face got serious except for a faint smile in the corner of his mouth.

"So you see him?" Jared asked Natasha.

Natasha paused before turning the handle on the door. She concentrated as if trying to burn a hole through the door with imaginary heat vision. "Yes, I see him." She said as if a little proud of herself.

"Good. He will scan minds once we enter the hallway and announce ourselves. Make sure everyone sees us where we stand and move. Once I have entered his mind, then you can move the rest to a room and knock them out."

"Okay Brat." Natasha replied.

"What do I do?" Jean asked, thinking she could help.

"Nothing. Adam will sense you, once you use your powers, so keep them ready for him alone."

Jared motioned Natasha and she opened the door outward. Jared stepped into the hallway which opened up to a corner of the floor as in most hotels and office buildings. The cyber lock was carefully closed with an electronic brush as not to trigger the alarm when the real contacts reconnected.

A well built man wearing a black security guard uniform came from their direction wanting to see who was down the hallway.

Jared closed his eyes, but walked quickly as if he could see where he was going. “We’re looking for Magi Adam. It’s important we talk to him.” Jared yelled down the hall while the illusion of Dan, one of the men who was in the bus accident scene was already permeated into the security guard’s mind. Jared made the guard think the three of them turned the corner instead of entering the floor through the staircase.

“I’m sorry Mr. Liken, but all floors have been secured. Magi Adam, is not on this floor and no one is suppose to leave until the all clear is given.” The guard stated.

“Is there a secure phone I can use or some other way I can talk to him?” Jared came within arm’s reach of the guard who seemed to be okay with it since he recognized all of the three people in front of him.

“I can take you to Magi Luke, he will know what to do.” The guard replied and turned back down the hallway.

Jared looked at Natasha and nodded. Magi Luke was probably the controller and so far everything was well. The guard took them down the hall and into an open area which was the central point for people coming into the floor.

Another guard was behind a security counter monitoring five video screens. Two elevators were in perfect visual position from the counter, as well as every hallway entry being monitored on closed-circuit cameras. But that fact didn't prevent three people instantly appearing on a monitor and no one seemed to have remembered or noticed it. Jared's slight of mind made sure of that. Especially since Natasha was adding light illusions on top of his mental illusions.

Jared could sense Magi Luke's mental thoughts pulse into the floor lobby-like area. They were passive in nature, but enough to let him know that the controller was paying attention to the security monitors or at least the minds of the security guards.

The mentalists talked to one another with thought projections and many disciples were required to mentally speak while in the station and complex as a training event. Jared knew that this might be a problem and perhaps it was expected they communicate in like fashion. So, when Magi Luke started to enter his mind, Jared allowed it with a projection of fear.

'What is going on? Who are you?' A cool and sinister voice asked within Jared's surface thoughts.

'I'm your worst nightmare, Luke.' Jared replied, but an image of Mindseye was revealed to Magi Luke instead of his mental attributes.

An elderly man with gray hair sat in a meditation chamber three rooms away from the trio. Magi Luke instructed three disciples with him in the room to go to the security counter. The mental attributes of a person normally tell a telepath a mental picture of a person's concept of themselves as if looking at a mirror. A person knows themselves so well after many years of living that even if they were psychic and thought they were another person or spirit, their mental attributes would reveal who they really were. Luke was a magi and very experienced in mental warfare, but Jared was also a very experienced and powerful mentalist.

Jared could sense Luke attack him, Jean, and Natasha with a paralyzing mental command. Luke's mental attack was perfect, but it wasn't a perfect world since Jared had already entered the Magi's mental perception of reality. All three of them fell to the ground as would be expected when the mind is shocked into a form of a vegetated state. The monitors showed the security guards running to their side and securing them as the three disciples arrived to assist them.

The scene however was opposite of what the monitors showed in reality and what Luke mentally sensed. Natasha and Jean ran around and knocked people out by injecting them on the neck with a chemical compound, and tied them up to include the disciples. Each person was oblivious to the activity of the three intruders as if everyone was in a different section of the twilight zone with nothing abnormal occurring.

Magi Luke stood up and moved out of the chamber thinking the intruders had been neutralized and subdued. He approached the security lobby and froze in his tracks. He sensed five people on the ground with their minds resembling a person's mind who was passed out from alcohol or other drug. He saw Dan Liken and the two women behind them, waiting for him to appear in the corridor to the lobby. Luke concentrated on Dan, Mindseye, or whoever it was, walking towards him but instant darkness fell on him. His limp body fell to the ground as a bullet bounced around in his skull.

The semi-loud thump was muffled by a short but very thick silencer on Jared's pistol. He holstered the weapon and stood above Magi Luke, looking for any signs of life in his mind. Not that a hole in the man's skull was enough confirmation, but mental tricks were his specialty and the best way to know the truth was by sensing mental activity or in this case, complete inactivity.

Jared and his team quickly hid the bodies in the meditation chamber Luke had exited from. The plan was to get someone to lead them to Adam, but now they had to improvise. "Okay, let's go up one floor since Adam isn't on this one, and see if we can get someone to lead us to him before anyone finds these people." Jared said.

"We need to hurry. There'll probably be a security check and the guards won't be able to answer it." Natasha pointed out.

Jared led the way to the staircase and preceded upward one flight. The bottom floor was primarily filled with machinery and considered a location Adam wouldn't ever think of visiting. They made it to the floor in a similar fashion, the only difference was the security force was larger and more people were present. But all were easy to fool with their illusions, and instead of trying to silence all fifty-nine people, they bypassed the floor and moved up an additional floor.

The three entered the floor with caution as both Jared and Natasha sensed a controller and a more powerful mentalist probing around the complex. "They know we're here." Jared said.

Jared walked out of the staircase as if nothing had occurred. The spherical security camera bulbs were telekinetically smashed into the ceiling as they walked down the maze of hallways. Men and women walked passed them unaware of their presence or if they did notice them, they were ignored as Natasha's illusions covered their identities.

Jared concentrated on the controller and confirmed that Adam was the other mentalist.

Adam was fairly young for a magi at the age of thirty-two, but his hair was brittle and gray from extensive use of his mental powers. His eyes were grayish black and his skin was pale. Jared didn't really understand why the metabolism and aging properties of certain people were accelerated, but he ventured to guess it was due to chemical or alpha wave experimentation. His own eyes had turned gray in color, but it was a natural effect when his powers grew stronger as a teenager over a decade and a half ago. The genetic trait came from his parents who were partially able to keep him away from the Magistrate's influence.

The controller assigned to Adam was a female named Sarah. She was a magi and much older than Adam, but probably not as powerful. Power wasn't everything and Jared knew she was more experienced and would be the one to contend with first.

Natasha spun her web of illusions slowly shifting room locations and people. It didn't attract the attention of Adam or Sarah. Her illusions were passive in nature and didn't attack the reasoning side of the brain and focused on altering the perception of what the person knew or sensed at that moment.

It took a few minutes but the only people who had not really moved locations were the people sitting at a desk. However, they were not facing their desks and were sitting on their chair in the middle of open space.

Jean walked behind Jared seeing people act as if they were extras in a movie milling about their own business ignoring the cameras. Natasha was falling behind as she concentrated on the activities of all the people on the floor.

Jean tapped Jared on the back of his shoulder blade.

Jared turned his head back to see Natasha who was now stopped in her tracks with a thousand mile stare on her face.

Jean put her hands up and opened them to heaven with a 'what now' type of expression on her face.

Jared motioned Jean to follow him in a hurry. He jogged lightly on his feet towards the room Sarah and Adam were at. Jean prepped herself, knowing once they entered the room she would need to be careful to use her ice powers at the right time. Otherwise she might freeze Jared by mistake since they would be in the same room.

Magi Sarah stood in the corner of the large office as Jared entered. Jared felt a heavyweight of dizziness swell in his ears. He lost his balance and fell to the cork tiled floor. Jean didn't enter the room but she too fell to the ground.

Jared took rapid deep breaths as if about to dive underwater in a very cold body of water. He shot out a mental pulse of darkness into anyone who was near him.

Adam and Sarah felt the darkness, but they both ignored it as they perceived mental activity and knew where Jared and Jean were. In addition, the illusions Jared was projecting were weaken with Sarah's mental domination command, which would have knocked out a normal person into a deep coma.

Jean thought she was in the room, but knew better as the edge of the doorway marked her arm with pain. She could feel the dizziness but was able to stay on all fours looking at a single spot on the floor which was now only a big blur. Darkness suddenly replaced the blur for two seconds, and she knew it was her turn.

Jean sat on her heels, but kept her hands on the floor and shot out a wave of cold in all directions two feet above the floor. The intensity of the wave instantly dropped the temperature to below ten degrees Fahrenheit in all the rooms around Jean.

Jared was laying flat on the floor, but the bitter cold was still very uncomfortable. He was expecting it thou, and focused on taking mental control back from Sarah.

Adam was sitting back waiting to pounce on Jared after Sarah had her fun, but the instant freezing of his body from the knees up took the air from his lungs. His eyes froze along with the air he was desperately gasping to breathe in. The light green magi robe wrapped around him did keep his unexposed skin from frosting over, but it failed to stop the abrupt initial shock to his body.

Sarah felt the numbing freeze and battled to control her body. In almost an instant she regained control and the ice berg effect on her body felt like an experience she had while in the northern arctic wasteland of Greenland. She squinted her eyes as if wanting to see what was happening in the room. Jared was walking towards her with a pointed gun. She concentrated on him commanding him to stop and shoot himself; but the attempt failed.

"You're not in control anymore Sarah. You're as good as dead." Jared said as he stopped three feet from her and fired the gun straight at her head.

Sarah stood there paralyzed unable to move as if she were stuck in a nightmare. The reality of the situation was death as the gun shot rang into her ears, but it was more of the feeling of the round forcing its way into her skull and brain for a microsecond that made the moment permanent.

Adam didn't hear any gun fire even with a silencer, but instead felt the dramatic difference in temperature rising as he fell to the floor along with his armchair. His position in the chair, and body convulsions inadvertently helped him fall sideways. He focused on his body and controlled the reflexive muscle twitching and lung contractions. His face and ears were numb, and the drastic change in temperature caused needle pinching all throughout his exposed skin. He clenched his teeth in anger using the emotion to focus on his surroundings, and ignore his great discomfort.

His cold eyes stayed opened as he saw Jean walk into the room which seemed to have become the inside of a frozen ice cream cart. He couldn't think straight, trying hard to enter her mind.

"This is for my sister." Jean said two yards away as she focused her powers on his body alone.

Jared was now standing up from the floor and walked slowly to Sarah who had collapsed in the corner of the room.

Adam's body froze into a murky blue and reddish pigment.

Jared pulled out his pistol and shot the mentally dead Sarah in the head without mercy.

Jean stepped away from Adam and faced Jared who was now next to her. "Didn't you already kill her with your illusions?"

Jared pointed his pistol at Adam. "This is called a double tap." The round went through Adam's head, almost shattering it completely off his body. Bloody ice particles splattered on the floor and top of the chair.

Jean smiled as the thought of avenging her sister seemed to be coming true. "What now?"

"That's my girl." Jared replied and deeply kissed her without warning.

Jean relented but after a moment broke it off. "What's that for?"

"Just trying to get warm." Jared smiled as he made his way out of the room.

"I'll get you warm later. But you still didn't answer my question."

"It's time to sign the calling card."

Jared rubbed his hands together and blew warm air into them as he approached Natasha. She was sitting with her legs crossed in the middle of the hallway. "Someone doesn't need to pay the AC anymore." She said with a slight chatter of her teeth.

"Are you ready?" Jared asked while he sat down in front of her.

"Yes, but the people outside will not be easy to corral."

Jean stood along the wall between the two, watching them as if they were mediating or holding a yoga session. The plan was to quickly ex-filtrate, but it seemed they had something else in mind before leaving.

Jared's mental projection went throughout the floor they were on and the floors below. The disciples who were put under in dreamland were his first targets. The drug used to put them to sleep would wear off in an hour, but the mental illusion Jared gave them put them into cardiac arrest and mental death. The humans who worked there out of ignorance or coercion were left alone to sleep it through.

Jean saw people enter the hallway lining up along the walls at the position of attention as if waiting to be inspected by a Drill Sergeant. She saw one security guard and wondered where the others were.

Jared and Natasha both opened their eyes and stood up, surveying the formation in the hallway. Natasha handed Jared her backpack and headed to the elevator with Jean following her. Jared went to the far side of the hall and started to shoot pairs of people in the head. The disciples and collaborators were positioned so one round would kill two people at a time. Jared packed ten extra magazines in the backpack, but it wasn't enough so he had to optimize ammunition usage.

"Why are we shooting people so much?" Jean asked Natasha.

"It's very messy, but my Brat knows what he's doing."

The elevator was operational, but no one in the complex was aware that anything was amiss even thought they were temporarily shutdown. Natasha and Jean entered the elevator holding the doors from closing. Jared quickly walked towards them with a wave of dead people trailing his wake of ruthless executions. He stopped at the last person and ripped the woman's shirt off. He then shot her and cleaned, as best he could, any blood splatter on the handgun and his person with the cotton shirt.

"Eighty-three people so far, but much more to go." Jared said as he entered the elevator.

Natasha pressed the upper floor button, and took the backpack from her brother. The elevator door opened and a long double column of people were already waiting at attention. Jean could count twenty-seven from what she could see.

Jared walked down the path as before shooting them without second thoughts. He got to the last person at the other end, but only stared at the young man before him.

He seemed no older than fourteen, but Jared knew he was younger. He took a relaxing breathe and hit the youngster on the collar bone with a karate chop, breaking it clean. The young man screamed in pain, fell flat on his butt, and woke up from

Natasha's illusion. Jared was ready and entered his mind only to knock him out as the youngster attempted to make sense of his environment and newfound pain.

He picked up the teenager over his shoulder and brought him into the elevator.

"We're going to take him with us?" Natasha asked wondering how far they would be hauling a limp body.

"Just up to the street, we'll let our people take him in and care for him."

"So, do we just go to the first floor then?"

"I'll carry him, you two can finish what we started." Jean interjected and cradled him with care.

They continued to the next floor and in like manner executed another fifteen disciples. The following floor was on street level, and Jared led Jean to the street while Natasha maintained the elevator from moving around. The controller on street level was sent on a wild-goose chase on top of the academy building. The other disciples were lined up in the gutted training building.

Twelve people were stationed around the block as lookouts giving Jared notice of new people in the area. The electronic implant in his head received the information instantly, but what it didn't do was give him an idea of whom was a mentalist and who were normal EMTs or firefighters responding to the intentional accident. The scene had been cleared of debris and the bus was already leaving the scene in tow when Jean carried the teenager out through the large hole in the corner wall.

Jared concentrated on his distractions and four people came out of recruiting station and waited for Jean on the street. Jared knew exactly where the last controller was and made sure none of his people and Jean's thoughts would betray them.

Jared was sure the controller was catching on to something being wrong because all communication with the people in the underground complex was too quiet. Natasha was able to use her illusions to get people to call in status reports and normal chatter on the radio, but now that everyone was asleep or dead, it left a mental void they couldn't fill. Jared could make the controller think everything was normal after the bus accident, but it would be a matter of time before he would know that he was in an illusionary world.

Jean handed over the teenager to four of Jared's people, and turned back. "Go to the rally point, we will be there no later than thirty-five minutes from now." Jared instructed.

"Okay." Jean replied and walked with the group away to the east. She had dyed her hair dark brown, but for good measure she covered her head with the hood of her coat sweater. She was not elegantly dressed but more like a wanderer matching the people Jared had hired to accompany her.

Jean breathed peacefully as if nothing had happened; but if she were nervous it was worrying about Jared and Natasha who were still in enemy territory. Over a year ago, she had no problem killing them herself, but now she loved Jared and trusted Natasha to have her back, for Jared's sake.

Jared quickly returned to his sister, and they went up the

building killing people as quickly and efficiently as possible. It wasn't long when a few disciples in the recruiting building started to notice irregular aspects of their fake environment. Either Natasha was getting tired or they had accidentally hit too many sharp objects or things causing pain or strong discomfort. She had less people to influence now, but the duration of the fake reality was taking its toll on her unique mental powers.

Jared was down to his last magazine when he mentally instructed the actors still in the area to start leaving as quickly as possible. Natasha followed him through the recruiting station entrance. Five police cars had entered the area and it was possible another controller had arrived. Jared focused on the eight people in the security entrance of the lobby and in less than a minute they all were breathing their last from shock and failed organs.

Natasha positioned the controller to come to them in the elevator. As soon as the door opened Jared was already inside his mind and made him believe the elevator had failed, plummeting him to his doom. Jared shot the controller in the head, making sure he wasn't somehow able to withstand the illusion which was strong and real enough to make him feel the sudden stop at the bottom of the elevator shaft.

The disciples on the second floor were corralled to the windows where they were made to dive head first into the concrete below; except for one who was led to the street.

Jared and Natasha walked back outside surveying the damage, Jared shooting two hurting disciples who had survived the fall.

The disciple, who wasn't harmed, was standing in the mist of the carnage as if in a hypnotic trance oblivious to his surroundings. Jared took off the disciple's upper clothing while Natasha withdrew a small and lean vest from the backpack. It was a form of a smuggler's device for hiding money or drugs. This vest however packed a special brew of eighty dark green crystals and finger size composite explosive bars. Natasha dressed the disciple covering the vest while Jared placed a deep command into his mind. Once both were satisfied with the new makeover, Jared elaborately commanded the man to personally tell Michael it was Jared who killed Adam. The disciple woke up from the trance and ran off to find his masters.

Jared and Natasha ran back behind the building and across the metal fence line across the railroad tracks to the river's edge. The boat which had brought them was let loose to drift downstream when they first crossed. Instead of trying to return to the staging area across the water into Canada, they ran eastward parallel to the river and railroad tracks. They ran a mile and a half to link back up with Jean who was waiting for them in an SUV.

"I assume all went well?" Jean asked as they entered the vehicle and drove off to a pre-designated location.

"Michael would have been persuaded not to get involved even for Adam's death; but for the death of one hundred sixty-seven followers. Yes, I think we left a lasting impression." Jared stated, but didn't smile.

He wasn't happy about killing so many people, and maybe some of them were innocent who fell with the wrong crowd under bad situations. People could change and it was one reason he allowed the teenager to live. The teen's future was still up in the air and his mind was altered by Jared's powers to make the teen permanently forget about the Magistrate. Jared would ask his trusted associates to take the teen in and raise him, with a modest fee of course. A change is his life might give him a new start. At least that's what Jared hoped for the young man.

Chapter Five

❖---⁂ ✪ ⁂---❖

I Want Him Dead

He talked about knowing your identity, but there's more." John paused.

"Jean Lorenz authorized the assassination attempt on Elizabeth. I'm assuming she knows who we are, or someone who knows our true identities, probably Jared." John stopped as he waited for Richard to ask questions.

Richard walked towards the elevator wanting nothing more than to see his wife and son. "Where are Liz and Alex?"

"They're on the way down right now. How are you father?" Erica's 3D hologram of a twelve inch tall woman appeared in front of Richard at chest level blocking the way to the elevator. She was not completely solid, but clothing like a greenish skin tight diving suit was keeping her from seeming naked.

Richard caught himself. "I'm sorry Erica for wanting to

only see Liz and Alex right now, but I hope you understand?"

"I understand. But remember that we all missed you too." Erica's seductive voice digitally echoed throughout the room.

Richard smiled. "What have you been up to?"

"I have been very busy since John gave me the information about the CEA and Eibren Milows. SIA has been trying to access their files and apprehend the director; but she has disappeared along with most data related to their existence. I am confident since they have abilities to affect minds that information was erased from several unknowing human sources with access to the data."

"Hmm, how is Eibren's interrogation going?" Richard asked more for John to answer than Erica.

"Susan should be back soon with everything he knows, but for now…" John replied and motioned to the elevator doors opening several yards from them.

A tall and very attractive woman with long brown wavy hair was carrying an almost two year old boy resting on her forearm as she hugged him close to her body. Elizabeth's very wide smile showed her perfect white teeth as she quickly walked out of the elevator.

Richard's face glowed with happiness even his totally black eyeballs seemed to reflect a gentle sense of joy. He ran to them and hugged both of them, kissing his wife and son. Alex was very rigid for a two year old and his skin was hard as steel as Richard took him from his mother. "So, did you miss me?" He asked him as he let the kid squeeze his fingers.

"Yes, I missed you." Alex replied and giggled slightly.

The pressure on Richard's fingers was like a crocodile's bite. He looked at Liz and then at John. "I hope he doesn't do this to everyone he meets."

John smiled. "Don't worry Richard; he knows you can take it. I had to enter his mind several months ago and instruct him on many things like his powers."

"Really?" Richard looked at his son's face and smiled... "Yeah, I see you like your mom's teal colored eyes."

"He can change outward appearance for a few days so far, but has problems with his skin." Liz said as they moved to the center of the battle room where there was a large sofa table and three sofas in a U-shape formation facing several large monitor screens.

"So that's why your skin's so hard." Richard stated and placed Alex next to him on the sofa. "Has mommy been taking good care of you?"

Alex didn't know how to reply to that question. "Yes, Mommy is always taking good care of you." Liz quickly replied for him and sat next to Richard with Alex on the other side.

They spent an hour talking and laughing before Susan and the rest of the group joined them. Robert and Becky, two of the live-in employees who knew of and assisted the superhero group also attended the reunion. It was a relaxing and joyous occasion as they all ate and toasted to family, friendship, and happiness.

The following morning was the start of Richard's work schedule revolving around the CEA and the Magistrate. Elizabeth, but more so Richard was very upset about the assassination attempt on Liz's life over two years ago. Not that it brought up bad feelings from the past, but the facts of the matter were never revealed until now.

The group as usual set their efforts into finding Jared, Jean, and any information on the Magistrate. Richard spent most of his time doing research in the battle room while the rest of the group maintained the farm or took care of errands out of costume. Cindy shadowed Larcis for a while, but she ended up by Richard's side trying to help as best she could. She was used to spying on people and watching Richard work fascinated her. Richard was talking to Erica and typing away information into his wireless super lightweight keyboard as if he himself was a super fast computer.

Videos and documented reports popped up in corners of the main screen and four other screens around the room. Cindy noticed that the information Richard was gathering was chronically grouped to specific screens; but other than that she couldn't see anything except a massive collage of information covering all topics and people.

"I know you told me we're looking for information, but what exactly are you doing." Cindy asked after seeing Richard slow down in his baseline queries.

Richard looked at her with a smile. "I'm looking for a pattern or a link to Jared."

"Huh, can't Erica find patterns faster and better?"

Richard leaned back on the sofa. "Super AIs are great and all; but my gut can find what they or other people can't. No disrespect intended."

"None taken Richard." Erica replied from the surround sound system in the room.

"So what does your gut say now?"

Richard looked at several piles of printed documents on the battle room table. "My gut says we're looking for the wrong person."

"So we should focus on Jean or someone in particular in the Magistrate?"

Richard flipped through papers. "No, there's a mystery person or people helping Jared. See here; it states he worked with teams in the past, yet recently he went solo. I don't buy it. If he's the mentalist all the evidence indicates he is, he would have connections and knows people who will help him in the shadows. We need to look for a lifelong friend or relative."

"And how do we find an invisible person, especially if it's a recent friend or trusted person whom he groomed into being a follower or something like that?" Cindy smiled knowing it was a pun since she was an invisible and mysterious person herself. The only people that knew about her true identity were in the group, Joshua, and her adopted brother Lee.

"We ask the person who might know." Richard paused for a second. "Erica, tell John and Susan I need them here for a mission."

"I'm informing them now." Erica quickly replied.

Cindy was eyeing information about the death of Neutronium, the founder and ex-leader of the Emerald Legion, back in September of 1990. "Why are you going back almost 30 years?"

"I don't believe in coincidences. Everything is linked in some way. Even you for instance; you told me Joshua rescued you from the Founders eight years ago."

"Yes, that's right; and?"

"The Founders was a private foundation which led research in mental abilities. When they were destroyed and broken up, the CEA and SIA both seized resources and people that have turned into these groups of telepaths that roam and assist them as agents or whatever they use them for. Telepaths like these were probably around, but not consolidated or used for national levels until maybe four or five years ago."

Many thoughts of the Founders and Cindy's past came to almost haunt her. She was safe from them now that they were all dead. But what Richard was saying was the ripple of cause and effect which took a different form of danger to her and other people's futures, because of the actions her family took against the foundation many years ago. She thought of the possibilities, but in the end trusted that Joshua was always looking out for her. Things might be worse now if the Founders hadn't been destroyed, so there was comfort in knowing Richard was involved in fighting this new threat along with Joshua.

"Things are coming into place and I don't like it." Richard stated after he noticed Cindy was in deep thought.

Susan and John teleported into the battle room with uncanny precision as not to disturb objects except the air they displaced in an abrupt exchange of space. "Good afternoon, Cindy!" Susan greeted her.

"Hi." Cindy smiled.

"We got your call Richard. What's up?" John asked and nodded to Cindy as a noon day greeting.

"Erica, I need you to correlate all information you have on videos and account transactions in the DC and Virginia area, linked to all CEA missions, safe houses, and Jared's last known whereabouts. In addition I need you to search any information on Jared's childhood and where he might have traveled to the present. Link all people with missions and bank transactions. John and Susan will help you fill in the gaps." Richard paused for a second and played the video of Mr. Patterson.

"Can you mentally find this man?" Richard asked John.

"It's a shot in the dark since I haven't scanned his mind before or know him very well, like in person. If he were a famous person, I could by chance find him, if someone was thinking of him because they are with him and then I could pin point his location. But considering most people don't think about themselves or people with them all of the time, this makes it very hard. Plus there are more minds I would have to scan because of the size of the area, and it would take me a while, if not impossible."

"I understand all of that; but what if I could narrow the search to a state or city?"

"Yes, I might be able to do it, but it might take me a day, and if it takes longer than that, it will probably not happen."

"Okay, once Erica has identified my mystery person you will look for that person to include Jared."

"Jared is probably blocking mental scans which is why we probably won't be able to find him even if we know the city. So, what are we missing here?" Susan stated.

"I'm betting a person Jared's age, a relative or very close friend is working with him and Jean. Jared would have protected Jean's mind and his own, but the other person not so much because he or she is off the grid."

"And if it's another mentalist with powers to be about to hide themselves?" John countered.

Richard looked at John a little frustrated. "It's a bet, you know a gamble. If all fails, we need to find the Magistrate leader and minions before they find Jared and Jean."

"You know, I didn't think of it that way. But, the Magistrate might have already found and killed them." John stated.

Richard smiled. His friend was right, he never considered that the Magistrate might have already silenced the situation, but the fact that Jared and Jean disappeared from the face of the Earth was an indication to him that they were in hiding. The Magistrate would probably not hide the deaths and instead make an example of them so others would fear them even more. “I haven’t lost a bet yet.”

“Yeah…” was John’s only reply since he had already lost hundreds of dollars betting against Richard, not once winning against him in the past five years.

“So how long are you going to take Erica?” Susan asked knowing the answer.

All of the screens in the room changed to show fifty photos of over twenty different women. “I think I have found our mystery person.” Erica stated as her twelve inch 3D hologram appeared above the battle room table.

Richard quickly scanned the information. “You think, or you know?”

“I think I know. These photos and videos were taken at specific times and locations during Jared’s mission parameters of three years since today. I was able to link these women to account information and also access to local police stations, and stores. I was able to link audio information to most of these women as being one person, so it is highly probable all of these women are the same person.”

“Could it be a shape shifter like Richard?” Cindy chimed in.

“It’s possible, but most shape shifters can alter their vocal cords to some degree and they also take on an appearance they are familiar with, like a photo of someone else. Only two of these women are known by facial recognition, the rest have appeared into existence as if they got completely new faces or never existed.

I am confident these are some form of light illusions which is why they fooled the cameras, but not the audio recordings."

"Can you identify where this woman comes from?" Richard asked.

"Her accent puts her in the region of Poland, but she could have been raised by Polish people anywhere in the surrounding countries."

Richard turned to John. "I hope you like the cold weather this time of year."

"Poland?" John asked.

"I always wanted to travel there." Susan smiled as she grabbed John's arm.

"Erica will keep us in touch. I need to go to SIA and get some information; Cindy and Larcis will keep Liz company."

"We'll take fifteen minutes to pack some things and then we'll start our search in Warsaw." John stated and the couple vanished, teleporting to their bedroom several levels above the battle room.

"How did Erica get this information so quickly?" Cindy asked.

"I instructed her to bypass all legal barriers and also use federal authority to scan all databases nationwide."

"So some of this fact-finding is illicit?"

"Erica is not one to abuse her knowledge and power, and neither am I. Do you have a problem with this?" Richard calmly asked.

"No, I was just wondering when I can get a piece of the action." Cindy smirked.

Richard changed his eyes to normal hazel blue human eyes and looked at her with earnest. "When I let you loose, I need you to just find information, not take them out."

Cindy stared at Richard a little surprised. "What has Joshua told you about me?"

"I saw what you did to Ego, and Joshua told me enough to know you can easily kill them all, but I promised him I would look after you, so don't put yourself in harm's way just to kill people. Please leave them to me and the rest of the group."

Cindy didn't really know what to say. It was true that she could kill people quite easily by dematerializing their body or parts of their body infusing them into other pieces of matter, without them being able to see it coming or be able to prevent it. But it was a time when she was full of anger, revenge, and killed out of a need for survival. She had changed a lot since then, and killing was something she wasn't timid about, but was at the bottom of her last resort list. "I'm not that same woman anymore."

Richard smiled, knowing she was engaged to Glenn Seber who was a Federal Marshal in Seattle. "Yes, I know; and that reminds me. Does Glenn know about your powers and past?"

Cindy almost blushed, but showed more surprise than anything else. "So is Joshua giving you a facebook or twitter play by play of my life?"

"No, Erica told me. But, I'm sure you would've told me

sooner or later, right?"

"We have been busy and I was going to, but okay. I wanted to ask you a few things." Cindy sat on the adjacent sofa so she could face Richard while she sat.

Richard paid all of his attention to her, blacking out the screens and muting them.

"You had girlfriends who weren't superhumans and didn't know about you. Did you ever come close to marrying any of them?"

"I guess you only heard of my time in the university, when I had three girlfriends. I ended the relationships on the first two, and on the last one, she left me for some other guy. I also didn't pay too much attention to them or the relationships, so it was mainly my fault. But, they weren't relationships that I would rate as a bonding experience for marriage or anything close to it. Having said that… I was married once, back in 1943. My wife wasn't a superhuman and she knew about my powers and history. She had two children when I met her, but they all died in a V1 buzz bomb attack…"

"Yeah, Larcis never told me that." Cindy filled in the pause.

"Larcis doesn't know the details, and his head is always in the clouds when it comes to girlfriends."

"So if your late wife and children were still alive, do you think it would have lasted?"

"Huh, would of, could of. I probably would be living in England right now, and could still be in love as before; but the question you should be asking is why would it have lasted? Evelyn would have aged and I would have aged in appearance with her until she would've died. She was willing to live with me and love me for who I was, and I was willing to give her everything I could. It was a mutual agreement, and she knew about my powers before we got married, because I told her and showed her. Then we told the children, and they all accepted who I was."

"I'm sure your past wasn't like mine." Cindy stated.

Richard half grinned. "No, my past was laced with death all around me because of several wars, and superhumans weren't popular or known back then; but people have fears and the unknown is one of them. Evelyn took a leap of faith with me because she loved me, and she knew I loved her. If Glenn is the man of your dreams, then I highly suggest you tell him everything before you say any wedding vows."

Richard answered her most important question, but she knew somehow he would. If she would have asked Joshua, he might have given her a parable, but it really didn't matter because she wanted to pick Richard's intuitive mind. "I will take that advice to heart once I get back to Seattle."

"Good, in the meantime, I might not need to eat, but you do, so what do you think about joining Liz and I for dinner, before I talk with SIA?"

"Yes, thank you." Cindy happily accepted the invitation.

The two headed to the main house level to join Elizabeth and Alex, while Erica continued to search for everything and anything in all the digital airways.

SIA Headquarters, New York City

The security guards at the main entrance to the complex waved the SIA agent through without delay. Nick Phamos was a veteran agent, at least that's what the SIA Super AI indicated on the guard's identity scanner. Nick was middle aged with fine ebony black short hair. He was clean shaven, but a thin scar lined his outer jaw across to his right chin. He wasn't fine toned as sleek bodybuilders, but the guards only saw a perfect African-American Soldier with no scar or distinguishable marks that attracted attention. He wore the standard agent uniform which consisted of a two-piece suit; his being dark blue. The dress shoes were specially made to muffle sound and protect the feet from extreme temperatures. The clothing at his disposal was impressive and common among SIA agents, but it wasn't earned; it was stolen property.

Nick moved into the containment wing without incident; but he was stopped at the control center check point.

"Identification please." The guard on the other side of the glass screen directed.

"I don't know Elvis, but Summerfield hates trespassing." Nick replied.

Both guards in the control room didn't flitch as they authorized entry and one left his station as if he had forgotten all of his training or common sense.

Nick turned on a scrambler on his belt as he entered the fifth corridor and walked up in front of cell 512. The guard at the control room opened the prison door automatically allowing Nick to walk unrestricted into the cell.

Eibren Milows was lying on his fixed bunk, but jumped up in fear knowing something was wrong. The African-American agent had no business in his cell, and he was alone, which meant only that he wasn't who he seemed.

"How are you Eibren?" Nick casually asked.

Eibren recognized the voice feeling a gruesome chill run through his body, ending in his extremities. "I told them nothing that they don't already know."

Nick smiled a wicked smile. "Yes, I know, but I'm not here to find out what you said or didn't say."

Eibren collapsed on the floor hitting his head on the edge of the metallic bunk. His heart raced, but the ruptured artery near the heart is what caused the fatal damage, not the now large bloody gash on his forehead. Thousands of burst blood vessels in his head also contributed to the overkill of his early demise.

Nick concentrated on Eibren's head and with a telekinetic twist broke his neck at a right angle for good measure. Nick exited the cell without touching anything except for the soles of his shoes to the floor a few meters in and out.

The cell door automatically closed behind Nick, and he retraced his path to the control room where using his telekinetic ability broke the necks of the guards who had assisted him. He made his way outside and past the complex outer perimeter before the three dead men were found.

Collin's Estate, Serenity Community, Chicago

A middle-aged woman robed in black linen cloth entered a dimly lit large room. The windows were tinted, and black automatic shades ensured the room was dark even in the brightest of summer days. An array of small candles surrounding the far walls provided the light for people to see. A single beam of white light shined down from the fifteen foot ceiling to the center of the room. The hallway the woman came from was also dark, so when the doors opened, the room maintained its gloominess. Eight long semicircular shaped cloth sofas were positioned facing the center. In the middle was a flat one-piece linen covered cushion with a foot tall backing. About a dozen people clothed in like manner as the woman sat on the sofas in what seemed like deep meditation.

The woman's blonde hair was very long, but was covered by the monk like robe and hood which draped partially over her ears. "Master, Lord Phamos is entering the community now."

An older man in his sixties wearing a red robe with black and silver designs sat on the center cushion. His eyes were closed as he sat with his legs crossed and hands intertwined at his waistline. "You interrupted me to tell me one of my servants is approaching?"

"Master, Disciple Ralph from Detroit has also arrived and wishes to speak with you; he says he's from the recruiting center."

Michael's eyes opened revealing dark gray irises, but the normally white eyeballs were severely bloodshot as if he had not slept in ages. "Come closer."

The woman had stopped about eight feet from her master, but now she quickly closed the gap and knelt in front of Michael's face.

Michael touched her cheeks with both hands. Her mouth dried as he entered her mind. Michael saw how Disciple Ralph was insisting on seeing him to give him a message. The mentalists who tried to mentally read his mind were unable to, which was why she came to give him the news. Michael lightly pushed the woman away from him.

"How inept are my soldiers? Bring in the shadows and Disciple Ralph." Michael commanded.

"Yes, Master." The woman replied and quickly left the room to gather the escort of shadows and Ralph.

The shadows were the Magistrate equivalent of SIA guards. They carried side arms, but their main weapons were their ability to fight against mental manipulation and withstand large amounts of bodily harm.

The woman traveled through the mansion up two levels and met the shadows who were detaining Ralph. Nick Phamos was already in the room when she entered, which filled her with mixed emotions. Nick asked what was going on, and the shadow in charge started to tell him what had happened, but her presence silenced him. Nick's anger was felt in the room instantly, but she quickly reported what Michael had instructed.

"The Master commands Disciple Ralph be brought to him at once."

"I'll take it from here." Nick commanded and led the way

to Michael's meditation room, leaving the woman to return to her duties in the mansion.

Disciple Ralph was constantly fidgeting with his robe which was given to him once he entered the community entrance. The community was occupied by Magistrate personnel as families and followers covering a hundred fifty acres of land and houses. Jared knew the community would be too difficult to infiltrate and fighting against a thousand or more mentalist wasn't his idea of good strategy. But the community was an attractive place to be for any proven follower or want to be mentalist working their way up the ranks. Ralph had always aspired to eventually live in the community, but now his future was uncertain as something inside of him plagued his mind and soul.

Nick, six shadows, and Ralph entered Michael's chamber. Nick was still angry by the fact that he didn't have an opportunity to find out what Ralph was doing here. It was unorthodox for a young disciple to even enter the community, let alone see his master without more notice.

"Master, with your permission I would like to find out what this disciple has in his mind?" Nick asked as he took a step into the room.

Four figures emerged out of the darkness from each corner of the room. Their robes were green and black veils covered their faces. They were controllers, but knew their place as Nick Phamos was the Archmagi of the entire controller sect. Their duty was to protect Michael, and having six shadows escorting a questionable disciple into the room was enough cause for them to be on guard.

There were three entrances into the room, but the two entrances opposite the main door were open to hallways, leading to other rooms like bathrooms, a kitchen, and cleansing rooms.

"Sit him there to the right." Michael instructed as the escorts grabbed Ralph and sat him on the first sofa corner from the double doors.

Nick stood a few feet from Ralph with his left side towards Michael.

"Master, I have a message…" Ralph started to speak.

"Silence!" Nick commanded and Ralph's tongue and jaw froze as if some invisible strong hand had just gagged him.

Ralph had no idea what had just happened, but it quickly dawned on him that Nick had entered his mind and commanded his own muscles to stop talking.

Nick started to look at his past and saw Jared greet him in a world without shape or form, almost as if in an unending blue sky with white cirrus clouds in the distance.

"The Magistrate is a virus that needs to die, Detroit is only the beginning; you and your master will die a painful death." Jared said and disappeared like a ghost permanently leaving its haunted location.

A jolt of mild pain went through his head as Nick backed off. "Master, Jared is behind the killing in Detroit. He has sent this weakling to tell us we will suffer a painful death." Nick reported.

"What else does he know?" Michael asked not wanting to spend any effort to enter Ralph's mind.

"His mind is blocked, but not for long." Nick replied and entered his mind again.

Ralph shook his head as if having a dreadful migraine and grabbed his head with both hands. He would have screamed or moaned, but Nick's mental command didn't allow Ralph to willingly control his mouth.

Nick saw Jared and a few dozen people on the street in front of the recruiting station, but it was a glimpse of Jared commanding Ralph to leave the area, nothing more. If there were other memories Nick couldn't find them. He withdrew out of the man's mind only to see Ralph pounding on his chest. In a microsecond, Nick saw Ralph's current mental thoughts and knew the explosive vest he wore was armed and about to explode.

"Bomb!" Nick yelled and flung Ralph away from him into the double doors with a telekinetic push.

The explosion wasn't extremely large, but it was big enough to shred Ralph to pieces and vaporize a large portion of his upper body. The dark green crystals packed along with the explosive bars shattered into millions of inch sized or smaller splinters. The concussion was strong enough to push four shadows and five disciples on the sofas several feet backwards on their backs. Nick was pushed back a few inches, but it was his telekinetic powers that created a force field around his body protecting him from harm. The crystals that would have penetrated his clothing and skin turned to liquid, poured downward, and the now blackish green acid like small puddles started to eat away at the floor tiles. The others weren't as fortunate as half of the people near ground zero were paralyzed or dead from the venom and acid properties of the crystals. Even the shadows who could normally withstand major physical damage were unable to counter the venom properties which attacked the nervous system through the open wounds caused by the acid and splinters.

The controllers converged on Michael and attended to the injured people. Michael's hand trembled with pain, and shock as a few splinters had made their way into his exposed skin. One of the controllers touched him and changed the chemical composition of the acid and poison. The dead cells were moved to the outside of his skin, and the toxins along with dead cells fell on the floor and cushion where Michael sat. The controller balanced his nervous system almost instantly, but it would have been much harder to do if Michael had been exposed to more than twenty splinters.

Anger filled Michael's heart as the pain subsided. Nine people were dead, to include Ralph, and it seemed Jared's calling card had made its way to him as if Jared were playing a game. His ego was hurt most of all, but he knew Nick felt the same way. They were Archmagis and Jared was only a tainted disciple a long time ago. Now Jared was defying them as if they were less than novice mentalists.

"Get the rest of the elders and controllers down here. I want Jared and everyone helping him. I want him dead!" Michael screamed with everyone fearfully clearing out the room and preparing for an emergency community meeting.

Chapter Six

Murders in the Streets

A heavy toll to pay, I would say." Beth commented.

The late night show audience paid close attention to the interview with Keith Brown, a legal consultant and best seller writer for celebrity criminal trials and investigations.

"People might think it is, but historical trends show that technology and the supernatural are always trying to catch up or pass our legal procedures and state of moral justice and reasoning. When DNA evidence first came out for instance, it was not considered strong enough to determine proof all by itself. It depended on handling of the evidence, how it was obtained, and if it was exclusive or unique to one person out of millions. As technology improved, DNA evidence also became a strong source of consistent accurate findings which have convicted and exonerated many people today." Keith explained.

“But what keeps telepaths from manipulating the system and people for that matter? I mean what keeps us from going back in the dark ages and witch hunts?” Beth Carson asked.

Keith looked at her with almost an awkward pause. “Honestly, the good guys and faith that good telepaths are strong and determined enough to keep everyone honest. The supreme courts are under the gun now that they have to rule over the use of telepaths to an extent they more or less deflected for two decades by allowing the status quo to keep telepathic evidence from being found untrustworthy, until now.”

“But aren’t Pandora and Mindseye being telepaths a conflict of interest when they started this precedent?”

“Here’s the problem Beth. In all the research I have done, telepaths or in some circles, mentalists; one or more can manipulate one and as much as five or six people. But evidence would be left in their minds. Now if one person were being mentally controlled, to use as an example, then it would be possible to not leave evidence of tampering. But Mindseye and Pandora are far beyond any other mentally powerful superhuman, at least that I could find with my research. Over three hundred people were brought into a mental conference, at the same time their bodies were controlled, and over a dozen were telepaths themselves. Mindseye showed who was doing the manipulating, and what was actual original mental processing, memories, and emotions at the time. Forty of the people included in this trial or mental conference were not even in the state of Florida. The current Supreme Court judges were included in the evidence. And no telepathic evidence can be seen as manipulation in the minds of all of these people. So either there was manipulation like mind control and it can't be detected, or what is there in the minds of the 300 people is what is, without a need to alter free will. No one knew this until later when I started my investigation."

"You mean that Creator's verdict will probably not get over turned by the Supreme Court?" Beth interjected.

"Beth, all of these legal statutes have been molded from many centuries of good people trying to uphold justice and the freedoms we cherish as Americans and citizens of Earth. The Supreme Court will have to take the Constitution and what the court rulings in the past have said, along with a need for justice in the minds of people, and not just what is spoken in the witness box, in order to come up with a clear procedure in telepathic evidence. I also want to add that telepathic evidence and use of telepaths in courts is being done in three continents. There has been proof of misuse of telepaths, but over ninety percent of the court rulings have a strong foundation of evidence that is not just memories."

"What do you mean by that?" Beth interrupted.

"In many cases, telepaths have entered an accused person's mind, and even though the criminal wouldn't admit it, they could find the physical evidence like the buried body, weapon, or proof that the person was innocent or guilty. There are times when the criminal volunteered the information so that a telepath would not enter their mind, and in some cases their sentences were reduced. Telepaths are also used to reform criminals, which I think will not happen here in the US for a while, because it involves an active role in manipulating a mind and the freedom of belief or free will as I would put it. Bluntly put, it's someone else's wishes and desires, not your own." Keith explained.

Richard looked on at the televised show with interest, not because he was mentioned in the comments, but because it represented one of many pathways to change. SIA wasn't taking their passive stance anymore; they were heavy in diplomacy on getting agents to assemble allies in law enforcement to fight the Magistrate and the underworld of telepaths they underestimated or were ignorant of. EFL was also making their presence known all throughout northeastern United States. They didn't have the mental abilities as the Eternal Champions, but they all were experienced investigators and assisted local and county police departments with great effectiveness. Police departments gave EFL's SAI, Bob, permission to run through cold case files and identification databases which linked thousands of people, times, locations, and statements in a matter of hours which would have taken a team of investigators days or weeks to accomplish.

The four Super AIs in the country were unique to the world and were not permitted to be used as a legal means of obtaining and declaring evidence since the AIs were considered thinking entities by law. The possibility of the invasion of privacy was greatly feared and weighed into the idea that they would take over the country. The Killer computer virus a few years ago had helped in reinforcing these ideas, but at the same time making it clear that the SAIs were needed to maintain social order. Erica was recognized as saving the world economy from the destructive virus which halted several civilizations worldwide and almost put them into the prehistoric age. Many people lost money in the blink of an eye, to include medical and identification histories. Even though the SAIs were able to reconstruct most of the information, Richard was certain that people with the means, used the opportunity to keep their criminal records or physical existence lost forever. But now, telepathic evidence would change all of that.

John walked into the battle room, seeing Richard sitting on his favorite leather sofa in front of the very large main screen. The Beth Carson Show was playing on the left side of the screen, while rotating news clips showed discussions of the trial and people acting up as some people do after their favorite sports team loses a championship game.

"I thought you were still in the danger room getting rid of some stress?" John stated.

"I thought you were in Poland."

"I came back after Erica told me what happened to Eibren."

Richard didn't turn his head to answer. "I'm not stressed; it's just lack of exercise in jail that got me a little sluggish."

John sat on a side sofa. "Yeah, I guess they don't have the one-hundred ton weight sets like we do in the danger room… Or force fields… or anything heavy at all, except maybe the building itself."

"I'm really tired of this cloak and dagger stuff." Richard said, leaning back on the sofa and looking up at the ceiling. The ten foot tall metallic carbon structure was light gray at the moment, but it could have easily been white as snow upon command, through Erica's interactive wall energizers. The black glossy dome was still there and still black as it was the source of Erica's projection abilities in the room.

"I thought you were over all of that guilt stuff after the trial?"

"No old friend, I'm talking about the way we are tossed around like chess pieces." Richard was able to crack a smile as he thought of John's one tracked mind.

"So you think we're just following some master plan and don't have a say in it?"

"Have you ever wondered how we came together? How South America became a superpower, or how telepaths are now influencing everything we do? How you and Susan became leaders of an alien empire?" Richard looked at John.

"You know I can tell the future?" John said out of the blue trying to make a joke since he didn't have a good response.

"You can now, but two years ago you couldn't keep from getting drunk, let alone call heads or tails without better than fifty-fifty odds."

"You have a point there, but what am I suppose to answer? We were put together for a reason, and honestly if it was for an evil purpose someone messed up, cuz criminals fear us and good people can live free and safe because of us."

"Do you remember when we were looking at Colombia taking over South America in the Caribbean War videos?"

John recalled the days they spent catching up on major events in history after they completed the construction of the Eternal Domain. "Yes, I remember."

"The Ramerize brothers were in Vietnam. Eduardo or Edward as some would call him; worked his way up the ranks up to full bird Colonel. His brother, Estabon, was also in Special Forces. He was a Major and they both had their own units. I never personally met them or even got close to them since I was on CIA missions with Mark as my shadow. But the reputation these brothers had on a very large piece of land in eastern Laos and North Vietnam was completely controlled by them. If you wanted to be in a safe zone, being near the brothers was it. Casualties to all allied military in the region was a fraction of a percent compared to the rest of all Vietnam and Laos. The men loved them, and as you can guess many of them helped in the takeover of Colombia and South America. It was rumored that Eduardo went against direct orders from higher… not sure why and the documented information was destroyed before the war ended, so very few people really know the true events that helped end his military career. Eduardo and Estabon both left the military before the war ended, and it was rumored that they roamed the world for years. They ended up in Colombia and before you know it, they organized a coup and the rest is legendary history…" Richard paused in deep thought as if waiting for John to respond.

"And you think all of this has to do with a master plan?" John doubted.

"No, I'm saying they're superhumans and more are coming out of the woodwork. Now that telepaths are going to be given more latitude here in the US, the bad guys will be exposed."

"I still don't follow."

"It was always at the back of my mind, but for some reason I wasn't able to make the connection until now."

"Are you sure no one's messing with your head anymore?" John asked a little worried now.

"Ever since Joshua saved Cindy's life, things have changed. The movie, Escape from New York, is not my favorite, but it's too similar to what happened in Complex San Francisco. We just happen to meet two other members for the group and then Susan becomes queen of an alien empire. Then you become king with powers to match. Now that telepaths are being allowed to legally fight crime, I'm sure they will also be used to uncover all the secrets that many people are not ready for. Like aliens or what Australia and South America are up to. Someone didn't want me to make the connection, at least not then, but now things are beginning to come together for some reason, and this is the cloak and dagger stuff I don't like."

John thought carefully about the new revelation. It was true, now that he thought about it; the John Carpenter movie did seem to be the inspiration for the events which brought the entire team together. "You don't suppose Joshua did all of that?"

Richard breathed in deeply out of habit. "I don't know, and if he did, what of it? Am I suppose to tell an all powerful superhuman; to not play match maker, use old movie plots for settings, or leave us alone to our own future? I'm pretty sure Joshua didn't alter the past, but maybe he did alter the present and future, I'm logically saying that only because we know that the Argonian Empire had already been around for thousands of years. Or maybe that's what Joshua is making everyone believe."

"It wouldn't hurt to say something?" John said, but he knew it wouldn't change anything. If Joshua was behind it, he had set things in motion and no matter what happened, people did have free will; or at least that's how everyone would see it. John had Elizabeth's and Susan's precognition powers, but he knew that even they had limitations, unlike Joshua. It didn't mean he could force or alter an event on someone if he were to tell them their future. He tried not to use the power because it became too annoying to him since he could see the future, but it was hit or miss. It reminded him of weather forecasts that sometimes were reliable, but sometimes caught him outside without an umbrella.

Richard stood up and extended John a hand motioning to help him up off the sofa. "Come on, we need to go see Rebecca and Lynda."

John took his hand and stood up. "I was wondering when we were going to go up state. Oh, by the way, I forgot to ask you, but how did you know Cindy was in the room back in Tallahassee?"

Richard smiled. "I asked Joshua a long time ago to allow me to know when she was close to me or when she was in danger so I could help look after her."

"Hmm, I didn't see that coming." John said in awe of his friend who was always one step ahead of him, no matter how gifted or powerful he himself was.

John and Richard changed into their superhero costumes almost instantly just before John teleported them out of the battle room.

SIA Headquarters, Randolph Maximilian's Office

Max sat at his desk reading the report on the death of his men, Eibren's death, and the breach of security to his complex. "Computer, why are files missing from the databases?"

"I don't recognize files as missing from the databases, Director." A high-pitched female voice answered.

Max breathed calmly in thought. "Computer you will run a diagnostic and once you are done, you will contact Erica from the Eternal Champions and allow her to examine your files to include core programming. In addition, you will suspend all control and give control to the main computers in the situation room which will be manned by human operators. Initiate please."

"Initiating." The SAI replied without contradiction.

"Hmm..." Max mumbled knowing that the SAI was too submissive and clearly wrong by the looks of the data or lack thereof. As an artificial intelligence, it would have asked if there was something wrong with her. As a super AI it would have asked something else, which Max could have only have guessed at; but the SAI was being more like a robot performing whatever command it was given without question.

A knock at the door interrupted his concern. Normally his secretary would have called him on the intercom, but the knock meant it was serious enough for her to allow whoever it was to get inside the office quickly.

"Enter!"

The agent of the deck entered the office with an almost pale face. "Director, there are reports coming in with people going on crazy killing sprees and committing suicide afterwards; as if they were being mentally controlled."

Max swung out of his chair and ran outside towards the situation room. The forty or so agents were busy as in an emergency crisis center in full activation. Twenty screens across the longest length of the room showed videos and live news reports of mass killings, meaning three or more people at one time in one location. Two suburban moms in two different cities drove their SUVs through a crowd of pedestrians and then intentionally crashed their vehicles, beltless with disabled airbags. "Sir, A Wall Street broker went postal in KFC downtown New York. A nurse killed six patients before taking her own life in Chicago. A school bus driver ran his bus off a cliff far from the scheduled route. A Texaco worker started a chemical spill in Denver…" The agent reported, but was cut off as Max took the report from his hands.

Max looked at the eighteen reports time stamped less than six minutes ago. "What have our field agents been able to find out?"

"There's no concentration of incidents, so our telepath teams haven't been able to assist the agents on the ground very well, but they indicate that the people were not acting as themselves by preliminary witness statements."

Max scanned the list again. "Get me in touch with Creator. Also instruct the telepath teams to rove the city downtowns to include nuclear power plants and look for telepathic assassins or people under telepathic influence."

"Sir, what about chemical and other high target areas?"

"We don't have the resources to cover everything. But I need the Eternal Champions quickly, before mass riots start nationwide."

Max went to the main screen to see more postings of incidents; not one of them occurred in Florida or Georgia, however, every major city in the rest of the eastern states were under attack. The telepathic assassins seemed to be avoiding Pandora and Mindseye, but Max knew better than to jump to conclusions.

Underground Maze, 15th Street, Detroit, Michigan

Jared's fingers raced across a six foot wide virtual console. The information he'd retrieved was now gone as Jean and Natasha entered from one of many intersecting control rooms. The women were laughing over some story Jared had missed. His concern was changed to happiness as he saw them acting as if they had been lifelong sisters.

"Brat, all of the rooms are secure and we're all alone." Natasha reported.

"Yes, and we are so happy to be stuck down here in the dark." Jean joked.

"I'm sorry about that, but it's a necessary evil."

"Nat told me, but I would like for you to explain why, so we both understand." Jean stated as if Natasha was not very convincing as to why they were underground and locked in.

Jared rolled his chair backwards and rested his hands on the chair arms. "Mentalists seem to be weird, but they do things for specific reasons. Michael on the other hand does everything for many reasons, one on top of another. He will expect us to be underground; not too deep and not aboveground. Ideally, he would want us to be on the surface or in a high building. I could make him or others walk off the edge of a tall building with rigged walls or doors, or even collapse the building on top of him, but he could do the same to us. If we are too deep underground, he will just bury us and take his time in killing us. So as long as he thinks we can escape because we are close to the surface he will hunt us down. If we were out on the surface there is less that can be used in a real physical sense to substitute as illusions. Even though we could have snipers and things like an airstrike, he would be ready for this and the numbers are on his side. His followers would have a field day if we were caught out in an open clearing. So, here we are, in a maze of hallways, corners, and rooms; of which have been booby-trapped, forcing Michael to come to this particular room. If you were thinking, this room isn't booby-trapped and there's no self-destruct button to take them out if we fail, because they could use it against us if we did. We lure them here, in which case I estimate he will lose ninety-six percent of his followers by then, which will place about three dozen people or less in this room and the adjacent rooms. The controllers he will have around him have telekinesis, manipulation powers that can heal or kill, and at least one with precognition abilities. We need to kill the precognition controllers first, they are elders and shouldn't be too hard to identify. If all goes as planned Michael will bring lots of guns with him." Jared paused, moving back to the console and bringing up a diagram of the complex which took him seven years to build.

"Why would he stoop to using guns? I thought the Archmagis saw people who used guns as inferior and undisciplined?" Jean asked.

"Wow, you did read my reports." Jared sarcastically countered.

Jean frowned. "I'm not sure if you wrote them now; being you're telling me do as I say not as I do."

Jared laughed. "I never said I was an Archmagi, and besides, Michael will bring guns with him as a self-centered arrogant response to the recruiting station. He will want his follows to shoot us after we're dead so they could all get the satisfaction of revenge. And he will make them feel they owe him for allowing them to wallow in their post achievement."

"Kind of like giving a treat to a killer pet." Natasha interjected.

"So why are guns so important?"

"Do you know the saying - guns don't kill people; people kill people?"

"Yes, so?"

Jared smiled and walked out of the room, loudly saying, "It's true. Nat, you and Jean need to read the instructions on the screen and get familiar with the areas I highlighted on the floor plan. Once you two are done, you can eat in the dining room with me."

Jean grunted under her breath and frowned to match. "Why do I love him so much?"

Natasha laughed. "You two act like a married couple."

Jean turned quickly towards her. Natasha seemed so innocent to her now, instead of an undercover operative or overly protective sister. Sadness filled her eyes as the thought of marriage wasn't a reality. They had been so busy, but yet she knew Jared had already bought the engagement ring. It was her secret, and she was excited that Jared was going to ask her to marry, but now it seemed short lived since she wasn't sure if they would be alive for more than a week. At least that's how long Jared estimated it would take for Michael to find them, if not sooner.

Natasha noticed the mixed emotions on Jean's face. "Jean, I didn't mean anything bad about it."

Jean tried to smile. "No, Nat, it's not you… I just wish things would have been different."

Natasha had moved into Jared's chair and pulled up another one for Jean to sit. "Did Jared tell you how I ended up here in the United States?"

"No, he didn't talk about your past at all." Jean stated.

"Really?" Natasha's wide smile showed that she was thrilled to be given the chance to tell Jean herself.

Jean sat down and looked at the screen with a long list of instructions. "Hmm, I feel like a schoolgirl who's going to get a pop quiz any second now."

Natasha laughed. "Would you like to hear about me and Jared when we were kids instead?"

Jean smiled with intrigue. "Yes, I would like that very much."

"I don't know if he told you, but our family used to be in a coven during the time the Magistrate was moving up in power. I was very young and remember my parents dying in a car accident. Jared and I were separated after the accident and I was hidden in Europe. It wasn't until I was seven years old when Jared found me and showed me the truth. He was very strong and told me what to do to survive. I lived in Poland for most of my life waiting for Jared to come and get me as he promised he would. Before I started in the university, he contacted me again and we lived together for a few years. He had joined the magistrate and learned about them, and plotted… and plotted." Natasha stopped talking as she lost herself in thought.

"And that's when he came to work for the CEA?" Jean asked.

Natasha snapped out of it. "No, he worked for the SIA, and they planted him into your organization."

"What?" Jean was stunned.

"Yeah, but don't worry he used everyone, except you." Natasha slightly giggled. "The SIA thought they were keeping an eye on things, but Jared was gathering all sorts of information from everywhere he could. He got me out of Poland with a new identity. I'm legally a US citizen and all."

"You mean he was a double agent?"

"Oh, no he's his own spy. The FBI, CIA, SIA, CEA, Interpol, and even the Magistrate thought that Jared worked for them until now. Jared's completely independent."

"So, he helped me because I wanted to destroy the Magistrate?"

"He's been helping you because he fell in love with you many years ago."

"Hmm, if everyone thinks that he works for them, how did he disappear in their databases or keep them from finding out he was working for someone else?"

"My Brat has been plotting to destroy the Magistrate since he was ten years old. I don't know how he does it, but I do know the Killer Virus a few years ago made his day. It is simple for him to erase memories from many people's heads, but harder to erase paper and digit memories since there're so many and the information spreads very quickly. There're also maybe a hundred people or less in the world that would recognize Jared's face, but even then not all of them would know or remember him as you or I know him. His face and stature would be different for most of them."

Jean didn't ask any more questions and waited for Natasha to continue her storytelling.

Natasha told Jean about her childhood in great detail, all the way up to the point where they both met. They were talking so long that they ended up eating late that night.

Up above, only Jared knew of the multiple murders and deaths in sixteen states. The Magistrate was trying to force Jared to come out of hiding, but as long as he kept Natasha and Jean ignorant; they would not nag or persuade him to expose them to Michael.

Martial Law was brought up before the President, but there was no epidemic or event like the economic breakdown of the nation that would warrant it. President Hanson authorized SIA telepaths to scan anyone they came across in an attempt to find the assassins or anyone already manipulated by the assassins.

The National Guard was mobilized to add security to high value target areas with the capability of causing a major disaster. But even with the precautions, two National Guard Soldiers on opposite ends of the country killed several other Soldiers and civilians before they supposedly committed suicide.

EFL Headquarters, 13th Ave, New York City, New York

Richard and John appeared in front of the main gates to the headquarters. John could have teleported them inside the base, but that would have set off Bob's automatic intrusion security system which would have added more unwanted drama to their lives.

The perfect 400 x 400 meter property was always maintained with immaculate simplicity. A fourteen foot brick wall surrounded the entire perimeter, keeping pedestrians from looking in or accidently walking into the area. The green artificial lawn was a buffer between the perimeter wall and mansion. The 60 x 50 meter four story rectangular structure in the center of the property seemed more like a futuristic office building than a home. A small blue metallic sphere flew out of the perimeter wall next to the gate and stopped in front of the two men, in midair.

"Welcome, Creator and Mindseye." The floating device greeted them.

"Hello Bob. We need to speak with the owners of the house."

"Of course, I will let Lynda know you're here, you can fly into the house and wait in the living room; or I can lead you to the forensics room where she's currently working."

"Lead the way." Creator said, and both men flew to the house entrance and entered the already opened doors.

They had visited the headquarters several times in the past and were familiar with the floor plan, so it wasn't long before they entered the forensics laboratory on the second floor.

Rebecca, known as Starfire, wasn't there as Richard would have hoped, but Lynda was there and maybe she could provide him with the information he was looking for.

Lynda was wearing a long white lab coat and had stopped working her cases in order to greet the visitors. Her long blonde hair was French rolled and covered by a head cap. Her bright blue eyes complimented her fine tan skin. "What a surprise and a pleasure to have you two visit us so soon."

"I was hoping Rebecca or one of the men were here but you might be able to help me." Richard said.

"Oh, I'm sorry I wasn't included in the first draft pick." Lynda joked.

"No, it's not that. The information I need is about things that happened before you became a member of EFL. Actually, probably before EFL became a group."

"Well, you lucked out, because Rick and Scott told me a lot about their past. I also had to read up on many things since I had amnesia decades ago. So, what is it you want to know?"

"Why did they as Quatris and Hellfire allow Colombia and later, South America to become a superpower?" Richard asked.

"Wow, I never thought about that. Rick told me he and Scott went to Colombia several times before the revolution. They also visited Colombia twice after the Caribbean War, but of course it was always covert visits. He told me that the human race had to deal with national and international policy without them getting involved all of the time. I think that they made a treaty of some kind with South America. But, why is this information so important to you?"

"Just a theory I'm developing; but I also wanted to know if you have any more leads on the Magistrate, before I go see Max.

"Unfortunately, we don't and Rick and Scott have been busy in space for quite some time. It would help if they were here right now."

"Yes, that's something I would like to talk to them about once they get back, when they have time." John commented as if requesting he be notified when they returned.

"I'll give them the message." Lynda assured him.

"Excuse me, but Erica has an emergency message for Creator." Bob interrupted on the intercom.

Richard looked at his wrist comlink, which was being blocked by Bob while in the base. "Bob, can you next time allow the comlink to work no matter if we are in a conversation?"

"My bag, I will allow encrypted secrets to seep into the radio airways from now on." Bob sarcastically replied for the first time when talking to Richard.

"Mmm, he's grown to like you." Lynda smiled.

"Arghhh, okay, can I talk to Erica now?" Richard signed.

"Creator, SIA is asking to talk to you. They are reporting nationwide deaths associated to telepaths. I have confirmed the incidents they claim. They urgently request you contact them." Erica reported through his comlink.

Bob's probe entered the room and projected the videos and information SIA had sent Erica on the nearest wall.

The three heroes quickly analyzed the information, while Richard asked Erica to patch him in to Max.

"Max, we have seen your data. What exactly do you expect us to do?" Richard quickly got to the point.

"If you notice, not one incident occurred in Florida or Georgia. I think they didn't occur there because of Mindseye and Pandora. If any of these telepathic murderers are caught by them, they could reveal all of the targets or methods they are using, and quickly stop this insane killing. But that's my gut feeling."

"Hmm, John will see what he can do. Having said that, have you considered that maybe they're trying to distract us or overwork us so we won't be ready for something else?" Richard suggested.

"I have an idea." John stated but kept silent afterward.

Richard looked at him. John was looking at the videos and reading information very intently.

"Any day now Mindseye." Richard smiled.

"Oh, yeah, sorry. But what if the Magistrate is trying to draw Jared out of hiding and keep us occupied at the same time?"

"And you think Jared would come out of hiding because people are dying?" Max asked.

"Jared isn't alone. If the information you have on Jean Lorenz and Jared are true, they may be seen as killers, but they also might have a weakness, a conscious, which the Magistrate is trying to exploit." John explained.

Richard smiled. John was being very logical and seemed to be thinking like a true leader by stepping away and looking at the big picture with an unbiased eye. "I'm impressed. But that still leaves us making a decision as to what to do before more people die."

"Creator, I think I can help in this situation." Erica added.

"Explain." Richard replied.

"I have been unable to trace the maker of the website and email, but an anonymous source provided a secure website that holds all of the Magistrate murderous telepaths, sleeper agents, and contacts. This information was provided a few minutes ago." Erica relayed the information to Bob's projection.

"Okay. John, you take that information and start cleaning house. SIA Headquarters first and then use the telepaths at your disposal to fix everything else. But before you do that, take me back home. I will examine the new information and see if we can find the Magistrate's base of operations." Richard instructed.

"What if it's a red herring?" John asked.

"No, I don't think it is."

"Why do you say that?" Lynda asked with interest.

"Because two of the sleeper agents on that list died during Eibren's assassination." Max stated.

"It's a good thing we're all in agreement." Richard smiled and bid Lynda and Bob good-bye.

Chapter Seven

❖---❋ ✪ ❋---❖

911, What's Your Emergency?

Detroit, Michigan

The speaker was turned on the cell phone as the 911 call came into the Detroit dispatching center. "911, what is your emergency?" A male voice asked.

A muffled weak cry came from the distance, but the dispatch operator couldn't make out what was said.

"I can't understand what you are saying. Can you tell me what the emergency is, your name, or where you are located?"

A very loud bang was the response and then silence. The call stayed open, and the only thing that could be heard was the dispatcher trying to get someone to talk on the phone. The nearby cell phone tower identified that the call was somewhere inside a ten mile radius of downtown, but the phone stopped transmitting after a minute. The phone belonged to Mayor Waters, but an investigation revealed that the phone was lost that morning. A body of a woman was found that same day in her own apartment with the phone in the other room.

These types of events were faced by police on a daily basis, and the information went into the backed up black void of computers and case files.

Jared worked at his computer console, but it wasn't any standard computer or terminal. The secure severs he used allowed him access to a network of locations, one in particular was the Detroit police department. He spent many years scouting out the city and people's passwords and secrets were just a small piece of his master plan and tools. Encrypted files were being transferred from one location to another. The major bank transactions were in the past; now all he focused on was the transfer of evidence and personal data to secure severs and locations. The Department of Defense was a very large pool he loved to swim in, but today the pool was local law enforcement databases.

The recruiting station accident and deaths were not reported on the news, or anywhere in police investigations, or emergency responders. The Magistrate controllers and contacts had made the incident disappear, down to the damaged building which was already renovated in record time. What the Magistrate didn't know was that Jared had arranged for two people to video tape the incident outside of the station with high powered cameras a good distance away. In addition, recordings of the reporting was cloned to a secure sever before it was erased at the source.

At the touch of a key he sent information to one of Erica's Eternal Champions superhero email addresses. He placed his computer to sleep and walked into the adjacent room where Jean slept. It was now a waiting game for him, but that didn't mean he was going to be idle. He eased next to Jean, and kissed her gently.

Jean and Jared walked along a New England grassy ridge line on the coast of Devon. The wind was moderate as if a storm were about to hit the shore from a far off very dark stretch of clouds. The sun was attempting to penetrate the misty cloud cover above, but it only made the scenery bright enough for a romantic encounter. Jean felt the slightly cool wind rush throughout her face and body as she held Jared's hand being led towards a cottage on the hillside. The grass was plush as if moss, but firm enough not to break apart if she decided to run and slide her feet along the fertile ground. She wore a light brown summer dress made of linen or silk, she couldn't really tell since it made her feel naked to the world as air passed through it.

Jared wore retro style nineteenth century light brown pants and a white linen long sleeve shirt. His short brown hair flowed with the wind, but not as elegantly as Jean's white long beautiful hair. Jared stopped and faced her. For a moment Jean was confused because she thought they were going to the cottage, but now Jared only had a wide smile as he hugged her close to him. "I love you." Jared kissed her.

Jean returned the kiss and they laid down on the dark green grass. Jean could feel the wind pick up and knew they would end up in a shower if they stayed there, but it didn't matter to her, she just wanted to enjoy her time with him.

They kissed for a while with Jean on top of him. Jared looked up and his attention was diverted to the sky. "What's that?" he asked with fascination.

"What's what?" Jean instinctively responded not wanting to stop kissing him.

"In the sky."

Jean moved to the side and looked up at the sky. The sky had opened up with three rainbows showing a very large blue spot and very white clouds in the middle forming the words, 'I love you Jean Lorenz. Will you marry me?'

Jared held a large diamond ring in his hand in front of her face as she turned back to see him.

She looked at the ring and at his face in the background with a very big smile and passionately kissed him. "Yes, my darling."

They enjoyed each other for hours, until Jean fell fast asleep. She awoke in her underground room which was dimly lit, instead of the cottage and knew it was a dream. But to her surprise she could feel Jared kissing her which felt at first like there was an ice cube they were sharing. Once Jean was fully awake, Jared broke away, "Good morning my love."

"Hmm, good morning." Jean replied feeling so happy with clear memories of the dream which seemed so real. "I had the best dream ever."

"Really? Was I in it?" Jared asked with an innocent look on his face.

"You didn't use an illusion on me, did you?" Jean asked a little unsure as to why Jared seemed to be so interested in what she dreamt.

"Now why would I do that?" Jared said and kissed her deeply. Jean felt a ring's shape and diamonds on her tongue, and quickly withdrew the ring from her mouth.

"I love you and want the best for you. I'm not perfect, but will you marry me again, and allow me to bring you joy for the rest of your life?"

Jean stared at the ring and then at Jared's gray glittering eyes. Tears swelled in her eyes which she didn't mind shedding. "Yes, I'll marry you."

They enjoyed the rest of the night in a lovers' euphoria, breaking the good news to Natasha late that morning.

Serenity Community, Chicago, Illinois

The order was given, and a small portion of the community population went out to lead and unleash a wave of terror across the nation. The other portion prepared to encircle Detroit and search for Jared and Jean.

Michael sat in his specialized cleansing room, consisting of a treated whirlpool, master bed, and air synthesizers. Natural concentrated aromas were introduced into the room to provide a relaxed and therapeutic environment. The quality of the air was also pure with a slight increase of oxygen per cubic inch. Michael lay on his bed with his hands on his chest. His recovery was complete after the bombing, and he was left along in preparation for the upcoming execution; but it was an excuse as his mind waited in a void of relaxation.

It seemed as if he floated off into a dream, but to the contrary; his dream of the ocean surface turned into a dark cold void of nothingness. A light appeared above and behind him, but no matter how much he tried to turn towards the origin of the light, it eluded him. A hooded figure like a medieval monk approached from the distance. The figure floated rapidly towards him with the light source above and behind him casting a moon like glare on and around the figure.

The figure stopped a few feet from Michael, but all he saw was a blue glow coming from where the eyes would be positioned on the face. A black grayish hood covered his head. His face was dark or was it the shadow created by the light above?

"My masters and associates have decided to terminate our agreement. Your carelessness in attacking the Eternal Champions and conflict with the CEA has caused too many variables." The hooded figure said with a hollowed low male tone.

"The Eternal Champions will not be a problem if I kill Jared and his followers first." Michael declared.

If the figure could smile it would have, but it only laughed a screechy groan. "Your destiny is death. The empire you have built will be restored by us once the Eternal Champions is done with you."

"You underestimate the Magistrate; I will take the country if I have to!" Michael protested, but the figure disappeared into the darkness never to converse with him again.

"You hear me! I will destroy them all, and then I will come after you!"

Michael woke up out of his mental communiqué. The Magistrate indeed was prepared to attack the country, with only the Eternal Champions, SIA, and now Jared to stand in their way. Three thousand mentalist lived across the nation, even though they were not as powerful as his controllers, they were powerful enough to attrite the country's sense of law and order. Only a few hundred were being utilized to commit mass deaths at the moment; but soon he would order full activation of his followers to kill and control all political, law enforcement, and military leaders. Once Jared was out of the way, he would order a country wide man hunt and destruction of the Eternal Champions. EFL would be dealt with through a renewed alliance to Australia, but that part of the plan was only theoretical, even though it was already a reality in Michael's egotistical mind.

Nick sent Michael a mental message indicating they had localized Jared to be hiding in Detroit.

Michael quickly left the room and prepared for the road trip with great enthusiasm. He ordered all followers within the Chicago city limits down to Detroit to converge on Ford Field parking lot; from there they would fan out and locate Jared, then destroy him and Jean.

Octavian Farm, Eternal Champions Battle Room, Ft. Lauderdale, Florida

John quickly dropped Richard off in the battle room and teleported away to see Max. Cindy was in the main house when Richard called her down for a mission.

Cindy was happy to do something else besides watching stream television, or even riding horses which she loved. It was a change of scenery which always brought her joy. Having a computer consultant job helped in keeping her going to various public and interesting places, but now she would get to go into secret places that people would normally be killed for should they be found out.

Elizabeth was speaking with Richard when Cindy entered the battle room. It seemed they were trying to decide which leads to focus on.

"What have I missed?" Cindy came into the room not bothering to wait for the elevator doors to open as she materialized through the doors as if they were made of air.

"We're trying to decide where to send you first." Richard said, stood up and walked towards the screens, but stopped in front of the work table.

"An anonymous tip gave use information about things happening in Detroit, Michigan. Richard thinks that it's either our mysterious snitch or it might be someone else wanting us to find Jared." Liz explained.

Cindy sat down and paid attention to Richard's briefing.

"A bus collided with a building next to a recruiting police station. Erica cannot find any evidence to that effect; but the information this source gave us says it did happen and it happened nine days ago. Watch as the bus collides. Pedestrians on the sidewalks rush into the bus, but they act like they were passengers. Erica, fast-forward. Thirty or so minutes later, people start to jump out of the recruiting station upper floors, head first into the pavement below."

Cindy had seen and done worse, but she felt the gruesome deaths as horrid nevertheless. "Are they really, what the hell." She commented.

"Yeah, wait for what's next. Minutes later, a man comes out and just stands there as an invisible force undresses him and re dresses him… But note." Richard waited for the right moment as the man left the area at a fast pace run. "There!" Richard pointed and the video was paused on a glimpse of Jared's face leaving the screen's edge towards the camera. Erica was able to find this image out of sync with the video speed. It would normally not be seen with normal vision.

"Who's that?"

"Jared." Richard said recognizing his face from John's and Eibren's memories.

"I guess I should have asked what was seen in the trial since John didn't know I was there, I never attended the mental conference." Cindy stated.

"Well, now you know how he looks like. Of course you know Jean's face; so after talking with Liz, I think you should go to the recruiting station and see what you can find out. They are covering or have already covered something up."

“What other leads are there?” Cindy asked seeing a lot of new papers on the table.

“In addition to the information, more information came in earlier giving us a list of over a thousand followers that work for the Magistrate. John is working on finding them and putting them out of commission. Susan reports that she has a lead on our mystery woman, so I haven’t called her back here yet. While you are up there, Liz and I will be tracking the names here in the surrounding counties. Oh, and Larcis will take you to Detroit.”

“Good, I was hoping when I could go on the roller coaster ride.” Cindy joked with a smile.

“One last thing, we don’t have any photos of the hierarchy of the Magistrate, I’m sure John will give us something once he finds out, but assume everyone is powerful. Call me if you run into Michael or anyone who seems like they’re in charge of something major.” Richard instructed calmly.

“Yes, Dad, I will tell you if the big bad wolf pops it head out.” Cindy laughed.

“I’ll take that sarcastic remark as a hell yeah.” Richard laughed with her.

SIA Headquarters Crisis Action Control Center

John as Mindseye instantly appeared on the main floor in front of the large screens. An agent barely missed him as he was range walking across the floor. Many people were startled, but the fear quickly changed to relief as they recognized the superhero.

"Erica, override SAI and computer control and place a GPS location for everyone on that list you gave us earlier, green for home addresses and blue for any other address like work." John talked into his comlink wristwatch. "Director, I need your telepaths to report here immediately." John shouted across the room.

"I'll do better than that," Max replied over the intercom which was linked to his collar microphone. He pushed a button on one of the agent's console. "This is Maximilian, all Valkyrie teams, report to the control room right now."

John smiled thinking of how Valkyrie was the code name for an assassination attempt on Hitler. And it also represented the mythological female being who chose who died and lived in battle.

John and Max met halfway as both walked towards each other once the order was given. The screens in the center flickered or turned off as if all the computers were being rebooted.

"What's happening?" Max asked.

"I told Erica to take over your SAI and computer systems in place. She found a problem with your AI, but we don't have time to have her take care of it now. Once the screens come back up, they will show were all these people are on the list, and make links to the mass deaths. I will weed out the sleepers here and instruct the telepath teams on what to do. I will teleport them to the key locations and they will subdue the mentalists. I need your field agents to be really to assist in making sure the mentalists are knocked out, drugged, whatever it is you guys do." John said.

Max smiled for the first time since the non-guilty verdict of Creator. “Thanks.”

“You can thank me later over a cookout with the President.” John nonchalantly said.

“Well, I will get my secretary to arrange it.” Max said, looking at the screens as they came back to life.

“Sir, Lieutenant Lee, reporting.” A female agent along with her team of three agents, approached the two men.

“Stand by Lieutenant.” Max ordered as he told one of the operators at the front terminal to scroll through the list of sleepers and mentalists’ names supplied by Erica.

“There, stop. Why isn’t the list alphabetical on this part?” Max asked hoping John could answer it.

“Erica, locate all those people in the headquarters please.” John commanded while Erica brought up a map of the SIA Headquarters.

All mentalists and sleeper agents were plotted in the headquarters.

“My agents don’t have personal trackers, how’s she doing that?” Max stated.

“All the names on the list are not the current names; people have changed names and a few have changed faces. The location of personal in the headquarters is currently being plotted by me using the security cameras. By the looks of activity the sleeper agents have no idea that they are sleeper agents.” Erica replied on John’s comlink.

"Valkyrie team Six is not responding to your orders, because Ryan Lester has somehow kept them from hearing your orders, or is mentally controlling them." Erica added.

John saw Ryan's plot, and teleported to him. Before Ryan could react to John's presence, John had nullified his mental powers, and the entire team was teleported to the control room next to Lt. Lee's team.

Everyone looked on in bewilderment. In less than a few seconds, a team of four agents appeared in the control room out of nowhere. "Can you get a security team to imprison this traitor, and keep him from using his mental abilities?"

Even Max was dumbfounded as John used his powers. He had never known John to be so powerful or able to teleport himself and others. He saw Susan teleport but he thought she was the only one that could do that since the encounter with the Argonian princess.

The third Valkyrie team entered the control room as five security guards took Ryan away.

"I assume these are all the telepaths in the complex?" John asked.

"Minus one, from these teams, and six from the psychological analyst section?" Max replied.

"Aah, please ask them to report here as well." John signed.

"Alright. Do as he says." Max ordered one of the communications technicians.

"In the meantime, I need all of you to open your minds to

me, so I can quickly teach you how to neutralize another telepath's mental control and penetrate mental protections. I will teleport pairs to these locations." John highlighted eight addresses across New York and Washington D.C."

"Max, they will need a team or more of federal agents to police up their targets. Each pair will continue to find and apprehend the sleepers and mentalists within the city limits. Please coordinate so teams near each other don't waste time on the same targets. Any questions before we start?" John asked.

"What do we do once we hit the city limits?" One of the telepath asked.

"I will be moving to other states and cities doing the same with other SIA telepath teams. The Director will give you instructions on where to go after your goals are met. It is probable you will be needed to the west, but if not you can make your way back home with his permission."

"What about the sleeper agents here?" Max asked.

"Get agents to arrest them and put them under so they don't hear, see, or think of any activation command. I will exam them after I drop off the last team. Lt Lee, you will be with two others. Your team will take care of the White House and Capitol Hill area." John said, but at the same time he was mentally speaking to the telepaths and instructing them on things to look out for.

'The sleeper agents you run into will have command memories which are hidden. The only way to get those commands and get rid of them is to look for sound memories linked to deep childhood memories. It could be phrases or sounds that would normally never be heard. It's not likely it will be a visual queue since those memories would be easier to spot by a mental scan which you guys have performed in the past. If you weren't able to scan for those memories before, you are able to now. I have given all of you the ability to block against mental illusions and neutralize mental blocks. This will allow you to scan anyone and see if they have telepathic abilities even if they are trying to hide it. Whatever you do, do not try to control or scan the mentalists for information, simply neutralize their power and knock them out. If you try to control them, they will be able to fight back giving them more time to figure out how to attack you and neutralize your abilities. Pandora and I will get to them in time, find the information they have, and take actions so they can't use their powers for evil anymore.'

'Mindseye, I noticed that one of the Magistrate mentalist on that list is a four-star general officer. What do we tell his security and other high officials - that they're under arrest?' Lt. Lee asked.

'You all have Presidential authority to arrest anyone on that list and anyone who is identified as a Magistrate mentalist or threat. Don't be shy to use your authority. There is no need to tell a lie, mentally show whoever; like the Secret Service or Marines, where your authority comes from, and exercise it.' John stated.

'Understood.' Was the mental reply of many of the telepaths.

Max was coordinating with the lead resident offices across the nation to fully support the telepath teams which would temporarily be put in charge of any federal agent, military, or police entity in the area. Before Max finished his briefing to the resident offices, John had teleported two teams to their locations.

Max made several calls to key personnel in Washington DC; in particular, the President and the Secretary of Homeland Defense. The summarized briefing was short and he knew once the dust settled, a viable plan would be expected by his agency to keep telepaths from undermining the country again.

John teleported to all of the telepath teams across the country in less than an hour, assisting them in their endeavor to stop the mass killings. Richard and Elizabeth were able to get a hold of a few unsuspecting mentalists in the Fort Lauderdale area. But news spread quickly and many of the Magistrate mentalists scurried into hiding to other cities or states. At the end of the day, the SIA telepaths with John's help rounded up over three hundred mentalists and deactivated nine hundred sleepers.

Richard and Max attended John's interrogation of the mentalists at SIA headquarters. John's report indicated the structure of the Magistrate underworld. The Serenity Community instantly became the prime target for SIA and the Eternal Champions, but it wouldn't be easy, even with John and Susan's powers. According to thoughts John forced out of the mentalists, there were over seven hundred mentalists in the community property. The top Archmagis all had powers strong enough to subdue and kill the SIA telepaths or agents. John, Susan, Richard, and Elizabeth were the only ones capable of taking on the Archmagis as a whole. But Richard wanted to minimize collateral damage so he instructed SIA to surround the community while his team entered and arrested Michael. Max was in full support of the idea, but he needed time to get his agents into position, and wanted a better recon of the community before letting Richard's team to blindly enter. It would be a day before SIA could have enough agents on the ground to lay seize to the property. Richard and his team waited patiently for SIA, but more importantly they waited for Cindy's and Susan's reports.

Chapter Eight

The Unseen Spy

A small black dot over Detroit quickly grew to reveal Night in his all black outfit and Mirage in her colorful camouflage skin tight suit. As they approached skyscraper altitude Mirage vanished, and Night stopped in midair. A moment later, Night flew off towards the southeast, with a few sonic booms being heard many miles up in the stratosphere.

Ten minutes later, Cindy flew above the recruiting station circling both buildings like a hawk looking for prey. She was satisfied with her aerial recon and flew down to the pavement in front of the station's entrance. She examined the pavement carefully. There was no evidence of blood stains or structural damage from heavy objects. But, the pavement and even the areas where the bus caused damage were clean; too clean. One concrete square was newly cured and the broken windows were not only new, but tinted with security film. 'Either they have very fast contractors in their pocket, or they made people do it by mental coercion. 'Well. It's time to see the inside.' Cindy thought with interest.

The outside of the station was quiet, and she assumed it would pick up a little once lunch started. But she wasn't going to wait for people to go for lunch. In fact she wanted to see people in their normal work duties and lunch time would only take them away from their desks or training.

Cindy flew through the double doors of the station like a cinematic aberration specter except she was totally invisible to everyone in the building. She stopped behind the reception desk and watched them work, listened and read what was out in the open. It was quite boring, listening to the guards talk about current sports events and gossip, but she was more interested in the names and offices on the phone directory and camera monitors. She flew up into the second story and entered the commodore's office. He wasn't in the office and his secretary was typing away at some spreadsheet.

Cindy stayed invisible but her body's molecular structure harden so she could touch matter and searched the desk with impunity. Drawers opened and closed as if they were automatic draws running through a self test mode. Paper files floated into the air and were replaced where they came from after Cindy read the jest of the information. She turned on the desktop, and it took her a while but she was able to hack into the Commodore's profile. It didn't reveal much to her, since it was unlikely the Commodore would be holding incriminating information on a computer which was easily exposed to law enforcement severs and agencies like the FBI or SIA. There was nothing out of the norm except for the cleanness outside. Now it was time to search the entire complex. She flew around the entire floor and worked her way down.

It wasn't long before she ran into the connecting underground hallways to the adjacent building. The scenery reminded her of spy movies where classified operations were being conducted or weaponry was being tested in a conspiracy theory underworld. She easily phased through the solid doors and entered the floors Jared and his crew had once roamed. But in place were different security guards and the rest of the space deserted of people. She could see that there was a totally different computer system installed, and the camera monitors showed different views than what the stations showed. In essence, the cameras were monitoring outside and inside of the entire complex next to the recruiting station. The slight scent of bleach or chemical was present in the underground floors which she didn't pay too much attention to, thinking the janitors were heavy handed on cleaning supplies. She also ignored the faint scent of new paint which covered plaster patches from bullet holes she couldn't see.

She flew around the floors only finding people, besides security personnel, in the first and second floors of the building portion above ground. They were conducting class training, but it wasn't the typical class setting she grew up with. The room she entered held ten recruits and two instructors. The instructors were on opposite ends of the room. All of the people in the room had their eyes closed and no one made a sound. Cindy floated in front of the students looking for facial expressions, but the only thing she could tell was they were all in a trance of meditation or paralyzing spell. A moan or deep breathing came from two recruits, but they returned to their emotionless state after a minute or two. The white board on the wall was empty as if it hadn't been used in weeks. She waited patiently for whatever they were doing to end. Almost an hour later, the people woke up out of their trance and all stood up as if an imaginary class bell had rung. The students left the room with the instructors following behind them.

Cindy flew above the group's heads listening in to their conversations. They talked about the adventure they just had that day. For a while Cindy thought they were talking about a video game or story in a book; but it finally dawned on her that they had experienced an out of body adventure in a made up world in their minds. She thought quickly and followed the instructors who broke off from the group and went into the lower floors she had recently scouted.

The instructors separated, but they were close enough for her to find out what each was up to by moving back and forth. One ate his lunch in a kitchenette, while the other man took a nap listening to what Cindy could make out through his earphones as sounds of nature. Many years ago, having to stay invisible and dematerialized caused her pain or made her very tired; but now she could stay invisible for close to two days. The instructors returned to their duties and the classroom sessions continued as Cindy had witnessed earlier. At times Cindy thought it was a waste of time by sitting in the classroom, since no one really talked at all. The only reason the students talked when they left for lunch was that maybe they were taking a break from the mental training; at least that's what she thought. But after staying with the students until the last classroom period, she realized that they all were talking verbally and mentally, having caught people speak in half sentences or verbally answer questions to unasked verbal questions. The more she thought about it, the instructors never spoke, even during their lunch break. Maybe she wasn't the best choice in spying on people who only talked with their minds.

Cindy moved back to the recruiting station and stayed with the Commodore who was now in his office. He seemed new to the leadership position, but yet it seemed that his files and wall decorations indicated he had been in charge of the training center for over a year. The end of the day came late for the chief, but to Cindy's surprise, he didn't get in his car and go home. The secretary left the building, but he got into the elevator and headed towards a room in the underground complex. The room was simplistic with a bed, a small desk with a computer and lamp stand. There was a connecting bathroom which he used to prepare for bed and without doing anything else he robotically went to sleep, that's if a robot could actually sleep.

Cindy stood next to the Commodore as he slept in the position of attention. She waited next to him for several hours. It was very weird to her as the man never moved to different positions or showed any signs of dreaming. The lamp was also left turned on, which was not too unusual, but it did seem odd to her since sleeping in darkness was something she was accustomed to doing.

She could tell it was very late, so she flew to where the security guards were on that floor. If there was any action that night, it would be there. There had been a shift change, and the new guards were somewhat different than the others she had encountered eight hours earlier. They weren't gossiping or talking about anything. They were watching Law and Order, besides the camera monitors, and seemed to be interested in the show, but the three guards never spoke to each other. Cindy had a flashback of the students in the classroom and now the security guards were doing the same. Cindy's body tensed and she cursed at the situation with frustration but no one saw or heard her. She had one last idea and flew around the floors looking for the server room. She could possibly look through the information, but it would take her a while and it would be detected. She might be invisible, but the active data retrieval would not. After a few minutes of trying to figure out other alternatives, she decided to go the server route instead of waiting for someone to expose some useful evidence by accident.

Jared's control room, Detroit, Michigan

The news of random public killings ebbed off as Jared expected. The pubic only saw the censored reports, but SIA had a live feed on the progress the telepaths were having with Mindseye's leadership. It was late morning after his proposal to Jean, and the women were in the kitchen area speaking of many things he would have liked to have listened to. But things needed to be monitored closely now that the Magistrate was feeling pressure from SIA and the Eternal Champions. The live feed from the SIA headquarters was not as secure as people thought. Not that he could have hacked security protocols or was using a mentally influenced SIA agent, but Jared liked to keep things simple. A few well placed cameras many years ago showed him what was happening in the SIA operations center. The feed was running along hard wired conduits to the outside, so there was no wireless transmission that could be detected by security measures in the complex.

The air filtration and ventilation system in the maze Jared had created was impressive. He scrolled over the touch screen and an additional ten percent of oxygen was injected into the rooms designated for their use. The clock was ticking and he and Natasha would need the good air for their illusions, when the time was right.

He sent out messages to his remote locations with positive replies. The building above him was empty, but automatic lighting, windows, doors, and sound systems made it seem as if people worked in it; but the lack of many cars around the building gave away the truth. It didn't matter to Jared, since the building had several hundred meters of empty open ground all around. All he needed was for drifters and pedestrians to stay away ever since he created the complex of mazes under the building.

Natasha entered the room with her hair bundled up prepared for a fight, but it was more of a trend for her now since things got tense several weeks ago. "So what's going on?"

"The stock market went up." Jared smiled.

Natasha looked at the touch screen next to Jared. "You haven't told me how much I've made in the past six months."

"Didn't you tell me you didn't want to know until you made millions?"

"Yes, but seeing that I might not be alive in the near future, I want to know now."

"Nat, you shouldn't talk so negative about your future. I told you we will survive this."

"Brat, how do you know?" She softly asked.

"I met a man a long time ago. He died, but before he did, he showed me a glimpse of the future." Jean entered the room as Jared told his story.

"He wasn't famous and he had a long criminal record. I thought he was a con artist, because if he really had precognitive abilities, then why would he be caught by the police so much. He showed me a vision of my future, and then I knew he was the real thing. I researched his past and death and found out other superhumans had been sabotaging his life, and no matter how much he tried to fix his life, he ended up on the wrong end of the stick. Precognitive visions aren't a hundred percent guaranteed, but so far he's been right." Jared explained.

"So you knew that we would be in this mess?" Nat asked surprised.

"No Sis. I knew the three of us would be here, Michael will die, but like I said, the superhumans who killed this man I talked about, are still around." Jared said as he tapped into Air Force and SIA space technologies platforms.

"Who are these superhumans?" Jean asked as she sat next to her fiancé.

"The last one alive is with Michael. His name is Oliver

Cox. We need to kill him first before Michael. His abilities stem from people deciding on actions, unlike Isis who sees the future no matter what's happening in the present. So as long as we don't decide until the last second, he won't know his death is coming until it's too late."

"Is that why you never mentioned him until now?" Nat asked.

"Yes, but also because now both of you need to know." Jared replied and a picture of Oliver and his personal data was posted on screen 2, out of four other screens on the eight foot desk/console. "This is Oliver, make sure you don't anticipate your actions if you do run into him; just act or respond without thinking."

Oliver was five feet five inches tall, with a large bald spot on the top of his head. His hair was gray mixed with dark brown from ear to ear. His three inch beard was well groomed, and whiter in color than his head hair. The characteristic mentalist gray eyes were dulled, and many mole-like splotches on his face made it look as if he had an undetermined skin disease. His lips were puffy and right eye was droopy which made him look as if he had an allergic reaction to something he ate. He was seventy-eight years old and had one son who was also a disciple of his in the Magistrate; but the son didn't show any signs of precognitive abilities. Oliver was an elder, and to Jared's pleasing expectation, would be with Michael when they attacked the deadly maze.

"What else have we been in the dark about?" Jean asked as if she and Natasha were being played.

"Well, thanks to your friend Randolph Maximilian and Presidential approval for moving satellite taskings, we now have eyes on Michael's movement." Jared said as a satellite live feed was being shown on vehicle movement west of Detroit.

Both women examined the screens and realized they were looking at SIA and Air Force Space Command footage of people and houses in a residential area, and vehicle movement on back roads twenty miles west of Detroit.

Jared pointed at a string of vehicles on Route 60. "I'm surprised they didn't travel at night, but I guess he wants to get to Detroit as fast as possible."

"Maybe the bomb helped him decide." Natasha smiled.

"So Michael is in one of those cars?" Jean asked.

"He's in one of these vehicles in this cluster. I'm sure his recon teams have narrowed the search to the west side of the city by now." Jared pointed at the screen with a specialized laser pointer.

"So how much time do we have?" Natasha asked.

"I would say one to maybe eight hours."

"Why would they know we're here?" Jean asked knowing they had covered their tracks to their specific location.

"I left clues so they would come here. But I couldn't make it too easy, so hence the possible eight hour wait."

Detroit Police Recruiting Station

Cindy flew down into the server room which was connected to the training building. To her relief the room was not being physically monitored at such an early hour. It was clear that there was an information systems security technician who monitored the server probably during work hours by the two workstations and personal items left there. But they were probably not needed all of the time since most of the operations were set on automatic. If something catastrophic did happen, it would alert the technician or security guards through a cell phone or other communication system in place. If the operation of the severs weren't so clandestine, perhaps there would have been a 24/7 IT specialist company monitoring the system from a remote location. She took advantage of the situation and typed away at one of the workstation. Cindy stayed invisible but turned solid and plugged in a USB connector from the computer to her wrist comlink. Erica took over from there and invaded the terminal with ease taking her less than a few minutes to create a valid user interface and permissions.

Cindy was very familiar with security systems and knew that what she was doing would have been found out if she were in SIA headquarters or the Eternal Domain. They monitored wireless communications, unlike the recruiting station which didn't have the resources to monitor all secure wave lengths which included cell phone calls and the like. Cindy could see Erica do her searching and altering on the monitor. It seemed very fast to Cindy as hundreds of files were opened up every few seconds to include secure files, read, and copied to Erica's memory banks. But to Erica it was very slow since the band width of the data transfer was extremely small for her liking. "Can you tell me any highlights so I know where to go from here?" Cindy whispered out of habit trying to be as invisible as possible.

The monitor locked up for a second and text displayed on it in a command prompt box, "I haven't found much more than what we already know from the tip. But perhaps this explains part of the cover up for the incident."

Erica posted an email to the commodore about how he needed to reassign the Necroes to the Lansing Police Academy with high marks, and the third precinct. The email came from Rueben, Director of Operations a week ago.

"Rueben seems to be an Archmagi filling the role of an operations officer by the looks of other emails to the complex. I also found evidence that the real commodore's name was Clairance Giggs, who had a record going back six years, but it seems he had retired a month ago and died a week ago from a heart attack. At least that's what's in public record, but according to the emails and files, he had been active here prior to a week ago." Erica texted on the screen.

"What are Necroes?" Cindy asked.

"I don't know, but it sounds like it's referring to dead people or bodies."

"Hmm, dead people meaning the dead bodies on the video or something else?"

"Considering we're talking about an organization that deals with mentalists and use words like magi in their lingo, I think it could be referring to humans without any mentalist powers. So the term necro or nekros in ancient Greek meaning dead body refers to powerless humans." Erica theorized.

"Do you know where the email came from?"

"It will take me a few minutes, but the initial view of the IP which seems to be altered is Denver."

"Of all places." Cindy said out of bad memories in her past.

"You don't have to go there, I can search the compartmented network from here since you gave me physical access through this workstation and server."

"Good." Cindy replied with relief. "Is there any data going to something local?"

"Now that you mention it. There is correspondence to several locations all throughout the city, similar to an all-points bulletin with a partial description of Jared and Jean."

"Why would they do that if the police have already put one out for them a long time ago?" Cindy asked.

"The APB wasn't sent to police stations, but rather to residents and businesses."

"Really?" Cindy thought about her next move. "Once you're done, I will leave here and you can direct me to the nearest location. I will investigate them until I get a solid lead on their progress in finding Jared."

"What should I do about this complex?" Erica asked.

"We could contact SIA, but leave it alone for now. We don't want anyone to know someone has been here at this time."

"I will tell the group. Oh, and I'm finished with the network."

Cindy removed the USB connector and dematerialized, flying up through the complex and outside northeast towards downtown and her first location.

It wasn't long before she arrived at a telemarketing business lot which was vacant at the moment. It was early morning and the place would be empty of employees for a while, so she moved on to a location which Erica had identified as a residence.

The four story mansion Cindy approached was impressively sitting on a hill like elevation in the center of tall buildings. It was the house of a minister next to one of the largest Lutheran church in the city. The hundred year old buildings on the property reminded Cindy of a horror movie scene in the medieval days. She phased through the mansion structure like an invisible spirit looking for victims to haunt, but at the same time observing the décor and upkeep of the place. If mentalists lived here, they were a different breed by keeping the place well maintained as opposed to the way the recruiting station was allowed to waste away.

She counted ten people to include the minister and his wife. They were awake in the kitchen eating and coordinating what seemed to her as a very early vacation trip. The church cover was ideal for them to be able to manipulate or make contact with other mentalists in the city, but that was Cindy's last concern. All of the occupants in the mansion were busy going through papers and items which seemed to be religious artifacts in nature but

Cindy knew better. She wasn't an expert in the occult, but the research revealed by Erica back in the Eternal Domain let her know that they were preparing for something big which involved combat or some important ritual. The minister was in his late sixties, but an older man seemed to be giving the orders as if he were going through a checklist in his mind. The man went through an itinerary and Cindy quickly knew that someone up in the chain of command was going to visit the city. She moved closer to see if she could see any documents of something that would give her more details. The old man paused in the middle of his sentence, and Cindy stopped a few feet from him and quickly flew above him with half her body inside the ceiling. She had seen this before and knew that the man had somehow sensed a presence or a warning of something. In the past. it was three superhumans with precognitive powers, but even they couldn't figure out it was her since she was invisible; and knowing that death is near and invisible is like knowing there is nothing you can do to prevent it. But this was different, because she had no intention on killing anyone in the near future, so how could he sense her if he did have fortunetelling powers?

The old man looked around and then up at the ceiling. Cindy felt a little uneasy, but she was sure he couldn't really see her, so she made sure and stayed above the old man wherever he moved in the house. The old man returned to giving commands and every now and then looked up at the ceiling, but that was all. Cindy didn't have to get close to any documents or cell phones as the words she was waiting to hear were said. Michael was arriving at Ford Field Stadium early in the afternoon and they were supposed to secure the area before 9:00 AM that morning. She had the urge to fly outside of the mansion and call in a report, but the old man's behavior made her stay with him until he would take a step outside. Once outside she would leave the area and report her finding to Erica. The old man would think it was a ghostly feeling that left him once outside the house, like a temporary spiritual haunting.

The group left the mansion completely vacant and moved to the sanctuary where slightly over a hundred people waited. The parking lots outside of the two buildings were almost without cars when Cindy arrived, but during her time in the mansion the large group had arrived into the church. Cars left the three parking lots with two police officers assisting the exit of the cars out onto the main street. Cindy flew straight up several hundred meters once the old man left the mansion, but she didn't call in the report as she witnessed the company size element militaristically move eastward like a line of ants. She followed the vehicles and on her way to the stadium she called Erica.

Richard came up on the comlink and instructed her to keep her distance and monitor Michael's movements once she spotted him. He wanted to see if Michael could lead them to Jared, but most importantly he wanted to know who was with Michael now that he was out of Chicago and assembling his followers in mass.

Chapter Nine

❖---✻ ✪ ✻---❖

Senate Inquiry

SIA Headquarters, New York City

Senator Harleigh Summers waited patiently for Max to gather his advisors and second in command. The secure conference room had three large rectangular tables setup in a U-formation facing three large screens side by side. Max was sitting in the center table with a technician handing him a small tablet which was linked to the data feed in the control center.

Three advisors entered along with his second in command, Paul Rohan. Paul was very young for his position, in his late twenties, but his reputation preceded him as an intellectual genius when it came to legal matters and agent management. It was because of him that SIA had been in the forefront of leading conviction rates and public policy development.

Max was at ease to have his deputy there, since his expertise would desperately be needed now that the Senate had called an emergency meeting. He was sure they would ask about legal matters since legal procedures were being strained if not overridden due to the unique circumstances. Max motioned for Paul to take a seat next to him, while the three advisors sat at the left table so they could see both the screens and their leaders face to face.

Congressman Kings, Senator Burns, and Senator Summers in the center could be seen on the conference room center screen. Both sides simultaneously un-muted their audio transmissions.

"Senator Summers, we're ready to proceed." Max initiated the conference.

"Thank you, Director. As you know, President Hanson is preoccupied with the cabinet and emergency media conferences; but I assure you that everything we say here will be heard by him and the Vice President shortly after we are done. I know you are busy, but a decision point has come and we ask that you explain the nature of the telepath teams that are arresting people to include cabinet members?" Summers was the youngest female Senator at age thirty, with attractive long black hair and blue eyes.

It was odd to Max that she would be leading the inquiry since she was not only the youngest but had also only been in her position for six months. He knew she had won a landslide election, but never really paid attention to her attributes, thinking she was just the prettiest new face ever with heavy political clout. But Paul knew why, and had written a quick note in front of Max when they sat down before starting. 'Senator Summers is the lead on Superhuman legal oversight, and has educational background to back it up, double PhD in Psychology and Public Relations... Oh and she convinced the President to authorize our guys to arrest people.' So when Max read the note, he gave Paul a quick glance, showing a very mild expression of being impressed.

Paul smiled, knowing Max was very rarely impressed by Senators or anyone on Capitol Hill for that matter.

"Senators, Congressman... the teams are being assisted by Mindseye so they can find and arrest the mentalists and people who have been controlled by them. They are being moved to Resident Offices where the victims will be de-controlled or deprogrammed, is the best way I can put it, and will be returned to their duties. The mentalists who are the real criminals will be interrogated and the organization known as the Magistrate will be legally dealt with. Currently, Mindseye is the only one able to assist in our efforts, but I have been promised by Creator that Pandora will join the effort shortly." Max explained.

"It has come to our attention that the leader of the Magistrate will soon be arrested. Is this true?"

"We have located where the leader, Michael Stockwell, has been hiding, but are working on apprehending him; he is surrounded by a sizable force of mentalists."

"Excuse me, I assume EFL or the Eternal Champions are leading this particular effort?" Senator Burns interrupted.

"Senator, the Eternal Champions are assisting in the effort, but it will be a day before we can organize a frontal assault on Michael."

"We're not going to ask for the methods in how you plan on apprehending Mr. Stockwell, but the top question which President Hanson wants to know is will apprehending him prevent future mass murders?" Summers asked.

"Mindseye and Pandora will use their abilities to find all of the Magistrate followers and any other conspirators."

"Excuse me once again Senator. Director, you mean to tell us that without this Michael, the Eternal Champions can't find all of the followers and any other conspirators?" Burns interrupted.

"We have already found over two hundred mentalist out on the streets. By us getting Michael and the mentalists around him, Mindseye can get all of the followers even if they scatter and try to go into hiding." Max replied, not revealing that they had a head start from a mystery informer.

"So, I can tell the President once Mr. Stockwell is apprehended, that all Magistrate members will shortly afterwards be apprehended as well?" Summers asked while briefly glancing at Senator Burns who was physically on her left.

"Yes, that's correct Senator; but the Eternal Champions have already demonstrated that they can stop the Magistrate for good, so what is it that you really want to know?

Senator Summers looked at Congressman Kings who moved his seat back and started to stand up. "I told you he would catch on. It's all yours Harleigh... Oh, thank you for the chat, it was a pleasure."

"Likewise, Congressman, Senator." Max replied while

respectfully bowing his head slightly.

"Sir, should we leave the room too?" Paul asked as the two male politicians vacated on the other end of the conference.

"No, I want you all to hear this so I won't have to play messenger." Max replied with a slight grin.

Senator Summers didn't mind that all of the SIA agents were still seated. Perhaps she knew the audience needed to hear what she had to say more than her peers who were there just for moral support and dispense any outside question as to how the senate and congress were involved in the decision process.

"It has come to our attention that very young mentalists are rumored to be living in this community where Michael Stockwell has been living. Should you find children, it will most likely be children who have been indoctrinated into the Magistrate. The President says we need to find a way to deprogram these children so they don't turn into our future enemies. I was hoping you could come up with viable possible solutions to this projected problem."

"That's a good question I haven't had time to fully research." Max replied.

"Sir, if I may." Paul asked.

"By all means, Paul."

"Ma'am, depending on the number of children, SIA is able to house up to four hundred children with a 1:2 telepath ratio. It might be possible to retrain and raise the children from babies to age ten without them holding on to the Magistrate core beliefs and end goals. The older children will have to be deprogrammed by Mindseye or Pandora before we can raise them in stable homes. It is also likely that a portion of the children are not currently being raised by their natural parents, which will make the deprogramming easier. The drawback is that most of the SIA telepaths will be used on these children instead of focusing on crimes and finding other criminals."

"Would it be possible for Mindseye and Pandora to just give all the children a new identity?"

"It's not that simple Ma'am, in accordance to Homeland legal statutes it could be legally done and successful with normal children. But that is not the case here since the children will likely be telepathic. A four year old could be given a new identity, but without constant telepathic guidance and development, they would mentally regain what they have learned in the past and revel. But in the methods I propose, the telepaths would in time teach them that what they learned from the Magistrate in the past was wrong. Instead of finding a hidden memory and rebel, they would accept a new role in society which we will teach them."

"What prevents some of the children, especially the older ones from disagreeing with the new teachings?"

"As much chance as a teenager challenging authority, but if they are monitored properly, they shouldn't fall into the life of hatred towards normal humans or our society."

"Sounds like a start for now, but we will need to develop this further. Director, I would like for you to put a team together to work on this and other options."

"You can call me Max, Senator. And I will get a team

together immediately."

"There's another concern the Vice President and I have, along with some of my peers, but to put it bluntly; the CEA is going to be disbanded; which means their telepaths and resources will be absorbed by other agencies. I personally think all of the resources should go to your agency. Of course, this will get a lot of flak and the SIA will become by far the most powerful law enforcement entity in the country. The breach inside SIA doesn't help in getting a vote to do so; but I need your help in you telling me what you need, want, and how the resources could be best used. I know that once the FBI or CIA get their hands on some of these resources, they will not share like before. Plus it makes it harder to maintain accountability for these dangerous resources if they're spread out in a bunch of agencies. So, Max... I could use your thoughts on this before I make a push for or against certain agencies getting resources."

"It's a good thing I have thought about this possibility, and I believe we should get all of the telepaths and other resources. However, I want to be able to augment the other agencies with whatever resources we approve with their input and needs. Not that they will abuse their resources should they own them, but yes, we can manage the resources better."

"And I was told you were a very humble man."

"I am, but I'm decisive and usually right, as well." Max replied with the facial expression of an analytical android.

"Senator, we have been assisting the other agencies for several years and having added resources will only allow us to assist them better." Paul stated.

"Max, will your deputy be available to organize my presentation to the President within the next 48 hours, and also the movement of these resources within the next few months?" Summers asked, noting that Paul was well versed in SIA operations and Max would be busy for a while.

"He's yours as of now. I'll make him work overtime when he gets back." Max smiled.

"Thank you. My assistant will be contacting you soon to arrange your arrival to D.C."

"I'll be ready Senator." Paul replied calmly, but his gut mildly tensed up in knots as if he were going to the first job interview of his life.

The conference ended and Max gave orders to the advisors to get started with creating a Think Tank. The advisors left the room while Max motioned for Paul to stay.

"I do need you but she needs you more. Take whatever you need with you, and use Erica to help you instead of our AI. I will let Creator and Erica know."

"I will try my best, but I wasn't expecting to go to D.C. all of the sudden."

"What are you worried about?"

"I just don't want to burn any bridges on the Hill."

"It seems like you know her, so tell me; is she married?"

"She's widowed."

"Does she have a boyfriend?"

"I think she's available; but why are you asking me these specific questions?"

"Well since you're available as well, I shouldn't be expecting a political scandal coming across my daily reports. Just make sure you're honest with her and keep the interest of justice in mind by not embarrassing us."

"A scandal is not an issue." Paul exhaled deeply.

"Paul... It's alright. I can tell you like her and see seems to like you so I have no problems with that."

"You can deduct that she likes me from a few words not even relating to our personalities?"

"She was looking at you for most of the conversation, and she specifically asked for you, instead of giving me a blanket request."

"Max, she was looking at you most of the time; how can you even tell?"

"Paul, you've lost your touch." Max laughed. "Her eyes were moving back and forth by a millimeter every few seconds, and they never moved at all when you were talking or she was responding to your comments. But its okay, you will see for yourself in a few hours."

"And I thought I was the expert psychologist."

A call came into Paul's collar clip. "Sir, this is operator five; there's a call from Senator Summer's assistant for coordinating your travel."

"You're an expert alright, just not in diplomacy and love." Max laughed and laid his hand on the top of Paul's shoulder as Max left the conference room.

Paul sat in thought as the operator spoke again. "Sir, should I patch the call through or do you want me to relay a message?"

Eternal Domain Battle Room

Richard played with Alex by showing him different forms of animals. Alex's favorite was a young white tiger, where he was able to huge the neck of the beast even though it was his father. Alex embraced him with the strength of a WWF wrestler bear hugging an opponent. Richard turned back to his own form and firmly held Alex's wrists easing the pressure. "No, Alex. Like this."

Richard softened his grip on Alex's wrists. "Softly, like this."

"Tiger!" Alex morphed his skin and head hair to white with tiger stripes.

"Yes, you like Tigger, don't you? Maybe you should be watching different cartoons." Richard smiled and stood up carrying his son close to him.

Alex giggled as Richard tickled his belly.

"Okay, that's enough you two. Daddy has to work." Elizabeth entered the battle room from one of the kitchens in the underground base.

"Really?" Richard looked at his beautiful wife, then at

Alex.

"One day you will meet your dream girl, just make sure you understand that when you do, you stop being the boss."

"He's kind of young to be hearing about a future wife and slavery." Liz joked and opened her arms to take Alex away from him.

"Evil doesn't care how young you are to be exposed to it; so why shouldn't I give my great wisdom to my son?"

"You're right for once." Liz laughed and softly whispered into Alex's ear. "Listen to me and you'll be fine."

"I heard that." Richard said as he walked into the elevator.

Erica's hologram appeared in front of Richard as he walked. "Richard, SIA's AI is extremely compromised with destroyed data. I don't know what to do at this time."

"It's really that bad?" Richard went down a few levels to the mechanics room.

"If I reconstruct the data and fix other problems with the SAI, I won't be able to perform other duties in pursuit of SIA's requests and finding mentalists at large. So, that's why I'm coming to you for guidance."

"Sometimes I wonder how you guys survived without me." Richard smiled while walking into a large room full of small to large specialized vehicles.

"Survival is a human trait, not mine, so I don't know what you're talking about."

Richard half smiled, knowing she understood the emotion and need to exist and live, trying to play an emotionless computerized entity. “Well for now, concentrate on helping SIA with their reorganization problem. I have a feeling that our mystery person, Cindy, or Susan will help us find what we want. So once Deputy Rohan is satisfied with your assistance, go ahead and get the SAI back to normal.”

“I will keep you updated as usual.”

“Thank you. But for now, I want to check out the new information you got in while I was gone.” Richard sat at a workstation with a fifteen foot squared platform at waist height in front of him. High above on the ceiling was an inverted platform which was lit up in a lighter shade of French blue. Richard touched the three foot wide console and the platforms started to dimly glow. The lights in the room automatically turned off, leaving the area between the platforms lit up. “Show me the schematics of the latest vehicle additions to the files.”

The console responded to his voice command and a holographic image of two aircrafts and a hovercraft appeared in the platform area. Richard put on a pair of synthetic wireless gloves and pushed the two aircrafts off of the platform with a wave of his hand. He moved the hovercraft to the center and expanded the size to fit the platform. He smiled as he examined the specialized machine for moving cargo across swamps and lakes.

It was his way of leisurely working while waiting for SIA to move their assets into position to enter the Serenity Community. Hours passed before he received a call from Cindy, telling him that Michael was no longer in Chicago, but Detroit instead. After instructing Cindy to monitor Michael's activity, he went upstairs calling for John, Larcis, and Liz to meet him in the battle room.

John was already in the battle room as Richard arrived. "Richard, Susan says she'll be here soon."

"Did she find anything?"

"Not sure, but I can go see her in person and find out if you want."

Richard almost laughed. "You're trying too hard, John."

"Is it that obvious?"

"You shouldn't force it. It will happen in time."

"Do you think our bodies are just incompatible?"

"If any two people are meant to be together in this cosmos, it's you and Susan." Richard said as he sat on his favorite spot on the sofa.

"The radiation from the nuke could have messed me up for good."

"John, I know you want children, but this negative thinking really doesn't help the fact that the Argonian doctors said there wasn't anything wrong with you or Susan."

"Since when do I believe what doctors say?"

"Well most people believe when they say bad things, so why not the good things… Besides have you ever considered that maybe you, Susan, or both of you are subconsciously not having a baby because it's not the right time?"

"So instead of being radiated, I'm sabotaging myself?" John smirked.

"Weren't you the one who told me, you and Susan saw the future with children playing in the Royal courtyard?"

John looked at Richard with doubt. "How do I know if it wasn't other people's children?"

Richard looked down in defeat. "Well you're right... you're radioactive, self-destructive, and not performing to standard as usual."

"It's a good thing you're my friend, otherwise I would punch you and bruise my fist in the process."

"Okay boys, that's enough male bonding for now... What's going on, Honey?" Liz walked in from the elevator and sat next to Richard.

"We were talking about all the baby butts John is going to have to change. Oh, sorry the royal army of nurses and nannies will do that." Richard laughed.

"So you told him about my vision?" Liz asked before John could say a word.

"No, I was hoping to keep John thinking he was Godzilla except without the tail and all." Richard grinned.

"What vision?" John asked.

"You and Susan are going to have five children and a lot of

grand children." Liz happily reported.

"Really? When did you know?" John excitedly moved closer to the couple on a knee.

"Last night." Richard replied and put his arm around Liz.

"Wow." John's thousand mile stare said it all.

"For someone who can tell the future, you sure are surprised." Richard laughed.

John said nothing and stared into

"So why did you call us here?" Liz changed the subject as Larcis entered the battle room.

"Cindy says that Michael is in Detroit. So it bears to ask if we should move into the community now without waiting for all of the SIA agents to be in position."

"Do we know how many people are prepared to storm the community?"

"Erica says there're fifty-three telepaths and eighty agents ready."

"If we can wait about thirty minutes, Susan can join us." John stated.

"Boss, you want me to stay with Alex, so Liz can help you guys out?"

"Yeah, you can sit this one out, but I will still need you to monitor things. If we do need you, you can come to the rescue."

"Does Max know about moving the schedule up?" John asked.

"Not yet, but I can patch him in right now if you like?" Erica interjected from the surround sound system.

"Erica, tell Susan to come back home now. Michael will lead us to Jared and Jean. If SIA's analysis is correct we need the extra time to safely secure the children. Then we can go to Detroit."

"Sounds like a plan." Liz half smiled.

Max came up on the battle room main screen and Richard told him the plan, along with getting SIA agents in Detroit to start mobilizing to an assembly area.

Shortly after the communiqué with Max, Susan appeared in the battle room. Everyone looked at her eagerly waiting for good news.

She was in full costume ready to fight. "Well I found out her name, "Natasha Basara". And I assume Erica will make the link soon." Erica displayed a picture of Natasha on the main screen as Susan spoke.

"Natasha Basara is also Natasha Erickson. There is a record of US citizenship, but that is the only official record on file. She is probably using different aliases on other identifying documents."

"Which means she's a sister or wife, and still a ghost." Richard stated and motioned everyone to sit on the sofas around table, taking note of Natasha's unique facial photo on the naturalization certificate.

"Erica, display imagery of the Serenity Community."

Erica put up a green three dimensional map of the community on the table. “We need to systematically clear each house starting from three locations here in the north, eastern gate, and southern gate.”

Richard pointed to the three groups of houses for all three start points. The community was elevated and connecting underground halls and rooms appeared.

“Satellite and Ariel surveillance has uncovered these underground structures. Once we get closer, we can better determine the extent of the complex underneath, but for now this is what we have. If children aren’t consolidated we will have to spread out the telepaths to secure them as we move towards the western perimeter. If the children are consolidated, we will leave the telepaths with the children and neutralize all the adults without them. The telepaths will move the children to these collection points in the eastern and southern gates, and the adults will be moved to the eastern and northern collection points.”

“So how many agents and telepaths will be with each of us?” John asked.

“Ten telepaths and ten agents for each direction, the rest will stay outside of the perimeter to make sure people don’t escape. But, I don’t want agents to be injured on this, so the first priority before moving into the area is to destroy or disable any traps, security systems, and lethal devices like IEDs in case they know we’re coming.”

“We can take care of that.” Susan volunteered John.

“How is Cindy doing?” Larcis asked.

"She is monitoring from a distance, but I'm sure she will get up close when Michael makes a move for Jared. So we need to take the community quickly and as silently as possible. I don't want Michael to get spooked and command his followers to go on a death rampage in Detroit."

"I guess you guys better leave now then." Larcis suggested.

"Alright John, take us to the SIA staging area." Richard commanded.

John placed one hand on Richard's shoulder and the other on Liz's shoulder. Susan grabbed Liz's hand and the four superheroes instantly vanished, reappearing in Chicago nine blocks east of the Serenity Community.

The SIA staging area was in an auto body shop business. Undercover vehicles occupied most of the parking lot and inside of the building. The agent in charge greeted the four heroes, but the formalities were cut short. John asked for the names and locations of all the agents and telepaths around the community. He entered all of the agents' minds and gave them their personal assignments and plan of attack. Susan scanned the vehicles and equipment and passed on the information to John who task organized the three breech teams, collection points and perimeter force.

Richard and Liz led the eastern breech, John on the north, and Susan on the south. The noon day showed almost no activity in the community except for the security guards at the gates. John used his specialized vision to scan the community several blocks from the northern wall. The complex of underground connections was a little more extensive than what was revealed by the SIA surveillance platforms.

The information was relayed to Richard, Susan and Liz. Richard ordered all communications to be jammed, and telepaths on the perimeter blocked all mental projections from exiting the community. The electricity was cut off, but water was left on in case water was needed to put out fires and the like.

Richard and Liz flew towards the eastern gate as soon as the first SIA vehicle made the corner half a block from the gate. John teleported his entire team of twenty agents on the inner side of the community wall. SIA agents quickly spread out on the first target while John started his neutralizing attacks on adults in the area.

Susan likewise flew down on the southern gate while the SIA vehicles made the first corner to the gate. The gate guards were all paralyzed and before they could counter the mental attack, they blacked out.

Richard and Liz approached the gate, invisible to the guards as Liz's mental illusions showed only normal traffic in the distance. Richard quickly tapped the eight guards with a specialized SIA knockout injector. Liz confirmed they were unconscious while Richard scanned the area above ground.

"Mindseye, I see several people in their homes, but most of the buildings above ground are empty." Richard spoke while the comlink on his wrist automatically relayed the message.

The comlink on John's end only hummed as if the volume was set on its lowest possible setting. John however, heard it loud and clear. “Roger, I see about three hundred people scattered along the center of the underground structures. My team is in position to enter the first two houses. Going in to confirm they are unoccupied.”

Richard stood in front of Liz. “What do you see?”

“A few sniping attempts, and some mentalists will try to use the children as shields. Other than that, everything should be good.”

‘It’s too easy, unless Michael isn’t planning on coming back.’ Richard thought about why Michael would be so committed to getting Jared that he would vacate the community.

Ford Field, Detroit

Cindy sat on top of the roof’s edge of the Ford Field blue and white lettering. She didn’t just sit there looking in one direction. It wasn’t likely but she glanced behind her every now and then in case somehow someone knew she was there.

Parking was scattered around the stadium, but she knew the mentalists were everywhere. The baseball stadium across the front entrance and all the other structures were void of security guards and maintenance personnel. The advance party had occupied the area and whoever was already there left the area without a scene. Cindy could only assume they were mentally commanded to go home or to the other side of the city.

She looked on as a mass of maybe a thousand plus people gathered. The crowd was eerie quiet in all they did to include getting out of the many buses and cars that parked lined up as if in position to rapidly move out of the area. Not one person spoke and if they did, it was in a whisper which Cindy couldn't hear from her perched location.

The time came when all eyes looked on as a group of older men surrounded by hooded figures moved underneath the Ford Field sign. Cindy could make out Michael's face as one of the monk dressed men. His robe was red with dark green and silver line designs on the edges.

'Wow, this guy has more bodyguards than Tulsa Doom,' a reference to the Conan the Barbarian movie. Cindy counted forty-three people within twenty yards of Michael and about a hundred or more black and gray robed guards on the perimeter of the crowd.

"My children. We have found our prey and today will be the day we show the world a new era of life. We will be like gods to the humans who surrender to us, and those who oppose us will die without mercy. My disciples will tell you where to go. Jared and his followers will be taken alive and tortured to death. Afterwards, we will spread out and link up with our brothers and sisters to take control of this country."

The crowd roared in unison, "Praise our Lord Michael and the Magistrate!"

'Well at least I don't have to wait for subtitles.' Cindy joked to herself. The assembly all quickly dispersed into their respected vehicles. Cindy flew fifty meters above Michael and stayed with him as everyone left Ford Stadium and headed directly to 15th and Marantette Streets.

Two and a half miles went by quickly as the vehicles took the most direct route on the interstate. Cindy noticed the vehicles moving around a large portion of the block. Five undercover police vehicles placed their lights on top of the cabins and blocked off all traffic into what seemed to be a very large clearing with a five story factory sized building in the middle. It was midday, but the normal expected activity in the neighborhood was dead. As if everyone in the area were evacuated with the Magistrate followers being the only ones in existence. The partly dark cloudy overcast also gave the scene a gloomy feel of time being stopped. Cindy floated high above Michael who had positioned himself on the northern side of the large circular formation around the outskirts of the sixty meter long building.

Cindy could see in the distance to her left, another smaller office building three stories high. The followers spread around the area in a very organized fashion like an immense choreographed show meant for an aerial audience. A muffled bang came from the small building. A cloud of gray debris shot out of all sides as it collapsed into a pile of rubble. Followers on the outside were baked with building residue.

Cindy instinctively looked down at where Michael stood in front of the vehicle he had exited. She quickly flew down to within a few meters from him overhearing Michael's rebuke.

"... just happened? You're supposed to be able warn us of the future. There's no one in your mind, so what's the problem?"

"Master, I don't understand. The only way I didn't see it, is if somehow the decisions and actions are not intentionally known."

Michael looked at the large building, then at the mess to the east. "Send in twenty-five disciples from each side to clear the building."

There was no audible reply as twenty-five people from each cardinal direction moved toward the large building at a light jog. A dozen followers broke off to investigate the few parked vehicles around the building. The rest of the recon party made their way to the entrances and edge of the building. All seemed clear, but Michael ordered that people would approach the building at fifty people intervals.

Cindy watched with interest as two hundred people had entered the building, but one of the vehicles blew up as further investigation failed to find a boom. The intervals stopped and a mob of gray robed men and women converged on the vehicles to include the building.

The people around Michael had dwindled down to fifteen gray robed and ten green robed Magi. Most of the green robed mentalists were old in age, but they gave no indication they were physically challenged, and seemed very energetic.

The cars were announced clear for a second time, and Michael ordered a large portion of the people around the perimeter to enter the building. Cindy didn't see anyone who previously entered the building come out, and was about to fly into the building when loud explosions came from it.

The flat roof top of the building seemed to open up like a living Lego mechanism as flashes of lights and smoke covered the upper portion of the building. Thousands of projectiles looking like large black dots spread out over a little past the entire block, about a five hundred meter squared area.

'What the hell!' Cindy thought as the swarm of black tire sized objects dispersed and exploded above the ground, creating a cloud of total destruction. The hundreds of followers caught under the heat, shape charge fragments, and lung bursting concussion effects were plastered and grinded into the grassy and concrete landscape. The ground itself welcomed the mangled flesh and bones for a brief fraction of a second only to turn over and reveal whatever was under the topsoil. Cindy had seen death before, but this man-made weapon abused the laws of physics, ignored the laws of nature, and repugnantly violated the laws of morality. The military grade cluster boom droplets failed to penetrate the invisible force field surrounding Michael and his small group of Magis and controllers. The ground they stood on survived, leaving a circular impression of peaceful green grass surrounded by hell.

The fragment particles, heat and concussion effects also ignored Cindy's phased out body. But the extreme close up mutilation of several hundred people caused her to shut her eyes for a few seconds, as she flew straight up twenty or so meters. The landscape was covered with blood, red and black, shredded flesh and bone particles with no identifiable or live bodies in the kill zone, except for Michael's group. She forced herself to stop looking at the death and focus on Michael and the building.

The top of the building was the only area not on fire or grated into gored landscape by the anti-armor explosive cluster bombs. But it was clear to Cindy from her vantage point that the upper story of the building was set up as a massive launcher. The building itself was now covered in a large cloud of dark dust and smoke.

Cindy and everyone in the area heard a voice come from all directions. 'The weak shall live by the will of the superior race. Darkness is the salvation for all that exists, with light as the beacon for hell itself. All shall witness the day I step upon the carcass of my enemies… Those are the words of an arrogant fool who thought he could be a god in his own eyes, naming himself after an Arch Angel. But you have learned nothing and this is why the only carcasses you shall trample on are those of your own deprived followers.' Jared spoke clearly as if declaring a truth to all that were able to mentally hear.

'This must be Jared.' Cindy thought as she looked down at Michael who replied to the mental message.

'You are but a nuisance of a man who doesn't know when your doom is at hand.' Michael's mental voice was heavier which carried more of an authoritarian tone than in real speech.

Cindy wasn't sure why she was now hearing what was being said, but didn't question it too much since it could be Joshua or Jared who was allowing her to hear the open mental conversation.

'A mosquito can kill millions before accepting its death. Your lackeys will die, but not before they see you shit on yourself in death.'

Michael and his small group walked towards the building ignoring the massacre, concentrating on protecting themselves should another trap be triggered.

Cindy flew back down a few meters above Michael, but noticed that a dozen or more followers on the outer perimeter had survived and seemed to be busy securing the area once again. The one disciple that seemed to sense her presence was gone. The group in front of her didn't seem to sense anything wrong by her presence. The fireworks would definitely attract unwanted attention, which would have confused Cindy as to why Michael continued in entering the building even though a lot of law enforcement would be there within less than half an hour. But Jared's conversation might have added to Michael's commitment in ignoring the likelihood that police officers and superhumans would soon be there.

'You cannot win old man. You and your whimpering babies are woefully ignorant and powerless.' Jared continued to taunt.

'You were once a promising disciple, but maybe I should have killed your parents when you were much older; that way, you would have appreciated how they were sexually disfigured and tortured to death.'

'I will make sure you die quickly so their memory won't honor you... Oh, did I tell you that all of your other three thousand, two hundred, forty-nine worthless minions will all face death and justice in the hands of the Eternal Champions and SIA?'

Cindy saw Michael slow down the pace for a brief moment and then continued into the dark cloud of dust. The dust moved out of the way as if an invisible current of wind pushed and cleared a path for the group of twenty six. Cindy flew behind the last man so she wouldn't lose them in the mist of dust and smoke which swallowed them up.

Chapter Ten

The Community

Serenity Community, Chicago

The SIA agents trailed the four superheroes in column formation a foot or two apart. Their non-lethal energy rifles strapped around a shoulder, breech helmets, and protective fatigues were camouflaged in accordance to the main color scheme of the houses in the community.

Richard was not in his Creator costume, but instead was in a SIA agent uniform. He headed straight for the first target running through the wall, but just before hitting it he shape shifted into a large camouflaged block of steel; creating a large opening for the people behind him to enter with ease and not get bottle necked. Instantly Richard turned back into the SIA uniformed agent and sprinted through a hallway into a bedroom where two adult disciples were taken slightly by surprise.

The man and woman miserably attempted to mentally and permanently put Richard to sleep. Richard's arms extended out about ten feet to each of their necks and forced them to come together where he stood. "Your mind tricks don't work on me now."

Richard shot out a mental bolt of rage which knocked them out. He wasn't able to read or control minds, but he was able to shock most humans into a state of panic, confusion, or unconsciousness. It took a little bit out of him, but he didn't want to wait for the agents to come in to inject them with drugs. His injector was empty, so he dropped the couple and half flew and ran towards the next occupied house.

On the northern side of the community, John scanned the area for people as the agents entered and secured two houses.

"Sir, the houses are secure and we're ready for the next set." An agent reported.

John didn't turn towards the agent, but instead raised his hand indicating to halt actions. "You know, someone told me that these Magistrate mentalists didn't use weapons."

"Sir?" The agent was completely lost as what to say after relaying the halt hand and arm signal to the agents behind him.

"It seems someone didn't get the memo." John smiled as he gestured to the ground and one by one, three disciples were teleported onto the backyard. Three sniper rifles with the front end of the barrels missing also appeared with the two men and woman.

Three agents knocked them out and carried them away to the initial prisoner collection point, just over the wall.

John mentally alerted everyone in the assault. 'Sniper threat is gone, but they know we're here, so don't worry about stealth and move quickly.'

Susan looked into the nearest houses in an aching pattern and mentally attacked the few occupants in two houses. She pointed to the occupied houses as she jogged between lawns and fences. "Three people down in that house, one there, and three there!"

SIA agents spread out to the designated houses entering with impunity. Securing unconscious mentalists, they retraced their steps back to the southern collection point.

John's group moved slowest as John was scanning everything under the sun. Besides apprehending the three snipers, the SIA agents were starting to wonder what John was doing as he moved slowly and allowed the agents to enter and go through the motions of clearing empty houses.

Richard had encountered five other mentalists, easily subduing them with a telekinetic punch to the head and neck areas. Liz was hot on his heels, making sure there were no booby traps that John or Susan had missed.

Richard stopped his advance and looked intently for children in the underground sections. He found many clusters of little people, but then looked back only to see Liz's beautiful masked face, and her usual white Egyptian Isis looking costume. "The agents can't keep up. Mindseye, can you or Pandora make it so they can see what we see? That way the agents will just run straight to the people instead of stopping at every corner."

John and Susan heard the message on their comlink. "Yeah, why didn't I think of that?" John mumbled and a few seconds later, all the SIA agents saw the houses seem as transparent glass. The structures further away were not as vivid, but it was clear that they could see wherever the three superheroes were looking at as if they had a video game like special x-ray vision in multicolor.

'Agents and telepaths. What you're seeing is what Creator, Pandora, and I are seeing right now. Be careful not to run into a wall that seems like it isn't there. Look for the subtle discoloration and get to the mentalist and children we put down. Bypass all empty rooms and houses.

The agents to include the telepaths were awestruck as they viewed everything around as normal. But when they looked in the direction of where the Eternal Champions were viewing and going, they saw a world of transparent objects and partial skeletons, skin, and clothing.

The pace picked up dramatically as agents and telepaths raced through the community blocks. But there was a major pause once the surface structures were cleared and they waited for the go ahead to start entering the underground complex through access doors in the many mansions near the center of the community.

Several agents were jittery as they noticed large sections of the property foundations were rigged with plastic explosives. Creator had assured them that the explosives had been neutralized, but doubt crept in as not sure if the explosives were for use above or below ground.

Richard noticed most of the agents were eager to proceed, but he changed the plan in case the explosives did go off. He could have gotten Susan and John to teleport the explosives to a central location, but that would have taken up valuable time and also put all the explosives in one concentrated location.

"Everyone listen up. Agents break up into fourteen teams and guard the entrances to the underground complex. We will go in and clear the entire underground. In case the explosives do go off, we won't have to dig anyone up from being buried alive. Mindseye will designate the teams and locations. Pandora will teleport children to the telepaths at the collection point once we get to them. We will start in two minutes."

Susan and John joined Richard and Liz at the main mansion which Michael had resided in. The occupants left the mansion in a rush and it was obvious they didn't bother to straighten up as if they never planned on returning or thought they would return after their errand was completed. The basement entrance was wide enough to be able to walk three people side by side down the first staircase.

"We go as a group and make a clockwise circle. Pandora, you know what to do. Mindseye, you will knock people out before we approach them. Isis, you tell use if something bad is going to happen, and we can decide from there. I will direct our movement and lead the way."

"Sir, all agents are in position." The Captain reported.

"Thank you Captain." Richard replied and forced the basement steel door open with a strong push, breaking the four dead bolts as if they were made out of fragile clay.

Richard practically flew down the staircase ignoring light switches that were turned off. The other three matched his speed as they ran past rooms and forced their way through doors like dominoes unable to stop falling.

Richard could see a dozen adults two corridors and many rooms in front of him, but before he was in view from the men and women, they all fell to the floor as if all fainted from instant knockout gas. Richard quickly placed the bodies in semi clusters and piles as John teleported the mentalists straight up to the surface without he himself teleporting with them.

Richard continued to the next group of people. This time twenty children of all ages were in two separate rooms as if playing hide and seek. John didn't knockout the children, but instead Susan neutralized their attempts to protect themselves. The four adults with them were knocked out and teleported as the previous group. Susan ordered the children to hold hands or hug each other. It wasn't too hard to get them to cooperate as they couldn't do much else. She teleported the entire group to the collection point and returned to John's side.

Once Susan was back, Richard had already picked out their next destination and sprinted to a larger group of twenty adults.

"Stop!" Liz commanded. "Three explosive ahead will go off once you get under them."

John looked into Liz's surface thoughts and saw the explosives. With precision he teleported the sixty pounds of C4 straight up about two hundred meters above ground. He teleported with the explosives and with a concussive beam of heat from his hands, ignited the C4 in midair.

In an instant, John teleported back to his original location. The very large and loud explosion spooked all the people above ground, but it wasn't long before the SIA agents focused back on their task to guard the exits.

"Okay, what's happening?" Richard asked Liz, and waited for an answer before moving on.

"I don't know, but the future is changing the more we advance, so there must be someone who is igniting the explosives as we decide to move on."

"Right..." Richard didn't show any sign of frustration, but instead turned in the direction of advance and placed his fists on the sides of his waist as if in a classic superhero conquering stance. He scanned for someone who looked different from all the rest.

"Got you." Richard proudly announced. "John, take out that guy in the green robe."

John looked at Richard's target and abrasively entered the man's mind. Deep thoughts were revealed to him in an instant and he knew the man was a controller put in charge of protecting the community. Protection meaning die if need be to give the impression that they were defeated, while Michael pursued a higher calling. Once John was satisfied with the information he had forcefully gathered, he telepathically knocked out the controller with ease and teleported him straight to the prisoner collection point.

John disappeared with the controller, and the three heroes waited for his return. Seconds later, John returned. "The guy was ordered to make it look like a last desperate attempt to fight for their lives, but the Magistrate is planning on something bigger like the overthrow of the government or a massive civil war." John summarized from the memories of the man's past teachings and things he was privileged to before Michael left the community.

"So that means no more booms, and we need to move faster." Richard said and flew forward to the next targets.

Twenty minutes later all of the children and mentalists had been apprehended. Police officers were called in to occupy the homes and confiscate all computers, files, and few weapons. SIA investigators were to document the lifestyle in the community and find evidence for links to Magistrate mentalists still at large.

Richard and his team went to the children collection point. Some of the older children were sedated, but others were being mentally indoctrinated into a new way of thinking which made them more cooperative and open to the fact that the Magistrate had brainwashed them.

Richard didn't know the details, but it was hard for him to see so many children having to be mentally re-programmed to be able to start a new life without the same adults who had raised them in the past. He could tell by their clothing that they didn't play much outside and discipline was something they understood early on. The taskmasters of their upbringing were controlling, but now he wasn't too sure if the SIA telepaths would be much better. Being forced to put aside rules and coming to grips with being a care free child might also be a very harsh opposite for them to initially handle. Richard transformed into his Creator costume and walked amongst the children and telepaths. A hundred had already been driven off to resident offices to the south. But it seemed like another two hundred children remained.

Richard walked up to the telepath in charge. "I want all the information you have on each child sent to Erica and Max before you clear out of here with the agents. I also want to know if any of these children belong to Michael."

"Yes, Sir. We should be done in about thirty minutes, but to answer the last question. None of the children are his direct offspring. He does have five grandchildren, with only two of the parents present here in the community."

"Inform Mindseye on who these parents are so he can interrogate them."

"Yes, Sir. Is that all?"

"Yes, thank you."

The telepath quickly left Richard to find where the parents were with the help of other telepaths near him.

'Richard, Erica says a longer list of mentalists just appeared in the webpage. SIA telepaths are working on getting them now. Also, there was a massive explosion in Detroit. Police have been dispatched about fifteen minutes ago. We were in radio blackout which is why we're getting this info now. Cindy turned on her comlink, but she must be dematerialized now.' Susan reported into his mind.

"Okay, everyone come together, it's time we go to Detroit." Richard commanded.

The group was about to teleport when Liz backed off with a disgusted frown on her face. "What?"

Richard looked at her with concern. "What's wrong honey?"

Liz took a very deep breathe trying to calm down, but it was very clear she was angry. "You three go, I will stay here with the agents. Come back for me when it's all over."

Richard was at a lost as to how to respond. Liz was very angry, but it wasn't directed at him and there was no chance someone was messing with her mind at the moment with John and Susan being able to sense any mental activity in the vicinity. "Are you sure?"

"It's alright. I don't want to go through it a second time. Go, I'll be fine."

Richard stood there in thought. John softly grabbed his arm. 'Richard, she saw something in the future. I think it would be best to do as she says.'

"Alright, let's go see what more of mess we can get into." Richard half frowned and the three disappeared in a small flash of light.

Chapter Eleven

Natasha

Jared's Complex, Detroit

An alarm sounded and displayed on Jared's main monitor. But it was a not surprise as the three patiently watched Michael and his army move along the interstate and surround their building from a distance.

Jean and Natasha were sitting on either side of Jared, both a little nervous even though they had gone over the plan of attack many times over. The problem was the plan seemed to have a gap and the timing was off.

The small army of people surrounded the place and they were expected to approach the building, not lay siege to it. "So what's the alarm for?" Jean asked being the one to question what she thought was important to know.

"Well this is where things get interesting." Jared replied as a prompt on the monitor came up [Action initiated press Shift S].

Jared pressed the keys on a red keyboard he slid out from underneath the console.

A camera view of the three story office building to the east showed it collapse as explosions took out the entire foundation. A faint demolition sound could be heard by the microphone located in the main building of the upper floors.

"Nice… So what's next?"

Jared turned his head toward Jean. "I don't know. That's what makes this so interesting."

"What?" Jean's mouth almost dropped.

Natasha was also visibly dumbfounded by the statement.

"You mean you don't know what the booby traps are?"

"If I did, they would see them coming." Jared stated as if that was clearly and naturally obvious when he mentioned earlier that Oliver and possibly a few others could see the future.

"You know Brat, you're going to give me an ulcer." Natasha accused him.

"I want you both to know that whatever happens, you have to have faith."

"We'll need more than faith to get rid of an ulcer." Jean countered.

"Everyone has faith in something, whether it is a person, object, place or idea, they all want, no need… an excuse to do what they do or not do. My faith is in my friends, the people that I love, and people that I never met in person. That's how we ended up here with all of this." Jared waved both hands at the console and room.

"I don't know what to say to that." Jean rolled her seat back as if taking a break from an overcrowded worktable.

"Brother, I trust you with all my heart. But sometimes, I wonder if you realize those guys aren't playing around." Natasha pointed at the videos with Magistrate followers entering the building.

"What's those numbers on the top right corner?" Jean referred to blue, red, green and white digital numbers on the monitor screen.

"I told you I don't know, but my guess it's the number of people inside and outside of the building." Jared placed his right hand under his chin as if in a thinking or amusement posture.

[Press Shift L or Shift A within five seconds]

Jared pressed Shift A and a car bomb activated, exploding as three disciples came within four feet of it.

[Press Shift 9 or Shift 0]

Jared chose zero, and four hallways on the first and second floors in the building were filled with poisonous gas. The camera views covering the hallways appeared on a corner of the screen showing many mentalists falling dead on the floor and connecting rooms. The gas was invisible to the eye, but a prompt on the screen stated, [poisonous gas injected]. The red counter increased by 74, while the blue counter decreased by the same amount.

"There're still eight hundred sixteen people left." Natasha

stated with a hint of impatience.

"Can I press the next prompt?" Jean asked, wanting to do something besides watch the show.

"Sure." Jared rolled his chair away from the table.

The mentalists closed in on the building in large numbers and a prompt popped up as the green number on the screen hit 675. Jean pressed one of the two options in the prompt.

Eight video windows opened up showing all the scenery around the building out three hundred meters. In addition were two video windows of a vantage point high and far from the block which included the interstate. The complex shook as the cluster bomb trap fired off. A second set of tremors were felt as the bomblets destroyed the block.

"Wow. That's something." Jared said as the large cloud of debris started to settle on the outskirts of the outer perimeter.

"Yeah." Jean froze, thinking what else was in store for the people in the building.

"They deserved it." Natasha stated. "Now we just have eighty-four people left."

"A number we can manage. But it's taking too long" Jared stated, looking at the increase of red numbers by 689.

Jared closed his eyes and relaxed in his seat. A mental call went out with power and clarity. Natasha and Jean heard the conversation between Michael and Jared as if they were speaking inside the control room.

Michael and his group came to the front entrance of the building. The debris was still thick except around the group as they opened the double metal doors which locked behind them. Nick turned towards the doors and broke the seven dead bolt locks making sure the doors stayed locked.

Cindy was to the side of the group looking at the lobby and many connecting hallways. Most of the lights weren't working but there was enough illumination for her to see dead bodies in the distance. The hallways to the left were blocked with collapsed concrete from the floors above.

Michael stayed in the center of the group as they took the second hallway to the right. 'What made you keep your whore alive? Did she promise you power and my head on a platter?'

'No, you still don't understand. But I will tell you a story of a man who wanted to live in peace and happiness. He married a beautiful woman, a psychic, a wonderful person… He prophesized the coming of the mighty Magistrate and the Lord of Illusions. You know the prophet, the name you outlawed to even mention among your disciples; Magi Amos. Everything would have been peachy, until you decided to kill off the competition. So killing my father who was favored to be leader of the Magistrate wasn't enough for you… No! You had to kill Jean's parents, her sister, Amos's wife, several dozen other Magi, and in the end Amos himself. Did you really think you could murder so many people without consequences?' Jared told the story into all of the people on the block.

Nick and four other Magis stopped walking in the hallway, looking at Michael as if that information was going to undermine his control of the disciples, but Michael waved them on.

"Master, he's using the conversation to track where we are and if we use our illusions." Nick whispered.

"It works both ways." Michael retorted. 'What consequences are those exactly? I am the Lord of Illusions and those weaker than me were unworthy to lead.'

'Amos was never a threat, in fact he was just a reminder that you aren't and will never be the Lord of Illusions.'

Two controllers telekinetically opened a hidden door leading downward. A shadow in the group found the passage, but wasn't sure if they should continue until Michael nodded approval.

'And you think that fighting me will bring you some sort of closure for your misery?' Michael kept the conversation alive.

'No, I have accepted my fate, which is to see the Magistrate exterminated.'

'You're a hypocrite Jared. You have murdered more people than I ever have.'

The passage ended at another hallway, but this hallway was well lit and unused. The metallic hallways all looked the same without any signs, door markings, or change in color schemes. The colors being white and off white, except the flat black tiled floor. Fire sprinklers, light fixtures, and camera bulbs were all spaced out evenly without a discernible change in distances or intervals. The cameras bulbs were automatically crushed with telekinetic pulses by the controllers and shadows as the entire group entered the hallway.

'You still have no understanding Mikey. The murders I have committed will not go unpunished. But neither will yours and all those old men with you.'

'Your traps won't help you anymore. We're twenty six, and you are no match for even one of my Archmagi.'

'Numbers do make a difference, but maybe you should have brought ten thousand minions if you wanted it to be a fair fight.'

The shadows in the front stopped moving as twenty tons of liquid poured down into the far end of the hallway from trap vents in the ceiling. The black liquid stopped in front of the group as an invisible wall kept it at bay. One of the shadows turned to the center. "Masters, its acid, there's too much for use to change it into something harmless. We must find a way out of this hallway or to another floor."

An elder pointed to one of the metallic doors to the right. Nick telekinetically turned the latch and pushed it wide open. A large white room could be seen as well as two other doors on the other end. The group quickly scanned for additional traps and moved into the room.

Two controllers trailed the group as they kept the telekinetic force wall on the acid. Several hundred steel spikes came out from between the floor tiles and skewered the men in a microsecond. The men kept their facial expressions at the time, unable to change them in their sudden death. The shadows on the other end noticed the composition of the thin spikes which released fragments of poison throughout their bodies along with separating whatever they penetrated. The telekinetic wall fell and the shadows instinctively slammed the metal door close before the acid reached them.

Michael and Nick didn't turn back to see what had happened like everyone else in the group.

'Now you're twenty-four and counting.' Jared mentally smiled.

Michael didn't reply this time. He looked at Oliver who was getting nothing on future events. He stood still and mentally searched for other followers in the building. Many had already died shortly after the cluster bomb trap, but he wasn't overly concerned about their fate. There were twenty-two disciples incapacitated or trapped in the complex. Some had made it to the third floor sublevel. He focused on their minds and saw the paths they saw and took. The complex was an intricate maze, but Michael had already figured out where Jared was and how to get to him. It was a process of elimination which created a gap of empty space indicating where Jared would most likely be.

Michael pointed at the door to the left and quickly walked towards it as everyone else tried to surround him as he moved. 'My followers will multiply with every sacrifice. I will see you soon.'

Jared looked at the white number on the screen. It was twenty-four. The facial recognition and other sensors took note of Michael's every movement along with the elders. "It's time you two get into position." Jared told Jean and Natasha.

The women took their chairs out into another room and prepared for the final battle.

Jared watched the video screens showing thermo and x-ray figures of the twenty-four people moving through a path never crossed by the mentalists, nearing his position. The security camera bulbs the controllers destroyed where just a small part of the surveillance setup throughout the complex.

Natasha and Jean were in position when Michael's group entered their floor. 'We're ready.' Natasha alerted Jared.

"Thank you, Thomas." Jared solemnly stated while looking up at the ceiling, as if talking to a spirit in heaven. He walked through the eastern door, another room, and down a hallway waiting for Michael's group to come within his most lethal mental range of illusions.

The first six shadows and controllers in the group attacked each other with their most deadly powers. A shadow survived, only because one of the Archmagi elder next to him was able to heal him within a fraction of a second.

Oliver stepped up next to Michael. "He's going to attack the controllers first since they can neutralize most physical and mental based traps."

'Nick, protect them while I locate Jared." Michael instructed the shadows to take lead with a wave of his hand.

Jared's mental illusions dug deep into all of the controllers to include Nick. All of the controllers found themselves outside in a wasteland with high winds, the stench of brimstone intermingled with smoke almost suffocating them. They could barely see each other huddled in a ten by ten foot space. The sky was dark red with a blood red moon. "Focus on the hallway we were in!" Nick yelled over the swirling air.

A burning meteor streaked down on the group appearing out of a low dark cloud cover. Nick and three others put a telekinetic force wall up several meters before impact. The cluster bomb was easy for them to defend against, but this meteor was one large projectile traveling over several dozen times the speed of sound. It was also Jared's world which ignored the laws of metaphysics even thought the controllers trained for most of their lives in similar environments.

The force wall collapsed, taking most of the destructive effects; however, the group was sprayed with red hot rock fragments. Four controllers were instantly dismembered in various locations. The other five suffered incapacitating injuries to include Nick with his right foot smashed and scorched completely off.

Michael ignored the nine controllers who screamed and fell to the floor in death or agony. "I see you." He smiled and mentally projected a domination command into Jared's mind.

Jared felt the command, but expected it so the command to put down his defenses and stop attacking the controllers, failed. Jared focused on Michael, now that his intent was met in causing disruption and more fatalities.

'Down to fifteen. Mikey 0, Jared 9.' Jared mocked.

The Elders helped the controllers as Oliver turned to Michael. "I sense..." A .50 Caliber armor piercing round exploded Oliver's head continuing through a Shadow's neck and down the hallway.

Natasha and Jean looked at the thermo video of the sudden disappearance of one of the members' head. The picture of Oliver Cox automatically closed on the laptop screen they monitored in their small room.

"Do you think the computer knows who's dying?" Jean asked as they took turns on the computer prompts.

"I guess it does. I think this is Jared, because there's a yellow number now." Natasha pointed at the three remaining numbers: 1 yellow, 13 white and 11 red.

"Can he take that many?" Jean asked not knowing Jared's true measure of power.

"Brat, will be okay." Natasha hesitated.

The two women held each other's hands, making sure not to break physical contact in case they were mentally attacked. It was a beginner's method of keeping the weakest mentalist close to the stronger one. Jean wasn't a mentalist, but it was more for Natasha's sake that she could feel Jean next to her.

Michael partially entered Jared's mind, darkening his senses.

Jared saw the minds he tracked fade away as if a thick mist dropped down from the sky into the underground complex. The lasers and sensors in the floor however alerted him to the exact physical locations of the mentalists.

Michael spoke to the now eighteen disciples on the above

levels wanting to guide them to attack Jared as a distraction. None of the disciple responded.

"I told you that you're woefully ignorant. Did you really think your disciples were alive?" Jared spoke through the intercom system for everyone to hear.

Jared lured Michael to the floor through fake mental connections with the disciples. Michael swiftly calmed down rethinking his strategy. Jared would've had to know intimate knowledge of the disciples he impersonated and he was obviously more powerful than his father or the elders, but not him. The great detail needed for the illusions required precise knowledge of their surroundings which Jared was getting somehow even thought they had destroyed the security cameras. He would have to rely on his own abilities and those within the group. Michael entered the twelve mentalists' minds around him. "Open your minds to me."

Cindy stayed with the group witnessing them being picked off like eaten potato chips from a bag. But now, she was sure Jared was close, so she flew down the hallway through doors and walls. She found Jared standing in the middle of the adjacent hallway with a door to his back. He was wearing a black rubbery like suit. 'It must be some kind of protection against electricity, heat, or something.' She thought as she floated inches beside him.

"Jean and my sister aren't saints, but they don't deserve to die. Whoever you are, I ask you make sure they live… They will save many more lives in return." Jared looked straight as he talked, and then turned back to the door entering the main room planned for the final stand.

'Huh, how does he know I'm here?' Cindy followed Jared into the room.

The large room seemed very small as walls created a physical maze. Jared quickly ran through the maze and stopped in the center of the room. Cindy stayed with him, but now all she could see was the ten by ten foot empty space and many pathways into the middle of the maze. The more she looked around, it seemed like the maze funneled paths into the middle.

Michael was satisfied with the deep mental conference, and the group quickly walked to the other end of the hallway, scanning for and destroying all laser emitters they encountered. They were more organized now treating Jared and the maze with more respect.

The data feeding into Jared's microchip greatly decreased, but the passive emitters on the outskirts of the complex gave him a general idea of their locations.

"Well, I guess the gig's up." Natasha said as most of the video windows disappeared and a new prompt came up. [Critical proximity, prompt options terminated.] She closed the laptop and they both waited for their cues.

Nick and the remaining controllers were healed of their mental scaring as they moved with Michael. The controllers stayed in the front with the three Shadows behind them ready to instantly heal them should they encounter another trap or mental attack.

The seven elders and Michael knew where Jared was, but they couldn't overwhelm him with mental projections or commands. The group entered the short hallway and continued on to the door which Jared had used less than a minute ago. Nick opened the metallic door and six passages ending at wall corners were visible to them. To Michael and the elders, there were only two passages visible into sharp corners making the room seem very small.

Michael instructed the group to split up in two, keeping three elders and Nick close to him. The group actually split up into six separate pairs except for Michael who had one elder and Nick with him.

'Whatever happens, make sure you concentrate on their desires.' Jared mentally guided Natasha. Natasha nodded to herself, knowing Jared knew she received the message.

Jared sat down with legs crossed on the floor. He closed his eyes and breathed deeply.

Cindy stood a few feet behind him contemplating on whether she should fly somewhere to call Richard or stay with him, thinking she might miss something important in her absence. She decided to materialize and turn on her comlink so Erica or someone could hear what was happening. She quickly dematerialized when several mentalists appeared in three funnels toward them. She didn't want to stay solid with a possibility of providing a chance that her brain patterns could be sensed by the mentalists.

Jared opened his eyes and telekinetically flipped a switch on one of the wall edges near him. Water an inch in depth filled various sections of the path. The select areas were depressed slightly so the entire floor wasn't drenched. Eleven people were in view walking on or standing in water. Jared flipped another switch and thousands of volts with obscene amounts of amperage vibrated muscles and nerves with chaotic deadly results. The Shadows naturally fought the electrical shock and jumped off the water puddles, once the illusion they were standing on dry floor faded away. Six elders and two controllers were less fortunate as they died and burned where they stood. The current automatically stopped after ten seconds, being rigged for one usage only. Two shadows saw Jared in the middle of the room, but everyone else in plain sight of him saw more maze.

'You Shadows are truly loyal to your master, but it's time you know the truth.' Jared entered their minds with ease, showing them how Michael ordered the death of the older generations of Shadows, their parents and extended family. 'Unfortunately, you won't listen to your conscious and disbelieve a lie you were taught all your life.' The three Shadows fell into darkness as their own negative healing powers turned on themselves.

The gray robed men quietly fell to the floor. Jared looked at the other figures in the passage ways, but there were no distinctions between them. He jumped up and concentrated on his surroundings. Hundreds of invisible fingers pressed down all over his body. The suffocating pressure on his neck was easier to handle than the eye popping and ear throbbing pain he endured as he was elevated a few inches above the floor tiles.

Cindy witnessed Jared's rigid posture as Michael, Nick, an elder, and two controllers casually walked up to him. She floated inches from the floor, six feet from the group. The action was so intense for her that she didn't think of anything except the people in front of her, but it finally dawned on her, 'Where's Jean?'

The pressure on Jared's eyes and ears eased as Michael stood in front of him. Nick's telekinetic hold on him stayed strong everywhere else. "You shouldn't have concerned yourself with my Shadows. But I must say that you made quite a mess." Michael awkwardly frowned with a half smile.

"It's not over yet." Jared managed to heavily exhale.

"What, do you mean that whore of yours?" Michael laughed, as Jean ran towards them through the maze.

Natasha wasn't able to hold Jean back as she witnessed Jared subdued on camera, even though the cameras were destroyed. Jean was being mind controlled, which Natasha couldn't prevent from happening, except to herself.

Cindy's answer came quickly as Nick telekinetically subdued Jean's body as he did Jared's body. Jean was still under mind control by the looks of her emotionless expression on her face. Jean's body floated next to Jared almost touching at the hands.

Jean was also wearing a black rubber-like diver's suit. Her short hair was fluffy but the beauty of it struggled to attract any attention. Nick smiled as he held the captives in mid air as prized trophies.

"You're time is up. But before you die, you will see your woman torn apart. You will beg for it to stop." Michael moved away from the pair expecting much blood splatter.

"Amos was right, and for that I apologize. He said I was the Lord of Illusions… " Jared said as Nick saw Jared break free from his telekinetic control and plunge a knife deep into his chest.

Jean fell to the ground but landed on her feet, confused and unprepared. No one saw the blade except Nick who felt its tempered steel and serrated edge separate a rib, cartilage, and heart muscles. His telekinetic powers failed to protect him as his mind went dead.

Jared also dropped to the floor but was very alert and telekinetically ruptured Nick's neck artery into his esophagus. His telekinetic powers weren't nearly as strong as Nick's, but it was sufficient to double tap the Magi ensuring the controllers or elder couldn't physically and mentally heal him in time.

Jean froze Jared's left arm causing instantaneous frostbite. The elder and controller attended Nick with a quick scan and attempt to heal him, but their powers couldn't reverse death. Jean screamed inside her mind as she fought with all her willpower to control her actions to no avail. Michael's will over her felt evil and torturous as she knew he made sure she was fully conscious of what was happening around her, in high definition with several vantage points.

The cold attack was probably intended to cause Jared pain, but it was more numbing than anything else. Jared focused on Michael's mind. He exerted all of his mental disciplines to shock the Arch Magi into releasing Jean. Jean woke up out of her nightmare into reality which wasn't much better. She was free now and focused on Michael's head, but before she could release her freezing powers, she once again fell into a daze as the elder took control of her mind.

'Now Nat, hurry!' Jared told his sister, knowing it was over.

Michael sensed the mental message, but partially ignored it as Jean froze Jared's head unable to breathe his last.

The controller checked Jared's body and lack of mental waves as Jean wept inside, with tears reflexively swelling in her eyes.

Michael saw a shifting of reality all around him. It was a weak illusion trying to take control of his mind. "Nat… Is that you Natasha? I thought you were dead."

Cindy had been seeing things unfold, but really didn't know what was going on until Jean attacked Jared. She flew to one of the dead Shadows and quickly grabbed anything on his person that was loose. She found a keychain with several keys. Grabbing the keys, she noticed and touched a ring on his finger which dematerialized and dropped to the floor. She quickly grabbed it too, and flew back to the group. The mental combat was too fast for her, thinking Jared would still be alive, but she was too late to save him.

Natasha was in torment as she wept on the floor in front of the laptop and small table. 'You're going to pay for this!' Natasha screamed, everyone including Cindy hearing it in her mind.

Michael turned in the direction of the room Natasha was in. 'You're not strong enough to kill me.' Michael disgustingly smirked.

The elder stood still as if he was daydreaming, but the two controllers moved single file behind Michael.

Both controllers saw Jared escape the telekinetic hold, but Nick moved away taking back control. Michael ordered each controller to quickly take out their gun and shoot Jared in the head before Jared escaped again.

'You really are ignorant. What makes you think that I need to be strong enough to kill you, now that your armies of protectors are gone?' Natasha sobbed.

Michael hesitated in his tracks as the shifting illusion of everything around him vibrating, stopped. What didn't stop was a 9 mm hot metal round entering the back of his head. Red fabric fibers of his hood stained the edge of the entry wound. The exit wound was large but most of it was less noticeable as the mangled round tore through the right eye, spraying brain matter, bone and blood on the floor and maze wall several meters away. The single bang was really two bangs, as one controller shot Michael in the head, while the other shot that controller. The live controller turned to the elder, but the elder broke out of his fake environment and commanded the controller to move next to and aim his pistol at Jean's head.

Cindy flew above the elder and placed her hand inside the man's head. She retraced her hand and left behind the keys, keychain, and ring she had taken from the Shadow. The items instantly materialized into a solid state once they separated from Cindy's hand. The elder blinked his eyes for a few seconds and fell dead to the ground once the muscles caught up with his nervous system.

The controller lowered his weapon and stood there as if everything was normal. Cindy stared at him and then at Jean who was balling her eyes out, cradling Jared's defrosted limp pale body.

Natasha came running to her side. "What happened, this wasn't supposed to happen!"

Cindy stayed invisible, turned solid, and pushed the call button on her comlink.

Natasha moved to the dead controller and took his handgun. Without a second thought she shot the remaining controller in the head at point blank range. She flung the weapon away like a useless piece of trash. Tears still running down her cheeks, she sat next to Jean and hugged them both.

Above 15th Street, Detroit

Richard, John, and Susan appeared several hundred meters from Jared's building. They surveyed the area with their unique visions.

"What the hell happened here?" Susan fixed her sight on the living mentalists waiting to kill more police officers around the perimeter.

"It looks like several cluster booms." Richard focused his attention to the building, ignoring the carnage of people.

"I don't sense many living people, fourteen on the block." John reported.

Richard peered into the building and below it. The complex underneath was more intricate than the Serenity Community, and the materials used far exceeded bunker reinforcement standards which made seeing through the material harder for him. "John, look for live people underneath the building."

"Susan, knock out those mentalists before they kill more cops."

"Erica, tell SIA to get everyone they can up here as fast as possible."

"Already done. But Richard, Cindy turned on her comlink. She's not talking, but there was a gunshot and sounds of crying in the background."

"John."

"Gotcha." John found the comlink's signal, touched Richard's arm, and teleported them next to Cindy.

Natasha sensed the two men standing on the bloody floor looking at them. Her chest and eyes hurt from crying, her heart hurt most of all, so the Eternal Champions being there felt a little poetic. She had thought they were superhumans looking for fame and glory, but now it didn't matter. Jared might be alive if they had been here earlier, but then Michael would also probably be alive.

Richard looked at the dead bodies, and focused his attention on Jean. He walked up to her and grabbed her by the arm, standing her upright, almost standing Jared's dead body up in the process.

"Do you know what you have done?" Richard angrily asked.

Jean's watery eyes blinked repeatedly, realizing Creator's presence. She stared at her own reflection on Richard's sunglasses, but said nothing.

Susan appeared next to John, as did Cindy floating above the blood next to Susan. The three waited as the scene unfolded.

"It's because of you that innocent people have died." Richard pushed Jean back almost causing her to fall on the slippery floor. "Come on! You wanted me to go to prison, now's your chance! Fight me!"

'Richard, what are you doing?' John mentally interrupted, but knowing the future kept him from further interference.

Jean stood rigid, but relaxed as she stared at Creator and glanced at the other three superheroes. She concentrated on Creator's body and attacked him with all her strength. The room temperature dropped a few degrees, as Creator's body and clothes changed into duller colors.

Richard flew at her grabbing her neck with an iron grip. His costume and skin color quickly returned to normal with his body automatically adjusting to the forced metaphysical attack. "I can survive in temperatures colder than you can create. But thank you for your reply." Richard placed his free hand in front of her face and the air vibrated as his telekinetic bolt was about to leave it.

Natasha watched Richard with mixed emotions. She loved Jean, but maybe now she would be with Jared; not that she could prevent Creator from killing her. Jean also welcomed the merciless push of her head being torn off her body, wanting to die at that moment.

"You should split her in half as you did Malara and her son." A voice suggested, being heard by everyone in the room.

Richard stopped his attack a microsecond before the voice spoke, vaguely recognizing it. "Joshua." Cindy confirmed the identity.

"While you're at it, make sure you kill her daughter by aiming a little lower than her stomach." Joshua continued.

"What?" Richard said what everyone was thinking.

It was as much a surprise to Jean as well. She never experienced morning sickness, and couldn't remember if her menstrual cycle had passed.

Richard looked at Jean's reproductive system. Jean was two months pregnant by size of the fetus. "So, you're my conscious now, too?" Richard looked up as if Joshua were looking at him from above.

'No Richard, I'm telling you that Jean's daughter will become a world leader in the future and will save countless lives on Earth and in space.' Joshua solely spoke into Richard's mind.

The anger ebbed, but it quickly rose again, thinking of how his revenge had been taken away; revenge for him and Malara's family. Richard let go of Jean's neck leaving a red hand imprint on her tanned skin. He walked around the edge of the open space in the center of the room brushing against the maze's funneled wall edges.

Jean looked at Richard, the other heroes, and stopped at Natasha holding Jared on the floor. "I didn't know." Joy and anguish clung to her voice.

Natasha lovingly beckoned Jean to come to her side with a hand gesture.

"What do we do now?" Susan asked John.

"We wait."

John's eyes met Natasha's eyes as she wondered how much different they were in person. She dare not use her illusions now, Mindseye and Pandora were much stronger than Jared and the mentalists put together. She felt their mental power spanning the entire room as if they were encased with an aura of protection. She was sure they didn't project such an aura in the courtroom during the trial, but now they had no cause to hide their power. The data she retrieved from Seattle, Washington was positive about the Eternal Champions. Somehow she felt at peace and very safe with them in the room, even though she had committed multiple crimes which they would know about once they scanned her memories.

'So now, I have to decide if Jean and her daughter live. And if her daughter gets to be raised by her mom?' Richard thought.

A mental heaviness of approval could be felt as Joshua replied. 'Many people have died, evil and innocent. Both of the women have lost the one person they loved, and all because the Magistrate ruined their lives many years ago. Just do what you do best and listen to your conscious, not mine… Many people believe in you Richard. And so do I.'

Richard scanned the entire room and far beyond. Joshua was done talking to him. He got into his combat stance and with both fists in front on him shot out telekinetic bolts into the maze walls. "Aaghhhhhhhhh!" The bolts hit the ceiling, floor, dead bodies, walls; everything except Jared and the living souls in the room.

Cindy was alarmed as she witnesses Richard destroy the underground complex like a minigun gone wild except he was shooting 60 mm invisible rounds that penetrated out as far as she could see. "What's he doing?"

John stared at his leader and smiled. "He's doing what my idol would do."

Cindy's confused face held firm, tempted to ask a second time.

"He's getting rid of evidence." Susan said, levitating Jared, Jean, and Natasha out of the way as Richard moved in a circular pattern.

The ionized air and heat created by the constantly disrupted atmosphere made the stench of blood and flesh almost unbearable. Susan raised her hand up and the air around it vibrated. Over a dozen super air fresheners paled in comparison to whatever she did in less than a few seconds.

The maze no longer existed as thousands of holes showed

the limits of the room. Richard was tired but showed no signs of it as he quickly came up in front of Jean and knelt. His hand once again grabbed her neck. His glasses sunk into his head revealing his face and black eye balls.

"Your daughter will live and be raised by you. But if you or Natasha break another law, I will hunt you down. If your daughter is raised by someone else that's fine with me, but I promise you that you will use the rest of your life to help people, or I will kill you." Richard let go of her and walked off out of the maze. "Get them out of here and comeback and get me."

John glanced at Susan. Susan walked slowly after Richard, giving him some space, knowing John would take care of the two women and Jared's body.

John touched Jean and Natasha's shoulders. All four disappeared in a flash of light while Cindy dematerialized but stayed visible. The perfumed air lightly mixed in with digestive material, rotting and burnt flesh was still too much for her to handle. "What are we doing now?" She floated next to Susan.

"We will get SIA down here and start cleanup operations. Once they arrive, we'll go home."

ED was Cindy's second home, and the sound of home gave her peace. So much blood was spilt these past several days, and at least it was over, but somehow this reminded her of when she and her brother, Lee, started a new life after the destruction of the Founders. 'When will all of the bloodshed really be over?' She muttered in her mind.

Susan heard Cindy's thoughts, and an uncanny smile came over her. 'Soon, there will be lasting peace.' She thought to herself.

Woodbridge, Virginia

John and his three passengers appeared on top of a five story apartment building. John maintained his hands on their shoulders and concentrated. All of the dried and wet blood disappeared from their bodies, along with their suits; seasonal women's clothing instantly wrapping them.

"You will be reinstated, but the CEA is in the process of deactivation and your position is already terminated. I strongly recommend you heed Creator's words and figure out how to help people." John stated.

"What about my brother?" Natasha's tired eyes blinked slowly.

"I will take him to SIA for confirmation of death and keep his remains safe. I will leave his body at the Baker-Post Funeral Home here in Virginia. You can have him buried or cremated, it's up to you. I will take him there at 4 pm tomorrow, so make sure one of you are there. I don't want someone else stealing his body. Also…" John touched both their heads.

Natasha and Jean felt power enter them. "You will both need to be able to defend yourselves. I have given you added mental abilities and defenses, use them wisely." John waited for them to reply.

"Why are you helping us?" Jean asked.

"We're heroes, not executioners. Also because, I read your minds while Creator was letting off some steam; and I know everything. I'm sorry for your loss, but I need to take him now."

Jean looked at John with humility, and then fixed her gaze on Jared's face. She kissed his cold stiff lips. How much she wanted it to feel like before, even a weak illusion would have satisfied her longing for him.

Natasha waited for Jean to move her face away. She too kissed him, but on the forehead instead. "I will take care of them, big brother." She said in Polish.

"You have money in your pockets; get to wherever it is you want to go. I'll see one or both of you tomorrow." John said and disappeared with Jared's body.

Chapter Twelve

The Masterminds

Ministry Defence Installation, Snowy Mountain Range, Australia

rare thing indeed to have such an elegance and beauty but yet be so deadly." Dr. Lethorn Harlov softly said, as he inspected one of his many masterpieces of death.

The tantalum carbon liquid alloy was camouflaged by organic nanomaterials continually creating real skin, fluids and hair. The long haired woman was labeled Eve 42, stenciled above her silver-carbon barred cubical. The androids were far ahead of Earth's technological times but not alien technology, which gave the scientist the ability to create ultimate assassins with his added human ingenuity.

"Doctor Harlov, it's so nice to see you again." A tall brunette along with three security officers approached the team of scientists.

"Colonel, it is nice. I waited a long time for your return." The doctor forgot about his trophies and attended to the Special Operations Liaison.

The doctor and Colonel Plaxon walked away from the rest of the scientists, with the security officers positioning themselves as a human wall of privacy. "The situation has changed. Command Central has given your program a green light for several assassinations." Plaxon's middle aged green eyes were overshadowed by blue makeup. It was elegant, but more so that signs of dark bags were covered up.

"You mean I can pick my targets?" Harlov's lips and hands excitedly shook for a brief moment.

The Colonel smiled. "No, the South American company will be reassigned to the United States. Also, you can't pick anyone that will attract too much attention."

"Huh, arghh, the new androids won't fail in South America." Harlov disagreed with the reassignment.

"We lost twelve of them in the past decade, and we still don't know how they disappeared."

Harlov stared into her eyes and slowly exhaled. "Thank you for now saying destroyed."

"Yes, well, may I suggest that since Central wants to test out the latest androids and place our own operatives in place at the same time; pick some superhumans living under the radar."

Harlov's eyes widen with joy. "I will search the databases and give you the targets for your approval within an hour. He quickly walked off towards the main data room.

Colonel Plaxon watched Harlov's backside. The man was tall and strong. His curly hair was perfectly black even though he was in his late seventies. The nanotechnology used by his division kept him young and vibrant, but there were complications and his present immortality was linked to a certain death at the age of 150. He was one of the very few who survived the nano-strain engineering wonder. Even though she was given an opportunity to participate in the trials, she declined hoping to naturally live out her life.

Dr. Harlov spent the full hour analyzing the best targets. Colonel Plaxon waited in his office looking at current performance reports. On average, the androids were stronger than most superhumans, but that was all Central wanted them to be. The AIs inside the android bodies could rebel against the Australian government orders and ideology so making them on par with most superhumans allowed for some semblance of control. The androids would also never be strong enough to defeat the very powerful superhumans, classified by the government as Alpha, Beta, and Gamma superhumans. The entire country was populated by superhumans, and the plan was to use the most powerful to fight EFL, the Eternal Champions, and Alpha rated superhuman loners.

The lone office was transparent to the laboratory floor being made of clear tempered glass. Dr. Harlov entered it as the glass door automatically slid open. "I've found four Alpha class superhumans." He placed a large electronic notepad in front of her.

Colonel Plaxon studied the information as the doctor

explained. “Sir David Lanhurst turned over his empire to these four superhumans. They have many aliases and all of their history is unconfirmed, but I think we have enough information on them to properly program the correct parameters. We least know about the leader, Fredrick Malleson, but a general purpose android should be able to take care of him.”

“We can’t send in the androids for four people at the same time. That will attract too much attention.”

“The group has been snooping around, trying to find some information on North Korea. We can plant some high tech equipment or person for them to steal or kidnap. We will be able to pick the location and time.” Harlov countered.

Colonel Plaxon thought for a moment. “That might actually work, but it will have to be out of the country and they won’t all leave the country. So we need to plan for Fredrick and Vicky Hammon.”

“How do you know it will be them in particular, and also not three of them?”

“Because Ms. Hammon is in charge of recruiting, and Fredrick will want to see the operation himself. The other two will make sure they run the empire as usual and possibly provide the two with an alibi if they need one.”

Harlov wasn’t the tactician, but he didn’t care as long as his androids were going to finally get a chance to redeem themselves by killing someone. His engineering department had a long failure rate, but Central fully supported him since 1990 with the first assassination of the legendary superhero, Nuetronium, succeeding beyond their wildest expectations.

"I don't know what will happen to the department if this mission fails."

"Don't give me that. There has to be some things already thrown on the table." Harlov retorted.

"That I know of… the programme might be accelerated or the entire department will transition into homeland defence. But I'm not authorized to confirm those options."

"Would it be better if we use two other androids to kill two targets in Asia?"

The colonel changed her gaze from the tablet to Harlov. "What did you have in mind?"

"I know Central is interested in country deterioration operations, so if we target and take out two political targets guarded by maximum security... Well I'm sure the androids can be used to topple many governments, to include the United States."

"Yes, it was on the table too. Lucky for you, it's being executed within the next ten months." Plaxon smiled.

"Really? When was I going to be informed?"

"Now, so congratulations Dr. Harlov. Two of the companies will go active soon."

Dr. Harlov grinned ear to ear. "This is wonderful news, and a great day." He looked across the floor and three hundred cubicles, each occupied by an android weapon of death for humans and superhumans.

United Federation Command, Bogota, Colombia

"Ladies and Gentlemen, the information is confirmed and our analysts indicate an imminent escalation of terrorism, assassinations, and/or extortion of political and military leaders. Our operatives in all countries have been re-tasked to counter these attacks. It has been suggested we mobilize our ground forces, but our space fleet is still not fully operational at this time. If there are indications of a war by Australia or North Korea, we will take advantage of the situation. In the meantime, I ask that you prepare our citizens to defend their home once we enter war operations. Thank you once again for attending." Eduardo Ramerize finished his speech to the country representatives.

The underground assembly room seated 29 parliament and senators, 210 representatives, 34 secretaries, and 5 council members. Fifty Soldiers guarded the leaders even though the underground fortification was secure and additional Soldiers roamed outside of the room. Thirteen assassination attempts in the past forced all leaders to be protected 24/7 by fully armored security details. Telepaths and special bio-scanners monitored cities and continental perimeter defenses looking for spies and other threats to the country and its inhabitants.

"The crowd looks brave." Estabon Ramerize whispered with Diego Gonzales sitting beside him.

"That's because they are." Diego smiled and applauded with the representatives.

"If only the world could be the same."

The monthly assembly ended with a confident note as the council members stayed or left the giant room, performing their duties as leaders of South America.

Jose and Andres walked out among the crowd greeting and addressing concerns. The other three council members headed through the back exit with many tasks still to be done for the day.

Eduardo walked by Estabon and Diego. "We need to work overtime and get the space fleet ready. Get the reserve units to help out anyway they can."

"I'll get with the generals, but what about the black fleet?" Diego replied.

"We can move them closer if the United States or Europe starts to fall apart. Otherwise, they can stay hidden for now." Estabon answered.

"Has there been any activity by the Argonians?" Eduardo asked.

"No, and we can't risk spying on the Eternal Champions, so we will have to wait for Hellfire or Quatris to return home." Estabon said.

"I miss the old days when the enemy was earth bound." Diego signed.

"I agree Diego, but it's a challenge we've taken for the sake of everyone." Eduardo smiled and placed a friendly hand on his shoulder.

2595 King Street, Alexandria, Virginia

The colonial style house was open from three street directions, a very easy target for assassins or police. Jean and Natasha didn't worry about it since their enhanced mental defenses could sense danger better than professional grade security cameras. The safe house was also never used until now. The bedrooms were unused as both women slept on the sofas in the living room. Not that they slept much at all, with Jared's ashes in a sheet bronze urn on the living room table.

They visited the funeral home and decided on cremation. Mindseye was kind enough to stay with them for the process which was done on the spot, an exception to normal scheduling and procedure, making it late that night as the doorbell rang.

Natasha scanned the outside, feeling one mental presence. Both women stood at the door when it opened revealing a fairly young African American wearing a modest tan overcoat, carrying a black metallic briefcase. His black Fedora style hat created a shadow over his dark glasses and face. The entrance light shone bright on his white teeth as he smiled.

"Good evening Ladies. My name is Thomas Keeper." He brushed the brim of his hat. "I wasn't sure you would be here, but Jared said you would."

"So, Jared sent you?" Natasha asked.

"Well sort of Ma'am. My father told me to come here if I ever received an alert on my phone. I did yesterday, so I'm here to deliver a message and this package from Jared." Thomas removed his glasses and stowed it on the inside chest pocket.

“Come in.” Jean said and completely opened the door.

Natasha nodded in agreement as everything seemed kosher.

Thomas looked around as he entered the living room. The house was modest, but desperately needed a maid. He noticed the very sad faces and bloodshot eyes, only able to imagine their lost as he recalled his own feelings when his father passed away. “I am very sorry for your lose. But I hope this helps you as one of these cases helped me.” He placed the briefcase on the living room table. He didn’t sit down as he motioned the two women to sit in front of the case.

Jean was hesitant, but Natasha wasn’t, as she recognized the briefcase very similar to cases Jared had used for many years.

“If each of you will please grab the handle one at a time, it will recognize your biometrics. It won’t open to anyone else.” Thomas explained as he took off the overcoat and sat beside the women.

Jean grabbed the handle last and the two latches on each side automatically released. The seal on the open case let out a small hiss of air. She completely opened the case, revealing a small monitor on the lid, a six inch mouse panel and two black compartments on the base. The monitor turned into a gold colored screen interface. “Speak full name to identify and initiate setup protocol.” Jared’s voice came out of the side speakers.

“Natasha Erickson.” Natasha said as a prompt popped up [Confirmed].

“Jean Lorenz.” Jean said, the prompt [Unauthorized –

Retry] appeared.

Jean looked at Thomas. "Is that your full name, or do you have another name you go by?"

Jean turned back to the case and thought. "Jean Erickson."

[Confirmed] The prompt disappeared as a video of Jared's face replaced it. "Well, it must be a surprise to you, but if you are watching this, your biometrics, voices, and images of your faces has activated this program. But first I want to tell both of you I love you so, so much. I'm also so happy that you are seeing this because it means both of you are alive… I will try to take this step by step. Jean, there's a compartment to the right, open it."

Jean opened the lid on the compartment. Folded documents were underneath a wedding ring. Jean picked up the ring and documents, revealing ten thumb drives in sunken slots underneath.

"I know we didn't have time to actually marry, but yes we did. The marriage is official, three months ago… I knew you were pregnant, and made you believe otherwise so our daughter wouldn't be targeted and you wouldn't freak out when things went bad. The ten thumb drives are videos of me talking to our daughter, you and Nat. The hard drive in this case is interactive and you can ask questions which hopefully I will be able to answer." The screen paused on Jared's face.

Both women wanted to shed tears as Jared told his tale, but their glands had been used up.

"Amos told me many things. I had to decide on the future, and I chose to pay for the deaths that we caused, and in return, both of you would live. It is hard to explain, but the future changed when Amos found me. I could have been the leader of the Magistrate only to have fought the corruption and die along with both of you. I had hope I would be next to you, but if it helps, I lived my happiest days with both of you. Amos told me I would fall in love, but he left out the details. I was only eleven at the time so it didn't register for a while. I loved you the first day I saw your beautiful blue eyes, white silky hair, and strict dominating face." Jared smiled. "Your wall to shun people away was my invitation to see you happy and love you even more."

Jean managed a tear and touched the screen with her fingers hoping she could feel his cheek and lips again.

Jared paused for a moment in recollection. "Thomas Jr. should be there with you right now. Thomas, thank you for everything. In the compartment to the left, there are three safe deposit box keys. They are labeled, one for each of you. There's information specific for each of you leading you to money, and documents. Oh, and don't worry about paying taxes, it has been taken care of, to include twenty percent to charity. Your father was an amazing man. I hope the best for you and your family. And of course, I wish the best for you my little sister, and my dear wife. Later our daughter can see these videos and interact with the computer. I hope you move on and live a life full of joy and peace."

Jared's face disappeared and a table of content came up on the screen. The standard start button was present to allow a person to log out, pause or shut down the computer.

Thomas accepted his key from Natasha. "Thank you. It

was a pleasure meeting the sister and wife of the man who saved my father, me, and my family. Should you ever need me, just call me." He handed her his personal card.

Natasha looked at the card. "Remark Industries. So your companies created the complex in Detroit?"

"My father did, it cost almost a billion dollars. That was one of the last things he did before he died." Thomas sadly replied.

Natasha almost smiled. Jared never intended on telling her she was already a multi-millionaire. "I'm sorry. Thank you and don't be a stranger." Thomas bid the women farewell with Nat seeing him out.

Thomas left the house and retrieved another case from the trunk of his car. He spoke to it, and it self-destructed from the inside. He rode off to dispose of the case, heading home; two states away.

The night and several days after were spent watching Jared's videos. Laughter and sobs were shared as the women envisioned a future together with Jared's encouragement and tutoring.

Chapter Thirteen

Goodbyes and Redemption

The director's office seemed different to Richard having been there not too long ago. "Did you change something?" Richard said as he looked around the room and then stopped at the bookshelf.

Max smiled as he sat in his armed chair. "I don't have the standard cleaning service, so yes I got a new calendar."

"No, that's not it. You got new books."

"Yes, The Indivisible Man is one of my favorite."

"You should get the Invisible Woman too."

"Yes, well I'll do that. Speaking of books, are you sure you don't want to change your story?"

"I'm sure the Magistrate framed Jean and Jared. I'm sorry

for destroying everything, but they used illusions and I had to shoot everywhere."

"Yeah you sure did that. If it wasn't for Michael's fingerprints and DNA, we would have never identified him, seeing that you took off his head."

"Yeah, sorry about that, he must have been laying down when I hit him." Richard said with a surprised expression on his face.

"Huh, what are the odds?" Max asked not mentioning that everyone on the bottom floor were headless. Oliver Cox and the controllers in the hallway were the only people with visible proof they weren't killed by Richard's onslaught.

"Everything around me seems to beat impossible odds." Richard smiled.

"You're sure Jean wasn't involved in any way?" Max half frowned.

"John told me Jared planned it all to destroy the Magistrate. Jean was one of his tools, and will need all the support you can give her. She has a new mission in life now." Richard softly said.

"Why did you let her go, Richard?"

"If I told you, I would have to kill you." Richard almost laughed.

Max stared at his friend, and best asset. Richard was unique, a born leader, and never ceased in fighting evil. If Richard kept information from him, it was to protect someone, not the mission or ideological cause. "You know she's labeled untrustworthy, and she's no use in undercover work or in the agencies."

"That's more of a reason for you to get her a position with the State Department as a criminal investigator or liaison of some kind."

Max stood up and walked around the table. "I'll see what I can do. I'll talk with Paul since he's with Senator Summers, maybe one of the politicians can take her in to run special projects."

"I have a feeling her children will go into politics so that might work, but I didn't come here to give you a personal report on what happened in Detroit. I assume John will be able to retrieve Jared's body?"

"Yes, he can have his body. But why is his body so important? We can secure it for decades until the allegations are forgotten." Max rested on the table ledge.

"John said he should be given a proper resting place like any other person. He also said that things will be different from now on, and we should focus on the future. The Magistrate was a very big organization which your agency didn't have visibility on for too many years. I have seen much in my life, but not like this. How many more people lurking in the shadows do we have to worry about?" Richard bluntly stated.

Max crossed his arms. "I know telepaths will change everything now that they can be used a lot more than before, but it bothers me too."

"Yes, I thought about that. Lies and secrets will become a

thing of the past. You know many people in high places will be at risk for scandals they can't outright deny. Private companies will charge for mental protections, and there might be a telepath war if things aren't managed correctly. But there's hope Max. I think South America has found a way to make it work. If they could do it, so can we."

Max smiled. "Do you know how much intelligence we have on South America?"

"A lot of nothing probably. And if you told me, you would probably have to kill me, right?"

Max smiled. "Well, let's just say they excelled in creating the perfect nation fully devoted for war. I have read many fiction and non-fiction books about people who dominated with technology and vast armies. Our analysts estimate they have over a thirty million Soldier army. I personally think they have more. Fortunately, they have been good to us. While we fight among ourselves, they're watching and waiting."

"It has crossed my mind, but what do you think they're waiting for?"

"The only thing I can think of is EFL and your group. War is coming, sooner or later. EFL and you guys will have to take sides, and I'm banking on the good guys winning."

"Thanks for the confidence in us, but it will take more than a group of superhumans and countries to change the world."

"Yeah, well I'm sure if Quatris or Hellfire wanted to burn the planet into nothingness, there's no one that I know that can stop them."

"And that's one reason you recruited them a long time ago?" Richard said what Max wouldn't openly state.

"Well they weren't known to have that much power back then."

Richard smiled. "Yes, but we were the same way. And now, if Susan or John wanted to destroy the planet, they could as long as other superhumans didn't try to intervene."

"Yes, it was a chance I had to take, to keep an eye on powerful superhumans like you. But honestly, I'm not worried about your team or EFL. Our SAI gave me an estimate on the number of extremely powerful superhumans, and out of over a dozen known and another dozen unknowns, the ones I worry about are the three in Australia." Max placed his hands on the ledge of the table.

"Well, let's concentrate on law and order here, before we go international."

"That reminds me. The Air Force made a special request after the trial was over, but we've been so busy, I just got around to it. They would like for you test pilot their latest experimental fighter."

"I'll take it."

Max's eyes widen. "You don't want to know for how long and where?"

"It won't take too long for me to find out the limits of the plane. I'm sure I can keep it from disintegrating into a great ball of fire. And as for where, I'm sure it's in Area 51, where the other fighter disappeared a while back. You can send the details to Erica."

"Thank you Richard, for everything." Max shook Richard's hand.

It was Richard's cue to say his good-bye. They would stay in contact and fight crime, where ever it took them.

Creator left Max's office and reunited with John who was waiting for him outside in the command center.

They teleported back home and went about their daily routine. John returned Jared to the Jean that afternoon. Cindy had left earlier for her home in Seattle, with the group seeing her off at the airport. She always wanted to do things as much as a normal human, and now that she wasn't fighting crime, it was her time to relax on the long plane trip.

Eternal Domain, several days later

Susan and John lay in bed both staring at the ceiling but their minds were inescapably linked in an intense conversation. It had been over a year since Toluvis had tried to take the throne for her son. Richard was not on trial anymore, and the Eternal Champions were more famous now than ever. The Magistrate and Jean's influence was not a threat to the group anymore. Elizabeth and Richard were successfully raising a future baby superhero. The time had come for them to join their destiny in space.

Erica had compiled information which John requested over the past few years on the Argonian Empire. Susan had shown him everything Queen Omia knew, but that was not enough for him. The EFL SAI, Bob, assisted greatly in this effort, but it wasn't until Lord Morinar came back to Earth when the Argonian scout vessels assigned to Earth were the major source of current information to them. The divided royal family needed to mend back into harmony. The Galactic Guardians had given the human race a good name in the empire; however, John and Susan being on the throne may have pulled that name and honor too far. "Things are going to get worse the more time we spend here on Earth." Susan continued to state.

"Darling, I agree, but timing is everything and we need to go with a good plan. Prejudices are never something to take likely since it involves change which many people are afraid of. I also think we should unite the galaxy instead of managing it."

"We know the Pylaxians are preparing to attack. The only problem I see is getting everyone in critical positions to accept us as king and queen." Susan replied.

John thought about all they had mentally discussed and let Susan see his reasoning and plan. In a matter of a few minutes, Susan understood what John was most concerned with, but he as usual had a plan to solve it. They came to an agreement and both enjoyed each other's physical and emotional sexual pleasures while they still could before they had to leave Earth to a new home.

The morning was gloomy with tropical storm Erin moving through the eastern shores of south Florida.

Richard gathered everyone in the farm's main house living

room area. Most of the employees were present as they said their goodbyes to John and Susan. The employees who didn't know their true identities were told that Susan and John were going to travel the world and probably settle down in the Fiji Islands for several years. Some of the employees thought it odd that they were leaving in the middle of a tropical storm, but they were known to do crazy travel plans like in the middle of hurricanes and worldwide computer virus attacks. But no one complained since all of the employees lived on the farm and were getting paid overtime for their time on call in case the structures or horses needed attention during the storm. The twelve employees were family as Richard always said when he got the chance.

The party started early that morning with John and Susan enjoying their time with friends. Food, drinks, video game consoles and multiple group games kept everyone entertained. Richard moved around talking to everyone, but he spent a little more time with the farm's secretary, Alexis Mora.

"How are you today?" Richard started the conversation.

The sandy blonde smiled, but this time it was different. "I talked to Max yesterday. I'm on suspension."

"It's a brave thing you're doing, and we're all proud of you."

"It would be brave if I were in danger." Her blue eyes widen. "Am I?"

"It all depends." Richard replied as her mouth opened in surprise. "If you start dating Larcis, you're heart might be in danger of breaking."

"What? He's not my type." Alexis' shock turned into a mild laugh.

"Whatever you do finally decide, we'll support you. Plus, you know I have connections and can write the best recommendations ever."

"If it's okay with you, I think Max knew my decision before I did. He gave me a way out of the agency through this suspension and my resignation… I already decided to stay here and work for you."

Elizabeth and John, who were listening in on the conversation, came over from across two rooms and hugged Alexis. Richard motioned her to a more private section of the room so that the employees wouldn't hear. "I understand that one of your specialties is analytical criminology and profiling."

"Yes, did Max give you all my information?" Alexis held a half empty wineglass in her hand.

"No, all he knows is your cover is blown and we are rehiring you. Besides, we got the information on you a long time ago."

"How long ago was that?"

"After your job interview, before we hired you." Richard said as if it was part of the course three years ago.

"What?"

"The SIA telepaths are good, and you got a lot of training, but I asked John to conduct a deep scan on you several times. I knew SIA would place a spy in the farm. To be honest, I thought it would be the butler."

Alexis laughed. "Who, Robert?"

Richard smiled. "Well, he is an ex-SEAL. But I guess SIA recruits them young."

"Yes, I was recruited out of high school. But, why the charade for so many years?"

"As long as Max thought he had an eye on us, it kept everything peaceful. I and the team don't have anything to hide, so it was fine with me… Until Mark died, I realized if Max had known he was here, then there was a possibility Mark would still be alive. I hate secrets, especially the ones that hurt people. But we kept the charade to see if I could trust SIA once again, and to see what you would do."

"What I would do?" Alexis' glass was empty now but she attempted to drink it being immersed in the conversation.

"You knew Erica was monitoring everything, and that passive surveillance within the farm was the only thing she would not be able to detect. You helped out more than necessary, and withheld information from SIA which proved to me that you sided with our actions. Thank you."

Alexis didn't know what to say. Her assignment to monitor the Eternal Champions was at first a provisional mission dependent on the success of the team. The addition of Elizabeth and Susan changed things and she fell in love with the group. She took on assignments on her own time, but it didn't prove to be what she expected it to be. Field agent work could be tedious and at times was exhilarating, but she didn't see criminals being caught like she dreamed as a teenager. But the Eternal Champions were catching criminals all of the time. Maybe she just wanted a piece of the action, or maybe she wanted to be a part of something bigger, besides SIA. "I will do my best."

"Good, because we'll need you more than ever with John and Susan gone."

"Where're they really going?"

"You along with Robert and Becky will get briefed once I get back from dropping them off. But for now, have fun and plan on reading a lot for the next few weeks." Richard said and walked back into the crowd.

Alexis smiled as she looked at Susan playing with Alex. Larcis was trying to get his highest kill score on Halo, and John was joking around with a small group. She was excited knowing that her new job with the Eternal Champions would change everything. She would meet Erica in person, something less than a dozen people in the world had experienced. She would get to be more than a monitor of superhumans.

The party lasted until noon, with luggage already waiting in one of the farm's SUVs. John and Susan said their last goodbyes with Richard and Larcis driving them to the airport. Elizabeth hated long farewells so having to attend to Alex, helped her cope in parting with her best friends. The airport was in the middle of nowhere deep on an Everglades side trail. Captain Allina's scout spaceship, the Tedious, waited for them while the four superheroes talked the entire way.

Erica II was Erica's extension outside the base. The small

baseball size blue probe hovered under the ceiling light of the car. “John, what will happen if the Argonian Empire can’t win this galactic war?” She asked as the SUV approached the linkup point with Erica’s voice coming from the probe, car speakers and their comlinks.

“I guess you guys will have to come and rescue the day.” John joked.

“Can you imagine Richard in space, what kind of chaos that would cause?” Larcis laughed.

“Do they have trials in space too?” Erica asked.

Larcis almost ran off the road with laughter. Even Richard couldn’t keep back the hilarious pain in his gut, even though it did bring up some sad memories.

John barely kept the SUV from running into a ditch with his telekinesis.

“You guys will have plenty to do here on Earth.” Susan stated with ending giggles.

“Yeah, thanks to you, we’ll be fine.” Richard looked at John and Susan sitting in the backseats. “If only you could take these two with you.” Motioning towards Larcis and Erica.

“One day my friend, we’ll all celebrate peace in outer space.” John replied.

“We’re here.” Larcis announced and quickly got out of the car. “Hey John, can I be a captain of a starship, like John Luke?”

“Not if you want a mutiny.” John laughed.

"Hmph." Larcis had their luggage ready in hand to the side of the car. "I will make you proud, I promise."

Susan smiled. "We're always proud of you Larcis."

Erica II floated next to Richard as he walked in front of the SUV. He waited for the three to stand next to him as he looked at the scout ship.

The Argonian ship was cloaked to visible sight and a few other frequencies, but he knew it was there by the heat radiating off of the tall grass. It was a very minor difference but it left a shadow like impression of a saucer like ship on the ground even though it was in the air. Richard smiled. "I'm impressed, the ship is there, and it isn't giving anything off."

John stood next to him. "Really, that's good to know. I'm impressed that you know it's there."

Richard grinned ear to ear. "I would cause a lot of chaos in space..."

"I can't wait." John smiled and hugged his friends goodbye. Susan followed suit and they teleported into the invisible spaceship.

The black ship turned visible seconds later. It spanned forty meters in diameter, floating ten meters above the ground. "Wow!" Larcis said, seeing an Argonian ship up close for the first time.

Richard only smiled as he recalled trying to break into Princess Navia's ship while underwater. Luckily he didn't damage the ship, which would have been a bad thing since he was definitely not going to pay the repair bill.

It was a sorrowful parting as Richard, Larcis, and Erica II watched the almost invisible blur of the Tedious' hull vanish as it moved towards outer space. The wind produced by the ship only complemented the tropical storm's wind currents, but the sound the ship made mimicked constant thunder which Larcis thought was cool. The two men and probe headed back with many ideas of the future.

To Richard's expectation, Larcis started the conversation Richard knew was on his mind since the party.

"Hey Boss. Do you think I can ask Alexis out on a date, now that she's on the team?"

"If you ask her and she accepts, and you break her heart. I will break your legs, wait for you to heal in a day or two, and break them again, and again until she feels you've been punished enough."

"Huh… So what happens if she breaks my heart?"

"I'll give her a raise." Richard laughed.

"And I'll be watching." Erica chimed in.

"Thanks a lot Boss." Larcis smirked.

"One day Larcis, you'll find the right person, just be patient and be yourself."

"I know Boss, Liz told me the same thing."

The conversation changed to stories of the past and the friends they already missed.

Alexandria, Virginia

Natasha showed Jean the display on her smart phone. “They’re looking for you. This is one of Jared’s SIA email account, maybe they think you would monitor it.”

Jean read the email from SIA. Max wanted to speak to her and arrange her retirement as CEA director. A proposal to work for Senator Summers was intriguing, but her daughter came first.

“I will go on the first flight out to New York. But if you don’t mind coming with me, we can go live somewhere in the Midwest until Isabella is born.”

“That’s my mother’s name.” Natasha smiled, as they packed up the car with luggage.

“Do you think I’m doing the right thing?”

“Jared would have wanted you to live free and help people. But I will miss pick-pocketing and all.”

“The country will go through many growing pains, and I want to be there to help. I’m sure your talents will still be needed. In the meantime, we need to start by getting you a cover as my assistant or something.

Natasha smiled and opened the door for Jean to enter. “Yes, Ma’am, it’ll be my honor.”

Jean sat in the Lexus and relaxed as Natasha drove to the airport, thinking of a new future for her and the country as telepaths were now the driving force in law enforcement. But being ex-Director of the CEA gave her a unique perspective. The Magistrate was only one of several organizations willing to attack the government. It would be a matter of time before someone else attempted to do what they failed to accomplish. Jared's words echoed in her mind. Maybe she couldn't become president, but she could still go into politics with the help of Senator Summers. The safe deposit boxes gave the two women access to a quarter of a billion tax free dollars. She could start a private business with that amount of money, but she knew that political connections were more powerful than money alone.

Jean looked at Natasha. Her hair was blonde now with a resemblance to Jordan, the Dallas Cowboy cheerleader. "I think you look better with black hair."

Natasha glanced at her for a second. "Really?" She thought about it for a moment and her hair instantly changed to her natural black color, length, and fluffy style. "Me, too." She smiled as the car made its way to the airport.

Author Notes

The storyline for the superhero epic series is setup in such a way that the action and events intertwine with each book. The fourth book "The Galaxy Is Ours" explains what John and Susan were doing before Richard was framed for the death of Malara, and after they left Earth. I tried to stay away from describing the characters as invincible; and show the underlying challenges superheroes face even though they may be bulletproof, have unique or very powerful abilities. Susan and John's powers stem from cosmic energy management and manipulation so that they can focus on one extremely powerful ability, develop new powers, or spread their energies to have more abilities, but not as powerful as they could if they focused on only one or two abilities.

If you have not read the previous four books in the series; I would recommend you do, so you can understand better how members of the Eternal Champion developed into the dynamics which are in this book and how Jared and Jean developed their romance which was firmly established from the beginning of this book. The legalistic ideas and events which occur for the most part are mirrored with the US legal system in the sense of structure and general procedure. But I hope you don't take the events as a mockery or factual with real legal procedures or ideology. The trial in a real situation would have probably been deemed a mistrial, and a new trial would have occurred. Obviously, the fact that mind reading is not in the real world so I had to imagine how people might actually react if they were shown the truth of other peoples' memories and thoughts in a trial setting. On the same note, I wanted to show how our heroes would deal with a justice system that is going through constant growing pains.

The final development and conclusion to Jean and Jared's relationship is sorry to say, short lived. But I hope you can see the complexity of the relationship and passion for a better future for Jean and Natasha. The underworld plot to increase in political and economic power is not something new in the world of fiction or real life; but in this case, the Masterminds are the ones who are trying to pull the strings. The introduction of large scale complex plots to take over the country is only the start of the next book in the series. As you can guess, book six "Superhumans from the Past" builds on top of what has already happened, toward the one villainous plot to take over the world by some and destroy it by others.

I thank my readers for your support and hope you enjoyed the book. Please look for the next three books in the series:

Superhumans from the Past - *book 6*

Ultimate Assassins - *book 7*

Last Hope for Earth - *book 8*

List of Characters

Richard Octavian / Creator - Leader of the Eternal Champions

Elizabeth A. Octavian / Isis - Member of the Eternal Champions

John Goodman / Mindseye -Member of the Eternal Champions

Susan M. Goodman / Pandora - Member of the Eternal Champions

Larcis G. Draven / Night - Member of the Eternal Champions

Cindy S. Owens (Samantha Brooks) / Mirage - Disciple of Joshua and Member of the Eternal Champions.

Erica - Member of the Eternal Champions (Super Artificial Intelligence computer)

Robert Dilinger - Head security guard for the Octavian Farm and supporter of the Eternal Champions.

Becky Ellington - Head veterinarian for the Octavian Farm and supporter of the Eternal Champions.

Alexis Mora - Secretary for the Octavian Farm

Randolph Maximilian - Director of the Special Investigation Agency (SIA)

Paul Rohan - Deputy Director of the Special Investigation Agency

Robert Thorn - SIA Field Agent and Lawyer, Superhuman Recovery Division

Senator Harleigh Summers - US Senate, (R - CA)

Jean Lorenz - Director of the Counterespionage Agency (CEA)

Jared Erickson - Special operative for the CEA

Natasha Erickson - Sister of Jared and special operative for the CEA

Eibren Milows – Mercenary and Special operative for CEA

Michael Stockwell – Archmagi/ruler of the Magistrate

Nick Phamos – Executor of the Magistrate, underworld of mentalists

Adam – Disciple prodigy of Michael, underworld of mentalists

Oliver Cox – Elder in the Magistrate, precognitive abilities

Starfire/Rebecca Emerson – Member of EFL and wife of Quatris

Starlight/Lynda Alexander – Member of EFL and wife of Hellfire

Judge/Deathstar/Fred Cider – Superhuman self proclaimed vigilante

Dr. Lethorn Harlov – Creator of Tantalumized Androids

SSG George B. Phoenix – US Army Military Police investigator

Malara Phoenix – Wife of George Phoenix

Honorable Judge Adam Cambridge – Florida Superior Court Judge

Charles Powell – Tallahassee District Attorney and lead prosecutor.

Joshua Marks (David) – All powerful Superhuman

Andrez Pobles – South American Councilmember of the Federation

Diego Gonzalez – South American Councilmember of the Federation

Eduardo T. Ramirez – South American Councilmember and Founder of the Federation

Estabon Ramirez – South American Councilmember of the Federation, and Captain of the Starship Andromeda

Jose Begestano – South American Councilmember of the Federation

CPSIA information can be obtained
at www.ICGtesting.com
Printed in the USA
BVHW050310211022
649809BV00001B/13